The Diary of William Harvey

JEAN HAMBURGER

The Diary of William Harvey

The Imaginary Journal of the Physician Who Revolutionized Medicine

TRANSLATED BY BARBARA WRIGHT

Rutgers University Press
New Brunswick, New Jersey

Rutgers University Press and the author wish to express their deep gratitude to Prof. Emeritus I. Bernard Cohen, Harvard University, and Alan McHenry, President of the Lounsbery Foundation, whose enthusiasm and generous support made this English translation of *Le Journal d'Harvey* (Flammarion, 1983) possible.

Library of Congress Cataloging-in-Publication Data

Hamburger, Jean.
   [Journal d'Harvey. English]
   The diary of William Harvey : the imaginary journal of the physician who revolutionized medicine / Jean Hamburger ; translated by Barbara Wright.
      p. cm.
   Translation of: Le journal d'Harvey.
   Includes bibliographical references.
   ISBN 0-8135-1825-3 (cloth)—ISBN 0-8135-1826-1 (pbk.)
   1. Harvey, William, 1578–1657—Fiction. 2. Medicine—England—History—17th century—Fiction. 3. Great Britain—History—Charles I, 1625–1649—Fiction. I. Title.
PQ2615.A227J6813   1992
843'.914—dc20   91-46771
                                                                    CIP

British Cataloging-in-Publication information available.

I write not my gests, but my selfe and my essence.
—Michel de Montaigne
(John Florio trans., 1603)

Contents

Preface

William Harvey is the most famous of all English physicians, and the British may well see him as one of their greatest heroes. But a man of such stature belongs to the whole world, and one does not have to be English to want to write about him. He was not merely a seventeenth-century English physician; he represents the adventure of medicine in all times and all countries, and also the eternal history of all men faced with the marvels and sufferings of the human condition. William Harvey is a man of the present; he belongs everywhere.

That is what this book tries to convey. It is *not* a biography, even though the historical facts are as accurate as possible. It is not simply the story of an exceptionally eventful life lived in the thick of the English Revolution and during a period of great unrest in Europe. Rather, through the thoughts I attribute to this physician, it is the story of all the struggles, all the distress, and all the amazement of men confronted with that strange thing: life.

I should not be reproached for having criticized Francis Bacon or René Descartes, for having caricatured the theories of Johann Baptist of van Helmont, for having defamed Oliver Cromwell and turned a blind eye to the king's weaknesses. Nor should I be taken to task for having made no mention of those who wrote of the circulation of the blood before William Harvey or for having declared without proof that, as early as his student days in Padua, Harvey already had a presentiment of the great discovery that was to make his name famous. For it is not *my* opinions that Harvey records in his diary.* He hated Bacon,

---

*Harvey's diary has been rendered in twentieth-century English—with a few exceptions intended to preserve the wonderful flavor of the language of his time.

whereas I admire him. He did not know the writings of Michel
Servet, whereas we know today that he testified to the circulation of the blood before Harvey, and so on. It is William Harvey
you are going to read, not Jean Hamburger, and if he makes
erroneous statements it is because, knowing him as I do, I think
that it was *necessary* for him to make them.

J. H.
Paris
October 15, 1990

The Diary of William Harvey

LONDON

1 April 1647

Today I am entering the seventieth year of my life. But it does not worry me to know that I am old. On the contrary: my trouble seems to be rather that I feel desperately young in spirit and in my secret desires. I swing endlessly between the interior world of my soul, which I feel is the same as it was when I was twenty, and the exterior signs of my body, which bear witness to my old age. I know very well that it is time for me to retire. I know that it would be reasonable to prepare myself for death. But I cannot bring myself to do so. On the one hand I am assailed by lassitude and by attacks of gout. On the other, I am still completely possessed by the recent memory of a turbulent, active life.

Less than a year ago my duties as Warden of Merton College, Oxford, were so onerous that I was working every day from dawn until late at night. Students and professors created incessant turmoil round me. King Charles, who had been residing in Oxford for three years, had entrusted me with this post. I was still his Physician in Ordinary, and I went to Court several times a week. My life was full of movement and contentment. By a disastrous reverse of fortune, everything changed in a few months. The Parliamentary Army surrounded the town, the King fled to Scotland, I was dismissed from the Wardenship. I had to come back to London.

Here, time drags, my days are empty, my nights interminable, and the memory of the happy times, far from relieving my anxiety, fills me with bitter torment; it is the heart-rending image of a lost paradise.

Tonight I am alone in my study. The house is shrouded in silence. I am sitting at my old oak table. I have opened the beautifully bound diary with the delicate fastener that my brother Eliab gave me as a New Year present. Between each month, dozens of blank pages are waiting to receive notes. Why have I decided to take up my pen and fill in these pages? More than once in my lifetime I have thought of writing a diary, but I never had the leisure to do so. Many of my compatriots record similar private memoirs, written whenever the opportunity presents itself, their sole desire being to leave a trace of passing time, a trace of men and events, of feelings and memories. In many cases such a diary is destined solely for the writer himself, and he sometimes requests that it should be burnt on the day of his death. My purpose is different; I would like to transmit some echoes of my struggle to the men who will live after me.

When I am dead, one not-far-distant day, I cannot tell whether some unknown man will take the trouble to explain and defend my life and work. I would like to know that unknown man. I would like to become his familiar, for him to learn to love what I love. Before I die, I must find time to record for his benefit the long path my thought has followed. If my notes are sufficiently coherent, I might even be able to extract a more disciplined volume from them, free from all personal irrelevancies. I already imagine myself bequeathing them to the College of Physicians. It would please me were this volume to remain there amongst their books, as a testimony to my attachment to the library in which I have so enjoyed working.

Today I received a visit from my brother Daniel. He is a man I admire. He is nine years my junior. I envy him because he has had ten children, whereas I have had none, and because he has a business sense (they say he knows more about the laws of commerce than anyone else in England), whereas I understand nothing about money matters. Since the death of Thomas, Matthew, Michael and John, I now have only two brothers left out of the great tribe of spice merchants who carried on the paternal tradition so well: I alone fled the art of commerce. I also envy Daniel his tall stature and the nobility of his features. There is no way in which I resemble him. I am not tall, my face has always displeased me and does so even more today: this morning I remained for a long moment in front of the Venetian mirror in the vestibule; my hair is greying, I am bald at the temples, my prominent nose has become more angular, there are lines on either side of my lips, my moustache and short, pointed beard are now completely white, and rebellious to the comb. Daniel seems to flourish in his maturity, whereas I have lost all hope that, with age, my own features might acquire a more serene harmony.

Daniel fully shares my fidelity to the King. It must be said that the Parliamentarians have done everything in their power to ruin him. They levied exorbitant taxes on his assets, they imprisoned him for debt, they imposed such heavy fines on him that he would never have been able to extricate himself from such dire straits without the help of his friends and employees. Despite his reverses, he remains one of the most active members of the Levant Company and the East India Company, and one of the chief importers of spices and silks.

April is a cold month this year. Daniel sat down in the big, well-worn leather armchair in front of the hearth, where several logs were burning. While he was telling me about his latest business difficulties I was looking at his face. The flame lit up his rather babyish countenance and his blond beard. No two faces are alike, just as no two voices are identical. There is nothing remarkable about Daniel's face and voice, and yet I could never mistake them for those of any other man. When I see and hear him, I immediately recognise the unique mark he has made on me once and for all, and every time I am seized by the same emotion. It is an astonishing thing, the marvellous diversity of men: each one's features are sufficiently original to rekindle in us, on every occasion, the same trail of specific memories and emotions—love, hate, or indifference. Listening to my brother Daniel speak, looking at him, I told myself that he was very dear to me.

I told him of the King's flight from Oxford under cover of night, his beard and love-lock shaved off, disguised as a footman, following the faithful Ashburnham, whose servant he was supposed to be. While he was taking refuge in the Scottish camp,

Oxford was surrendering to the Parliamentary forces (or, to be more precise, to Cromwell's clique), and very shortly afterwards I was forced to return to London. My brother had not seen me since that time.

This was because I had gone to the Scottish camp at Newcastle. The King had sent for me, saying that he was suffering from a state of fatigue for which he needed to see his personal physician. It is my belief that above all he needed to see a friend. I received a pass to go to the King on November 24th last, and immediately set out. On my arrival, I was conducted by a Scottish officer to the Manor where His Majesty was residing. I judged from the number of guard-posts we had to pass that the Manor was more a prison than a royal residence. As was his wont, the King's face betrayed nothing of his anxiety and bitterness. But his doubts, his inner turmoil, his chagrin, soon became apparent to me. The very next day after my arrival, he confided to me:

"I came here to take refuge with the Scots on the strength of an express promise. In London, the official representatives of Edinburgh had assured me that Scotland could restore to me the liberty of action that Cromwell's armies had taken from me. Barely had I arrived here, however, than I heard quite another story. The price of their hospitality was nothing less than the abandonment of the Anglican Church, the acceptance of the Presbyterian doctrine and the dismissal of the bishops. You will find it difficult to imagine the pressure they exerted on me. Their knavery confounds me."

I saw that he was heavy-hearted, if not in despair. I tried, clumsily, to bring him some comfort: "Despite all the misfortunes that have befallen England you must know, Sire, that the people's fidelity to their King is more enduring than ever."

On such occasions my natural timidity, and a feeling of absolute respect, render me totally stupid. I wondered whether the King was not hoping for some advice from me. I knew that the Queen and her entourage had sent messages to him from Paris urging him to accede to the Scottish demands and abandon the Episcopate to its fate. Perhaps I should have joined in these objurgations? Perhaps I should have begged him to think only of saving his own person, whatever the cost? But I kept silent. Besides, I know him too well to believe him capable of an act of renunciation that he held to be cowardice.

"And yet," I said to Daniel, "if he had capitulated in the matter of the bishops, the Scots would probably not have dared to betray him. They would probably even have wished to keep the King in their midst as a valuable hostage, a glorious standard for their Presbyterian combat."

The fire had slowly gone out. Night was falling, and the room was almost dark. My brother stood up, and left me on my own. But I was still haunted by the menaces accumulating against King Charles. I am proud of a King who is more attached to his convictions than to his life. But my pride is coupled with fear. A few days after my arrival in Newcastle, I heard from the King's own mouth that the Scots had ignominiously sold his person to the English Parliament for the sum of £400,000. A King, sold like a market commodity! We watched him leave for Holdenby, the first stage on the route to London, and that time I was forbidden to follow him. The King was smiling. He seemed not to see the impending dangers. For my part, I am convinced that if the London Parliamentarians lay their hands on him he will not escape imprisonment, perhaps even some sort of summary trial.

I am selfishly thinking of what kind of end to my life I could then expect. Deprived of his support, hated by those who are jealous of me, pursued by his enemies, the only course open to me would be to find some obscure retreat where I would try to be forgotten. I already refrain from being seen too frequently at the College of Physicians, where only yesterday my presence was a joy to me and, I think, to the others. Already I no longer feel entirely free to fight, with the necessary strength and voice, against the still-fervent detractors of my scientific work. If England loses her King, future generations may well lose the benefit of what I have contributed to the knowledge of man and the knowledge of medicine.

I remember the exhilaration that possessed me when I suddenly realized that the circulation of the blood had surrendered its secret to me and that I had understood what no one before me had succeeded in unravelling. I had not yet assembled all the experimental proofs necessary before making public a deep-seated conviction. But from that moment on, my ideas were

clear and my path assured. There is no greater intoxication than
that which overwhelms the man who hungers after truth when
he wrests from Nature one of her hitherto-unknown secrets.

I was in Padua, and I was twenty-four years old, when the
event occurred. Two years earlier I had been the first English
student to be admitted, at the beginning of this century, to the
University of *Il Bo*. Padua, for an Englishman, was a dazzling
city, even though rather dirty. I remember my first steps on the
shining cobblestones of the narrow alleys as I discovered the colourful palaces, the teeming arcades, the seven cupolas of the
Saint and, finally, the grandiose edifice of the University, its yellow stones contrasting with the violent blue of the sky, a sky
blue such as I had never seen in England. The porch was like the
door of a temple, framed by columns and surmounted by a
winged lion in bas-relief. I entered the square inner courtyard,
at the far end of which was a two-storied, balustraded *loggia*.
Architectural beauty, at once classical and exuberant, was here
at the service of science: the very opposite of the grey austerity
of the stones in which I had lived for seven years, in the buildings
of Caius College, Cambridge.

And I was soon to discover, in those walls and streets of
Padua, a fascinating effervescence of the spirit. Students from
the entire world, from France, Sweden, Germany, Poland,
formed, with the Italians, a world in microcosm, burning to exchange ideas on all the subjects that arouse men's curiosity. Almost all the professors were illustrious. Our relationship with
them was as respectful as in England but more familiar, more
personal. I studied in the Jurists' faculty, and at the same time
followed the courses in medicine and anatomy; I sometimes
even slipped into the crowded amphitheatre where Galileo lec-
tured on mechanics and astronomy. Everywhere the argument
was new and free, tradition was subjected to criticism, the student was encouraged to think for himself.

Outside the university, our encounters continued. The bookshops, the pharmacies, the libraries, even the taverns, were every
day filled with men of all ages arguing about beauty and ugliness, about the world, about women, about the secrets of the art
of living. I remember the Angel Pharmacy, where I often went in
the evenings. It was more like an artists' and scholars' club than

an apothecary's shop. It was said that the master of ceremonies, Giovanni Vincenzo Pinelli, possessed the most wonderful library in all Europe. He led discussions whose freedom of speech and thought were incredible. When he died suddenly, the entire city grieved for him. In the Italy of that time, which pursued heresy everywhere, Padua was an island of tolerance; any re-examination of the past was there greeted with jubilation, seized upon, bandied about, fêted; we exulted in the fact that we were living in the place where ideas were born, ideas which tomorrow would change the face of the world. It was in vain that the Jesuits had built a College to compete with our University in an effort to subdue the unruly city; its only effect was to exacerbate our horror of interdicts and our delight in our continuing evasion of the traditional paths. Padua, the thinking city of the Republic of Venice, was the most civilised place in the whole of Europe, by which I mean the most fecund womb for a new science. A little, no doubt, like Athens in the century of Pericles. Athens had transmitted the message to Rome; the Roman Empire, when it disintegrated, had allowed it to become extinguished. Then the Renaissance took up the torch anew, and Venice, fertilised both by the rest of the peninsula and by oriental Byzantium, had become the birth-place of a new scientific civilisation.

Strange dance of the living springs of science, unexpected errancy of the climates of discovery: why those hiatuses and those renaissances, those zigzag journeys of the centres of knowledge, that flame which becomes extinguished in one part of the world only to be re-kindled in another? No doubt the geography of the sciences simply follows in the wake of the wisdom of governments. Athens dies because the men who govern her do not know how to protect her from the Goths, the Heruli, the Normans and the Turks. Padua flourishes because the Doges of Venice have known how to preserve her from the desire of both East and West to conquer her; the Doges have even realised that both prosperity and peace are better defended by the glory of universities than by the force of arms. May my country learn this lesson, instead of wasting her time in fratricidal quarrels.

This wisdom bears fruit, and it is fruit that later tends to self-propagation. A centre of excellent men attracts other men naturally, and these, through association with the first, in their turn develop the taste for research and the ability to pursue it. One man's intellect fertilises those of other men. What a happy time that was, in Padua, when I had the good fortune to live in the midst of illustrious scientists and acute minds. What an invaluable influence was exercised over me by famous professors like my beloved master Fabricius of Aquapendente. He was already nearly seventy years old, but his ardour was still youthful. It was an experience to hear him describe how he had discovered the valves in the veins, which, in the interior of these vessels, seemed to prevent the blood from travelling to the extremity of the limbs. He had not yet published the little work in which he described these valvules. If I had remained in England, if I had not heard my beloved Fabricius speak of them at such length, I should have missed an essential pawn on the chessboard of my researches. At the same period, Fabricius unwittingly stimulated the spirit of contradiction in me, for he explained his own discovery to us and then interpreted it in defiance of all common sense. It must be said that Aristotle and Galen, and after them all the anatomists, had declared that the blood went to the extremities and did not return; the blood stream descended in the veins to the hands and feet and led the vital spirits to them; the whole of medicine was founded on this irreversible system; to overthrow its image was to annihilate a dogma basic to the development of medicine. And there was Fabricius, observing with his own eyes the valves that exist in order to impede the traditional direction of the movement of the blood; he had before him the obvious proof that an error had been committed over twenty centuries; he had within his grasp the chance to understand at long last how the blood circulates; but the ascendancy of the millenary tradition was too great; he hesitated before the enormity of the overthrowal; he strove in vain to discover—strange enterprise!—how the blood is able to pass through the natural obstacle that Nature opposes to it. He was to leave to me the great good fortune of being the first to discover the truth.

Towards the end of my stay in Padua, I was convinced that the enigma of blood circulation would be one of my main concerns. I began work on the project that was to occupy my life for twenty years: first, to make enough observations and experiments to find the actual movements of the blood in the vessels; and then, going farther, to discover the whole circuit of the blood and how it manages to refresh and renew itself, in order to irrigate each of our tissues and impart its vigour to them.

It was also at Padua that I saw the first demonstration that the venous blood does indeed travel from the extremities towards the heart, and not the reverse. I no longer remember the name of the student who, that evening, repeated on himself the experiment with the tourniquet which had been demonstrated in the Anatomy Amphitheatre that morning. He took off his belt and, using it as a ligature, wound it round his right arm. Immediately, the veins under the strap began to swell. This is what the physician does, before bleeding his patient, when he wishes to provoke a swelling in the veins in which he is about to plunge his lancet. I very quickly understood that the blood then exerted pressure on the veins and dilated them, for the simple reason that an obstacle had been placed in the way of its return route. And yet, our masters misunderstood this evidence: they declared that the swelling was a sign of irritation, a sort of vital rage on the part of the strangled tissues. What nonsense! Someone present told me that an anatomist in Rome, Andrea Cesalpino, drew the same conclusion as I from this experiment with the tourniquet; this comforted me.

I went back into the monk's cell that served as a bedroom. I appreciate solitude after an encounter. My rebellious spirit can only prosper in solitude. That is where I forge my weapons, where I imagine the probatory experiment. It was to be the observation of animals, rather than of man, that was to enlighten me about the circulation of the blood. From this period of my existence on, animals fascinated me, and I was sure that the study of small animals would teach me more about the secrets of life than the study of man. Alas, the anti-Royalists, who pillaged my Whitehall apartment last year, blindly destroyed all my notes on insects. All I have left are my documents on birds and I want, before I die, to assemble and publish my observations in order to contradict, politely but firmly, the posthumous work by Fabricius of Aquapendente, *The Formation of the Egg and of the Hen*.

Although apparently so remote from man, the bird has guided me in my knowledge of man. I love the bird, the conqueror of the air as well as of the earth and the seas. I remember long waits on the banks of a lagoon in the Venetian hinterland, a few leagues from Padua, in order to have the pleasure of seeing the blackish-brown curlews and the bluish grebes alight and take wing one after the other. One spring morning I had taken up my position at the water's edge, motionless, hidden by the tail stems of the rushes. Two buzzards were playing in the sky, seeking out invisible air currents to bear them along, and then allowing themselves to glide, like great, supple, inert objects, with an extraordinary economy of movement. Suddenly, from the south, a flight of purple herons came into view. There were several hundred of them. The whole formed a kind of aerial veil, at the same time very white and very colourful, each bird's outstretched body directed upwards in a northerly direction. Undoubtedly united by mysterious signs, the group traced the ideal lines of its journey against the blue background. I told myself that I had before me the image of the perfection which life can attain. Each of these birds was admirable. I felt exalted by such perfection. Birds are like messengers showing the way to a heaven that man cannot attain, but towards which he sometimes imagines that he in his turn will take wing after death, searching for terrible or marvellous places.

15 April 1647

The agitation of the present time oppresses me, I shall need courage to succeed in my project and organise my memories. Too many people know of my attachment to the King. Until he has recovered his lost sovereignty, I shall be like an outlaw in my own country.

It seems to me that, behind all the puppets in Parliament and the Army who are threatening King Charles, one single man is pulling the strings and calling the tune: General Oliver Cromwell. My feeling towards him is one of the strongest antipathy. He has the red face of the coarse-spoken boor, which as I see it is the exact opposite of the King's countenance. Just as Charles's noble features radiate honesty and discretion, so Mr Cromwell's appearance betrays boorishness, rigidity and ignorance. Alas, narrow-minded men are often conquerors, if they only have enough egotism and ambition; whereas those who, like the King, combine timidity and hesitation with their occasional demonstrations of strength, are only too likely to get the worst of it, to the great misfortune of the people. Thus in former days Caius Marius, a slow-witted but ambitious general, succeeded in plunging Rome into the bloodbath of civil war and in nullifying all the good works of the moderate rulers who had preceded him at the head of Roman society. A nation runs a great risk if it entrusts its destiny to a petty-minded, ambitious man, and it is our ill-fortune that such men of ambition often possess a force of attraction that wins them the favour of the common herd. A perfectly healthy nervous equilibrium does not facilitate the acquisition of power; for that, a more unusual temperament is necessary. All the world's ordeals, all the wars, all the miseries of the people may perhaps stem from the strange force that favours certain intemperate men but is lacking in those who are wise and well balanced. I fear for England, my beloved country, for I do not believe that Mr Cromwell's mind works normally.

My London colleague, Theodore de Mayerne, told me that Cromwell consulted him some years ago. He diagnosed a state of melancholy. His patient informed him that he was subject to strange hallucinations. In his youth, in Huntington, he had sometimes sent for his doctor in the middle of the night because he had had a vision of biblical personages who had come to announce his imminent death.

"This distressing temperament," Sir Theodore told me, "was inherited from his ancestors. His grandfather was so mentally unbalanced that, when he lost his wife from a decline, he accused a whole family of having caused her decease through practising witchcraft from a distance, and had them all tortured and put to death in public."

Bring up a child in the midst of such obscurantism, and you make of him a man prepared to become a passionate adherent of the most fanatic sect or the most intolerant religious faith. Mr Cromwell, with his simple, rustic mind, was pre-disposed to embrace Puritanism. I detest that particular fanaticism. It seems to me that for the last century my country has been following the path of wisdom in the matter of Christian faith. Anglican England allies the reconquest of a certain purity, which Catholicism has lost, with the tolerance refused by the Calvinist Protestants. And now, today, Calvin is contaminating England. Does a more inhumane doctrine exist, though? To declare that each of us is pre-destined, some to salvation and others to damnation; to say that everything has been won or lost from the moment of our arrival on earth; that it avails nothing to be an honest man or a brigand, charitable or evil-minded, generous or miserly, chaste or debauched; to accept, in short, that God represents a mere blind fatality—this, to me, is truly immoral. How is it that Cromwell and other English Puritans have been seduced by such immorality? Is it the blinding fascination of despotic disciplines? Is it a taste for the whip and for martyrdom? We doctors are well aware that the hair-shirt provokes unwholesome joys, under the pretext of mortification. It is possible that Puritanism subjugates by the same combination of suffering, humility and mortification. Perhaps Mr Cromwell derives pleasure from his Puritanism?

But mischief-makers suggest that he has many other reasons for calling himself a Puritan and arraigning our Kings for indulgence towards the Church of Rome. It is a fact that all the domains given by Henry VIII to the Cromwells, and which were the foundation of their fortune, had just been confiscated from the Papists. What would happen if, by chance, the Queen, who has remained a Catholic, were to manage to persuade His Majesty to revoke the edict ordering the despoliation of the Roman Catholic priests? The Cromwell tribe would lose all its property at one stroke. I leave these perverse insinuations to the mischief-makers. Interpreting political calculations has never been my strong point. I abandon this game to the professional historians. My natural tendency is to credit every man with sincerity. Moreover, it seems to me that men are almost always more sincere than is generally believed. But the sincerity of some men incites them to attack others, and I cannot forgive Oliver Cromwell for fighting against my King. For England's sake, may he lose this detestable combat. May all the world's madmen lose the desire and the power to take over the governance of nations, which they do to the great misfortune and impotence of reasonable men.

The Ten Plagues of Egypt were all sorts of ulcers, feverish swellings, epidemics, with locusts into the bargain. The plagues of our time are intolerance and prejudice. The religious believer is not their only victim. Science and medicine also find them their principal obstacle. Young John Milton (who, I am told, alas embraces Cromwell's cause) sent me his *Areopagitica* three years ago. In this work he recounts his visit to Arcetri, in Italy, where the aged Galileo had been assigned forced residence by the Inquisition "for thinking in Astronomy," writes Milton, "otherwise than the Franciscan and Dominican licencers thought." It is now five years since Galileo died in Arcetri. But I remember him as if it were yesterday. He was thirty-six years old and I was twenty-two. I was a timid young student, and he was already an admired master. For nearly ten years he had occupied the chair of Astronomy at the University of Padua, where I had just arrived. The students praised him to the skies. At that period he was still teaching that the sun and stars revolved round the earth. All the professors of Astronomy did the same. The earth was the centre of the world, because the whole of Antiquity had so decided. Ptolemy had confirmed it, in the reign of Antoninus Pius, in his *Mathematica syntaxis*. Respect for the Ancients allowed of no doubt on the subject. Today, alas, the fear of new discoveries has become an article of faith; religion has become involved, and intolerance hinders the search for truth. Rome transforms a doubt into a crime. The very same year that I arrived in Padua, the Dominican Giordano Bruno was burnt alive by order of the Holy Office, for having dared to call into question, in his work *Del infinito, universo e mondi*, the Ptolemaic system of astronomy. But, as far back as that year, I foresaw that Galileo would not allow himself to be intimidated. He already had the audacity to teach that Aristotle had understood nothing about the laws of falling bodies. Already, I am quite sure, he no longer believed that the earth was the centre of the world, even if he had some hesitation in announcing it publicly. Some of the students called him bizarre, others judged him imprudent, and yet others admired his freedom of thought.

For my part, the rumours I heard of this agitation only increased my certainty that the Aristotles and Galens of this world are not always right, and that doubt is the most important quality a scientist can possess. Excessive respect for the Ancients seems to me to be disrespect. For what is the lesson we learn from the Ancients? What do they teach us, if not that we must dare to have new ideas? They themselves would never have done anything worthy of admiration if they had restricted themselves to copying their predecessors. Men form a long chain of generations, they build up our knowledge of Nature throughout the centuries; this chain must not be broken, it is senseless to stop short once and for all at the knowledge acquired by the ancient seekers. If they were to come back to life, they would be the first to accuse of stupidity those who refuse to go farther than they did. This is perhaps the most striking thing I learnt at Padua. It is true that Padua is part of the Republic of Venice, one of the rare places in the world where new ideas and other men's thought are tolerated. Whereas Rome's intolerance condemned Galileo without even being prepared to listen to his truth, or examine his proofs.

My own researches have not escaped the rule. I have experienced all the honours of an intolerant criticism. In England, thank God, they do not burn scholars for their writings. But on the day of publication of my *Movement of the Heart and Blood in Animals,* a work that demolished the image Galen had presented and for the first time demonstrated the true paths of the blood and the true function of the heart, on that day I too raised a storm. When I look back on my life, I tell myself that it has been a never-ending struggle against fanatical traditionalism. If the great Galen fifteen centuries ago said that the blood does not circulate and if that is what everyone has been teaching ever since, it cannot be false. So many eminent personages cannot all be wrong. You are showing signs of a mutinous spirit, William, in daring to rebel against such respectable authorities. You say you have proof? Are not a reading of the classical texts, and correct reasoning, worth all the proofs in the world?

Am I wrong to ironise? Am I exaggerating? Come now! Did not my illustrious London colleague James Primrose, that perfect imbecile, write to me one day: "Are you claiming to know what Aristotle was unaware of? Aristotle observed everything, and none of his successors should dare to challenge him."

Unfortunately, I *have* dared to challenge all those wonderful people. Because experiment has contradicted the ideas they passed down to us. Because I believe more in observed facts than in systems born of the imagination and of "correct" reasoning. Nevertheless, in order to brave the storm, I should have been possessed of a combative spirit that cares nothing for lying critics, that knows how to fight on equal terms. Now it is obvious that I do not possess that gift. In physical exercises, when I was young, I was quite aggressive (perhaps because I was of small stature and wished to compensate for it by being great in courage and strength). But in the exercises of the mind, I cannot become accustomed to open warfare. I prefer to try to convince, sometimes even flavouring my arguments in cowardly fashion with excessive compliments to my contradictor. In Paris, Jean Riolan is still maintaining that I am completely misguided: I have decided to reply to him one day soon. Given what I know of his multiple errors, I should easily be able to make a fool of him. The fact remains, however, that in spite of his stupid blindness Riolan is illustrious from one end of Europe to the other, and I am certain in advance that my letter will be full of honey rather than of the vinegar it ought contain. I shall never rid myself of my foolish hope that gentleness may win the assent of the stupid and self-satisfied, although I would do better to tell them quite bluntly what I think of them.

28 April 1647

Of the King, of what he is doing, of what he is thinking, I no longer have any certain knowledge. They say that he is treated with respect at Holdenby House; he reads, writes, goes for walks and plays chess. But none of his friends is allowed to see him, his chaplains have been kept from him, his liberty is under constant surveillance. The sole reason for hope is that this situation is still dragging on: the King has been at Holdenby for more than two months, and the Parliamentarians do not show any signs of wishing to take possession of his person. Parliament is surely not unanimous about the decisions to be taken. Cromwell does not yet have the Commons under his heel, and the House of Lords does not much care for him. I wonder whether they will dare ignore the feelings of the inhabitants of this Kingdom: the people have never rejected their King, and remain greatly attached to him.

My powerlessness to intervene in the matter weighs heavily upon me. I have no difficulty in divining Charles's bitter meditations at Holdenby. I imagine him, in his solitude, perceiving at the same time the responsibility he accepted when England was entrusted to him, and the impediments which today prevent him from pursuing this great enterprise. His enemies array him in the garments of a tyrant, whereas he has never turned his thoughts to anything but England, never to himself. His mean-minded adversaries refuse to allow that a man may be generous by sole virtue of the functions with which he is invested. His monarchical attire forbids him any concern for his own person. His crown

requires honour and probity of him. This inner force, which in-
sists that *mission oblige,* is something I have myself experienced
in many circumstances in the modest course of my own life.
Every time I have been given a responsibility, it has divested me
of a little of my egoism, it has left me no other alternative than
to fight for my new purpose.

I remember the first investiture of my youth. I had been no
more than a few months at Padua when, on August 1st, 1600, I
was elected *Consiliarius*—councillor for the English Nation at
the University. In those days, each group of foreign students was
called a "Nation"; ours consisted of some fifteen Englishmen,
almost all of them, like me, members of the poorer division of
the University, that of the Arts, in which theology, medicine and
philosophy were taught. The other division was the law school,
aristocratic, rich and powerful. It was called the Jurist University. Now the Jurists voted for me, and I became the councillor
for the two Universities, the sole representative of England. All
the councillors were students. A university run by students
would have been inconceivable in England. Both Oxford and
Cambridge, like Paris, were "Magistral" universities, under the
sole authority of their masters and ancients. But at Padua, everything was always different.

My nomination had filled me with somewhat naive pride. But
I soon became aware of the responsibilities attached to my new
position. From the age of ten, from the time when England had
defeated the Invincible Spanish Armada, my father never
stopped telling me that we belonged to the most powerful country in the world. England, at all events—or so I believed at the
time—was the country of wisdom and of attachment to concrete realities; a country that preferred experiment to the *a
priori,* and evidence to dreams; a country that fought against
every Utopia that sought to overwhelm men. If Sir Thomas
More was beheaded, it was perhaps because he had had the te-
merity to give the title of *Utopia* to his pamphlet on the political
manners of the time (although the real reason he was put to
death was because he dared oppose Henry VIII's repudiation of
Catherine of Aragon). In short, I believed England to be one of
the nations most necessary to the equilibrium of the world. This
was the nation I was representing, and I represented it within

the bosom of an advanced and innovatory international society, the University of Padua. At each meeting of the councillors, I felt as if I were enclosed within the gravity of my mission, I no longer reasoned like the everyday William Harvey, I became another, whose mandate was to speak for every Englishman worthy of the name.

At the beginning of October in the same year I took part in the ceremony of the installation of the new Rector, who had just been elected by the councillors, with the aid of the preceding Rectors and some delegates from the various disciplines. The rite impressed me profoundly. We were in the magnificent cathedral, whose plans had been designed by the celebrated Michelangelo Buonarroti and which had just been completed. The whole University was present. There were certainly more than a thousand students present, crowded together like customers round a market stall. We councillors, enveloped in ample, dark-coloured *farraioli,* had the right to sit in the front rows. I watched a solemn doctor place the Rectoral cap on the head of a newly elected candidate, while an invisible choir sang declamatory motets. Then came the valedictory *mêlée.* For the first time I was present at the strange spectacle of the *vestium laceratio,* which consisted of the students rushing upon the new Rector and tearing off fragments of his robe. According to tradition, the Rector was required to distribute silver coins on all sides to prevent his toga from being entirely torn to pieces. But I believe that the custom is charged with another meaning. It signifies that it is not to the robe or to the function that respect is due but only to the man, if he later proves himself worthy of it. This is the classical *caveant consules* of the Roman Senate: "We appoint you Consul, but woe betide you should Rome suffer through your fault."

To conclude, the Rector invited as many people as possible to his house, where they were greeted by long tables covered with flasks of wine, plates of poultry, hams and fruits. My comrades continued their shouting and turbulence even in the midst of all this magnificence.

Two years later, I again encountered the same predilection for pomp and ceremony when, on April 25th, 1602, I received the Paduan diploma. It was in the great hall of the University

Council, which is decorated with mural paintings that resemble frescoes by Giotto. Between the frescoes, tall niches in the walls contain marble busts of illustrious men, most of whom were unknown to me. On a rostrum, a long table was covered with a red velvet, gold-embroidered cloth. Behind the table, dressed in great black robes, ermine cloaks thrown over their shoulders, ornamented caps on their heads, seven personages were enthroned in majestic, high-backed armchairs. In the centre was Sigismund de Capilisti, Count Palatine, representing the Most Serene Republic of Venice, and delegated by the Doge to sign the diplomas of the new doctors. Around him sat the Syndic of Brescia; the Notary Public of Padua; Georgius Raguseus, Professor of Philosophy; and my two masters of anatomy and surgery, Julius Casserius of Piacenza and my beloved Fabricius of Aquapendente. Their gravity showed clearly that this was a considerable event. The seventh man, whose name was Johannes Thomas Minadous, and whom I scarcely knew, was in charge of the ceremony. He stood up and asked me to approach. I then mounted the rostrum.

"The moment has come, William Harvey, for you to pronounce your request."

I knew what I had to answer:

"I present as a humble petition the desire to receive the diploma of the Doctor of the University of Padua and I swear that, in accepting this diploma, I will make the just use of it that my masters have taught me."

Then Johannes Thomas Minadous made an oration which demonstrated that I had been a most remarkable pupil (I knew that the formula was identical for every new recipient of a diploma), he gave me the accolade, pinned onto my chest the Doctor's insignia, which he had taken out of a jewel case, and then handed me several books on philosophy and medicine which he had taken from the table. According to the rite, the books were closed when they were given to me, but I had to return them at once, and they were immediately given back to me, open. Finally, Minadous put a golden ring on my finger, placed the Doctor's cap on my head, declared that it was a crown of virtue, and, to complete the ceremony, made a sweeping gesture resembling a benediction. Behind me, the whole assembly rose to its feet and applauded at length.

Hieratical acts and customs. Man needs rites as he needs bread. What is this craving for ceremonial but the desire to conceal one's nudity? Empty lives, lives of uncertain appeal, surround themselves with glittering ostentation, as the bird displays in the mating season. No doctor should allow himself to be deceived by it. The body is naked under the habit, and the flesh is perishable on the bones. The Bible says it, but the doctor sees it. All the ritual in the world cannot efface the image of the skeleton hidden under the *toga praetexta* or the *toga virilis*. My eyes will never forget Fabricius' Anatomy Theatre: at the bottom of the five circular tiers, on the central dissecting table, a corpse, the anatomical model, showed us all what becomes of a man at the end of his earthly history.

29 April 1647

England is inundated with pamphlets, almost all of them circulated by that band of revolutionaries the people call the Levellers. The Levellers want to level everything, and not allow anyone to own more property than his neighbour, to have more power, more knowledge, or more capacity for thought. They dream of a world where everyone would command, and no one would be obliged to obey.

A few months ago an unknown person left at my address the lampoon by a certain Overton: *A Remonstrance of Many Thousand Citizens and Other Freeborn People of England to Their Own House of Commons*. It contained affirmations of this order: "Our nation has not ceased to be kept in slavery by the force of the officers who are the repositories of our mandate— the King being foremost among them." Was it the same unknown person who yesterday left at my address another pamphlet of more than one hundred pages, which was even more virulent? The title, spread over the whole of the first page, begins with: "The Royal Tyranny Unmasked," and the inflammatory text continues: "After William the Invader, robber and tyrant, alias the Conqueror, the present King, Charles Stuart, deserves a more severe punishment than that suffered by the dethroned Plantagenets." These pamphlets spare no one; Parliament is indicted, the Presbyterian party insulted, the House of Lords condemned, and the whole is mingled with frenzied considerations about Adam and Eve, the prophet Hosea, and other biblical personages. The author, a certain Lilburne, known as "Freeborn

John," declares with great simplicity that he has a secret agreement with God. In the England of today God is pulled hither and thither, and every man seizes hold of him to call him to witness.

I find it difficult to tolerate these revolutionaries, their scurrilous pamphlets disgust me, they are a menace to my King. At the same time, I make an effort to understand them. What is a doctor, if not a man who tries to understand others? Behind the cries of the Levellers there is, I know, the wretchedness of the people, the same wretchedness that horrified me when I was first admitted to office at the hospital. That is something like forty years ago.

I had perhaps been near the image of poverty in the streets of my childhood in Folkestone or, later, in the streets of London, but I had not seen it. One does not see everything that is before one's eyes. My father and brothers, being men of business, had accustomed me to a life of ease, and ease is an effective rampart against the sight of other people's misery, in much the same way as fog blurs passing silhouettes. Misery only really impinged on me on that day in 1609 when, having been appointed Physician to St Bartholomew's Hospital, I entered the Great Hall where the consultations took place. According to the Charter of the hospital, not only the destitute sick were to be admitted but also every man or woman who was without food or lodging. Some eight or ten beadles were commissioned to scour the streets of the city and to bring in every vagabond wandering abroad with neither hearth nor home and who could not give proof of some means of existence. In the main, it was the old they brought us. A band of ragged unfortunates, either resigned or aggressive. And then there were the sick, who came either on their own or dragged along by their lamenting family. Every kind of disease or wound. On some faces I could divine impending death. But the Charter forbade us to keep the incurable, the beds were reserved for those whom I declared curable, and sometimes I hesitated.

It was probably at that time that I first experienced a feeling of revulsion against the injustice of poverty and sickness. Were I not sure that we must believe in God, I told myself, I would doubt his goodness. He commands us to be charitable, but what about him? There were occasions when I could not understand why so many men still had to pay so dearly for original sin. Seventeen centuries after an astonishing attempt at redemption. And, furthermore, the price to be paid differs greatly from one man to another. These heretical ideas remained fleeting, however. Long-drawn-out spiritual anxiety is not my strong point. But I found it well-nigh intolerable to have to send a young incurable home; I found it well-nigh intolerable that one of two children lying side by side in the same bed should die in spite of all our efforts, and that the other should leave the hospital ward cured.

Until that time, it had been curiosity that inspired me with the desire to understand man's body and diseases. But that curiosity was now strengthened by a feeling of responsibility. My life would only acquire meaning if I managed to become an actor in the progress of medical knowledge. Some physicians must do more than apply received ideas; they must harness themselves to imaginative research, and seek new human weapons against the injustice meted out to man.

I often reflected on the role I might be able to play in this matter. I wished to be a man of observation. Frightened by abstract theoreticians, attracted by the direct lessons to be learnt from a look, a touch, and patience, I knew that if I were to produce any enduring work it would be that of a naturalist, of an observer of Nature, that is, who had no desire to rush towards premature conclusions. I was convinced that in order to understand the mechanisms of disease it was first necessary to understand the mechanisms of normal functioning. I was also convinced that the complex beings that we humans are would be more easily decipherable if I were to examine the simpler animals first. I had transformed a room in my house into a kind of laboratory; there, I had a basin full of water in which I kept a few eels, those viscous fish with elongated, serpent-like bodies that English housewives cook or smoke and serve as a delicacy.

The heart of an eel seemed to me to be far simpler to study than the heart of a man. It contains only one ventricle instead of two. Once I had opened the eel, I could extract its still-beating heart, examine it, palpate it, and watch it live for a few more instants before it stopped for good. I saw this heart contract like a muscle, it hardened rhythmically, and, with each of its contractions, I saw it get whiter, because it was emptying itself of its blood. Whereas, ever since Galen, everyone had declared that the heart is only active when attracting the blood by its vacuity, I clearly perceived that the opposite is the case: the heart is active in the movement by which it expels the blood, through the stiffening of its muscular wall which contracts and lengthens its central cavity. It is inactive in the following phase, when it is passively allowing itself to be filled with blood. Later, I was to verify that this is indeed the action of the heart, not only in cold-blooded animals such as eels, serpents and frogs, but also in warm-blooded animals and in man. One image remains with me, which I recorded in my 1628 book: it is that of the heart of a dove which had ceased to beat. However, having moistened my finger with saliva, I applied it to the heart. This gentle warmth appeared to restore its strength and its life, which was on the point of becoming extinguished. And I saw the heart contract, and relax, and exercise the same expulsion of blood that I had contemplated in my eel's heart.

What the examination of the heart had shown me was confirmed in succeeding weeks by the observations of the arteries. It so happened that the hospital had admitted an individual whose neck was deformed, on the right side, by an enormous, pulsatile tumour, beating and swelling in time with the heart. I had no difficulty in recognising that it was a question of one of those dilations of the artery that have been given the name of *aneurysms*. Now this aneurysm became distended immediately after each beat of the heart against the chest, which is to say after the cardiac contraction. It was clear that each of these contractions injected blood into the dilated artery. And the certainty that this spurt of blood did indeed travel from the heart to the aneurysm, and not the contrary, seemed to me to be reinforced when I observed that the arterial pulse was only barely perceptible at the wrist: obviously, the large dilation of the artery broke the force of the blood spurt, which was then in a much weakened state when it reached the arterial segments situated below the aneurysm.

Returning to the vivisection of fish, I made a tiny incision in one, thus opening the blood channel that links the heart to the lungs, and I saw that with each contraction of the heart the blood gushed out of the wound. Even if one confines oneself to looking at the arteries without injuring them, they are seen to dilate at the moment of the cardiac contraction. Those who uphold the traditional teaching maintain the contrary, thereby betraying the ancient concepts. They have not read Aristotle with care; the master of the Peripatetics wrote that all the arteries dilate at the same time, because the vessels "are all subordinate to the heart," and because the impulse is transmitted everywhere, as the impulse is transmitted when one strikes a drum or the extremity of a long beam. So he had already understood, not the correct manner in which the blood circulates, but the fact that it is the heart that commands, and the blood flow in the arteries that obeys. For my part, I have preferred in my book to give the image of a man playing the bagpipes, for the heart blows the blood into the arteries as the piper blows the air into his instrument's leather bag and thus dilates it.

2 May 1647

A year ago today, my wife Elizabeth died. Silent, unobtrusive, always concerned to ensure that nothing should cause me disquiet; I watched her move from one room to another like a delicate shadow wishing to be unobserved. And yet I miss her transparent presence perhaps even more than I would had she been one of those bustling, noisy women with whom so many of my colleagues are encumbered. In Elizabeth's gaze I perceived a confident, gentle submission, which sometimes caused me a kind of remorse: I told myself that the life of a physician ought to impose celibacy. She was often alone, and I sometimes thought she seemed sad, in this house where no child had been born. She had desired the presence of a pet bird, a brightly coloured parrot, on which she lavished tender, child-like care. Elizabeth was a child-woman, but the almost over-respectful attachment she showed me for forty years was a source of happiness to me, and of strength on the days of discouragement. Her very weakness obliged me to be robust. Weak women, and they are legion, condemn men to become strong.

I think I have never really understood women. All I know is that they are assuredly very different from us. Men attempt to adapt their lives to their ambitions; women try to adapt themselves to the life they encounter. They espouse circumstances as the octopus espouses its prey. Even our Queens differ from our Kings by this trait. During my childhood I was always hearing everyone speak with admiration of our Queen Elizabeth. This Queen must certainly be counted amongst our greatest sovereigns. I remember that the Venetians, in Padua, used to tell me that she had transformed a small European island into the greatest country in the world. They jested that Pope Sixtus V, who died a few years before I arrived in Italy, declared that only three personages had been worthy of reigning: himself, Henry IV of Navarre, and Elizabeth of England. He added that he would have given a great deal to be able to spend a night with her, for he was sure that it would have resulted in the birth of a new Alexander the Great. Now what I understand about this great Queen is that she had the gift of adapting herself flexibly to circumstances, she yielded to events in order to dominate them, employing finesse and ruse rather than the conquering violence that is the usual mark of sovereigns.

Such is woman, both in the most elevated conditions and in the modest position of a loving spouse. And that is why women have always inspired me with a measure of fear; I did not flee them, but I have never approached them without remaining on my guard. I am certainly not the only man to experience this ambiguity, and consequently to entertain extreme feelings for women, from passionate love to indifference, and from indifference to hate. Three years ago I was taken to the Globe Theatre to see *The Taming of the Shrew,* which Mr Shakespeare had written fifty years earlier; all the men in the audience looked delighted every time the shrew was being disciplined, and the final declamatory speech, on the wife's duty of blind obedience to her husband, was greeted with cheers such as I had never heard at any spectacle.

Nevertheless, I have more than once thought that woman could surpass man, in the glory of the human species. I have assisted many women in childbirth in my life. Every time, although I gave no sign of it, I experienced the most lively emotion mingled with respect. At first, as a sort of prologue, one is confronted with the surprising sight of that child's head emerging from the parted thighs of the screaming woman. It is bald, dented, shiny with foul, dripping matter, but the miracle is there. A new being, a new generation, is about to be born from this obese stomach, as the fledgling emerges from the egg. A new life is beginning under our eyes. The miracle of eternal renewal is in operation.

It is woman who is the priestess of this mystery; man is but a minor officiant, and I do not even know how his semen intervenes. For a physician, who lives continuously in the midst of births and deaths and who is thus haunted by the image of the endless chain that unites the ancestor to the newborn child, woman is more important than man in the game of our life. It is true that I am no doubt influenced by my observations of insects, among which the female is queen, while the husbands are often fleeting, insipid creatures.

My mother Joan believed in virtue. And for her, virtue and devotion were more or less identical. Every day, she prayed to God at great length, never for herself, always for her husband Thomas and for her children, to whom she had once and for all dedicated her life. She was twenty-two years old when I was born, and from that time on she gave birth to a son or a daughter every two or three years. At the age of forty, having brought nine children into the world, she stopped. She remained on this earth for another few years and then she died, the year after my admission to the College of Physicians of London. I can see her in the ceremonial dress she wore on feast days, a long dress in dark green silk, with puffed sleeves and a black guipure-lace collar, which seemed to be supporting her delicate face. Round her neck she wore the chased gold necklace my father had given her on the birth of Eliab. Towards the end of her life my mother had a few white hairs in the long, curled coiffure framing her face, but this greying seemed to me to add to the sweetness of her features. My mother never raised her voice; it seemed to be natural for the household to obey her tranquil wishes. For she had the tranquillity of a woman who is sure of her mission on this earth, the mission of maintaining order in the house of Thomas Harvey. My father left the problems of its stewardship to her. He devoted all his thoughts to his maritime business and to the many responsibilities he had accepted in the administration of the town of Folkestone and its associated Cinque Ports. She was well content with this, for she had an unfailing desire for success, not for herself—she must have had a horror of feminine ambition—but for her husband Thomas and then, successively, for each new Harvey her body brought into the world. Women are either all egotism or all altruism. There is no middle way. My mother was a fanatical altruist. This she no doubt was for her own pleasure; it was vitally necessary to her that my father and my brothers should all occupy a high and worthy place in British society, and she was always full of plans for each one separately.

When she became aware that I was attracted to medicine and the sciences, she felt great pride. She considered the role of the physician to be inferior to that of the priest, but nevertheless to resemble it to some extent. She imagined me devoting my life to the poor as much as to the well-endowed, and this image fully satisfied the ideal of Christian morality that had taken total possession of her. I believe she had a special affection for me; mothers frequently have a weakness for their eldest son. I was not officially charged with caring for the poor, at St Bartholomew's, until four years after her death, and I felt sad when I thought she had not lived to see an event that would have fulfilled her expectations.

Mothers and wives are the same women; why is it that mothers have a better reputation than wives? My wife Elizabeth was perfect in all respects; it is probable that she was an exception. My mother was admirable; it is probable that she was within the norm.

I am thinking of another woman, Henrietta Maria, Queen of England, today separated from our King, her husband. It is already two years since she embarked for France with her children, to escape the Civil War. I heard that her sister-in-law, Anne of Austria, installed Henrietta Maria at the castle in Saint-Germain. She lives there, surrounded by a small court which, I fear, passes its time in plotting rather than in aiding her. Many of my compatriots do not like our Queen. They will never forgive her her Catholic faith. And it is true that the fact of having brought a Catholic wife to England did not serve the cause of a Protestant King in these difficult times. But the truth is that it was not the Queen, it was the French clergy who created the trouble, ceaselessly trying to use her to undermine Anglican stability from within. She, vivacious, laughter-loving, frivolous perhaps, only half-understood the role they wished to make her play. But I know her well enough to forgive her her blind spots. I have a thousand proofs of her devotion to the King and her attachment to the grandeur of England. When the King sent her to Holland four years ago to bring back soldiers and money, she even pledged her jewellery to buy 40,000 mercenaries. Last year she sent from Paris the proceeds of the sale of her last diamonds, and part of the allowance made her by the French Court, doing everything in her power to support the King's cause. Could there be any more conspicuous sign of her loyalty? When the King was in Scotland, she probably displayed a great deal of finesse and ruse in counselling him to appear to yield to the Presbyterian pressure: had he followed this line of conduct, the situation would probably have been far better today and, with his sovereignty restored, the King would have had no difficulty in recreating an Anglican equilibrium to his own satisfaction. Women, who are supposed to be frivolous, are often shrewder than men, who are supposed to be politic.

5 May 1647

I have known men who had the character of a woman, and women whose nature was masculine. When James Stuart, son of Mary Queen of Scots and father of our present King, succeeded Elizabeth, it was whispered in the taverns that the feminine was succeeding the masculine. It was maintained that James had an unstable, capricious brain. I remember having been invited to Court in 1609, thanks to my brother John, who occupied the position of "foot-man" to the King. I watched James making a speech to a crowd of courtiers. He was agitated, garrulous, he stammered, he even slavered. His Scottish accent rendered his words even stranger. I can understand that some people found him ridiculous. Yet I will not speak ill of him: it was no doubt his letter of recommendation to the Court of Governors that enabled me to obtain the post of Physician to Saint Bartholomew's Hospital, where I spent my life. Later, in 1617, he renewed his confidence in me by appointing me his Physician Extraordinary. I am therefore grateful to him.

But gratitude does not necessitate admiration. There was at least one trait of character in King James that displeased me (and which is happily entirely absent in his son Charles): this was a naive faith in the power of witches, a morbid terror of demons. He had written a book on the subject which was published, I believe, in Edinburgh in 1597, but which I read only many years later, at the time of the Robinson affair. I was looking for enlightenment on English law as it applied to witchcraft, in order to accomplish in a fair manner the mission with which

King Charles had entrusted me in that business. I found a great
deal more in it; enough to leave one wide-eyed in amazement.

The work is entitled *Daemonologie, in Forme of a Dialogue.*
The King was indignant at the blindness of Reginald Scott who,
in his book *A Discovery of Witchcraft,* had dared to cast doubt
on demonic powers, spells and other malefices. This incredulity,
the King wrote, is culpable, it constitutes an obstacle to the protection of the English people against witches, it prevents witches
from being put in a position where they can do no more harm.
Next, James wondered whether English law clearly defined the
methods whereby a witch could be positively recognised, thus
avoiding the condemnation of innocent women wrongly accused of sorcery. In James's time, English law was the King, since
the King receives his power and his delegation directly from
God, as James himself had written in *The True Law of Free
Monarchies.* So James decreed that the evidence of women and
children must henceforth be accepted in cases of witchcraft,
since this evidence had long been admitted in treason trials, and
witchcraft is a form of treason. (This clause made me shudder,
because it was precisely the evidence of a child that was in question in the Robinson affair and because, as a doctor, I knew only
too well that children are very natural liars and inventors of
fables.) A suspected witch, he went on to say, must be examined
according to the rules of the art, the said rules, as everyone
knows, enabling this species to be positively identified. They all
have, and they are the only people to have, callous spots on the
skin or on the head (they must always be shaved, so that the
head should not be forgotten), and these callous spots are insensitive; this is easy to ascertain by pricking them with a pin. Also,
they have—and they are the only women to have—aberrant
teats, shaped like a toad or some other animal, with which they
may nourish their familiar demon who serves as their link with
Satan. The text added that those who are inhabited by the demon are always lighter than other people, and that this can easily be determined by plunging suspected women into a large
pond and watching them float. No error is therefore possible,
and to avoid all injustice the examination will thereafter be carried out not by a single judge, but by an assembly of witnesses
aided by one or several physicians.

On June 29th, 1634, I received a message from the Earl of
Manchester, Henry Montagu, the Lord Privy Seal, requiring me,
by order of the King, to form a jury of nine midwives and seven
court surgeons in order to examine several women accused of
witchcraft by an eleven-year-old boy, Edmund Robinson.

The events took place in Pendle Forest, in a remote area of
Lancashire. In the month of February of the previous year,
young Robinson had asked permission to make a deposition before two local Justices of the Peace. Having been out gathering
wild plums, he declared, he had seen two greyhounds running
up to him. Each dog was wearing a gold collar attached to a
leash, but there was no human being with them. He tried to
chase the two animals away but without success, so he began to
beat them with some branches. Whereupon one of the dogs
turned into an old woman, and the other into a white horse. In
his fright, Edmund attempted to flee, but was soon caught by
the woman, who hoisted him onto the horse and led him off into
a clearing well known as a habitual meeting place for witches.
Shortly thereafter, Edmund recounted, sixty persons with terrifying visages arrived on horses of all colours. Edmund managed
to escape. But that same evening, while he was taking the cows
back to their stalls, a boy threw himself on him and beat him
savagely, a boy *who had a cloven foot.* Luckily, Robinson's father came up. His weeping son told him the whole story, together with a thousand other details of which I now have no
recollection.

Edmund Robinson's father took him from church to church
in the district, declaring that his son had seen many witches at
close quarters and was prepared to identify them among the
congregations, against some slight recompense for his efforts. It
so happened that the curate of the church of Kildwick, to whom
Robinson proposed the services of his son, was none other than
David Webster, a shrewd priest who was at that very time studying the frauds and trickery perpetrated in witch-hunting. The
curate notified the bishop, the bishop confided in the Secretary
of State, and the Secretary of State reported the matter to King
Charles. And that was how the Secretary of State was instructed
to speak of it to me. In the meantime, of seven women imprisoned as a consequence of Edmund Robinson's accusations, three

had died in their cells even before their trial began. Four remained alive, whom I could perhaps save from death.

I assembled the midwives and surgeons who were to have the mission of examining them. I told them very bluntly what I thought of the insensate rules established by King James. I told them the story of Anne Gunter, who had claimed to be possessed of the Devil and whom King James had sent to the physicians of the College. The physicians had suggested that it was a case of simulation; they even used the recent term *a state of hysteria.* The King himself then interrogated the girl, and finally made her confess that she had only pretended to be bewitched in order to revenge herself on a woman whom she hated. I am well acquainted with these delusions of adolescent girls who are in desperate need of love but who may be cured by hymeneal exercises. And James must have suspected as much, for he gave Anne Gunter a dowry, whereupon she married and found herself miraculously cured. I therefore recommended the jury of midwives and surgeons to bear constantly in mind, in their examination of the accused, the possibility that they might be simulators or hysterics. My remarks must have been convincing because they found no unambiguous signs of witchcraft and the four women were acquitted. Later, young Edmund Robinson was taken to London and re-examined alone: he confessed that the whole affair had been staged by his father, who had taught him his role and told him that they would make a great deal of money out of it.

Mad women, lying children, avaricious men—we meet them all in the world of today. But these tares would not grow to be so hardy were it not for the immense credulity of our time. There is no such thing as solitary imposture. There must be at least two people for one to deceive the other. The spectator is as important as the actor. These days, however, the spectator is prepared to accept the most extravagant affirmations. He is attracted by miracles, captivated by the bizarre, fascinated by the supernatural. Without the Devil, without thaumaturges, without fortune-tellers, without the scent of the inexplicable, life would become as insipid as a dish without spice. The spectator needs to believe, he feels a void within him which must be filled with mysteries whatever the cost. His credulity is an invitation.

The imposter cannot resist the pleasure of answering it; he is excited by the game he is about to play, he is delighted to be trying his strength against the human imagination. The spell cast by his own ideas is so powerful that he is himself bewitched by it, he ends by believing his own words—if he has ever doubted them, that is—he is swollen with pride, and everyone is delighted with the show.

My doctor colleagues, men who are often as brilliant as their resources are fertile, are not the last to succumb to the temptation of the histrion. The celebrated Swiss physician, who liked to be known as Paracelsus but whose real name was Theophrastus Bombastus von Hohenheim, gained fame by asserting that the health of the body depends on the harmony between mercury, sulfur and salt. What on earth does that mean? A Belgian physician, Johann Baptist van Helmont, whose death I heard of three years ago, taught that every man possessed two magnetisms, the one drawn from his flesh and the other from his soul, the first in the service of the Devil and the second coming from God: if the physician refuses the Black Masses of the first, and on the contrary directs the vibrations of the second into the body of his patient, he becomes infallible. In my childhood, everyone also spoke of a French physician who won fame not, as one might have thought, by teaching therapeutics at Montpellier, but by claiming to possess the gift of prophecy; his reputation as an astrologer became so great that Catherine de' Medici summoned him to her Court. I read some of his prophecies, and they always seemed to me to be sufficiently incomprehensible for everyone to interpret them in any way he wished, according to the circumstances (although my poor knowledge of the French language may perhaps render me unjust). The glory of this physician seems not to have faded even today, for I sometimes still hear talk of him. His name, I believe, was Michel de Nostre-Dame, but he called himself Nostradamus, perhaps because that has a better ring for so famous an astrologer.

I should like to be able to write that charlatans are only to be found in Switzerland, Belgium, France and other meridional countries, and that England is protected by her common sense from these exploiters of credulity. Alas, I have many proofs to the contrary. A few days ago Sir Kenelm Digby, who has taken refuge in France to escape prosecution by the anti-Royalists, sent me a copy of a manuscript he intends to publish. In an extremely courteous letter, full of false modesty and florid compliments, he made a pretence of asking my opinion of his work. It is entitled *A Treatise of Adhering to God; Touching the Cure of Wounds by the Powder of Sympathy*. Sir Kenelm is a strange man. I knew him well at the court of King Charles, where he was a gentleman of the bedchamber. In 1628, in order to demonstrate his attachment to the King, he played at being a corsair, chartering at his own expense a fleet which went to fight for England in the Algerian and Venetian seas. He married a woman of extraordinary beauty, Venetia Stanley, and he was so madly enamoured of her that he decided to devote all his efforts to the study of methods to preserve feminine charms intact. A few years ago he sent me his book *Secret Experimentations to Preserve the Beauty of Ladies*. It was said that he forced the beautiful Venetia to eat nothing but capons fed on dead vipers. But he had no luck; his beautiful lady died in the prime of life.

In his recent manuscript on the "powder of sympathy," he claims that the secret of this remedy was revealed to him by a Florentine monk who had come from the Indies. The powder has a base of vitriol. He declares that it heals wounds even at a distance, and he explains this extraordinary effect by the subtle fire of light, which detaches the active atoms from his powder and transports them wherever they are required.

With my habitual cowardice, I have not yet replied to Sir Kenelm's communication; correspondence with France has become difficult for me, perhaps that is sufficient excuse. Were I to reply, I think I would not be able to conceal my anger. If miracle-makers wish to give free course to their imagination, I can do nothing to prevent them. But that they should have the audacity to ask the opinion of a man like me—this passes all bounds. I know very well what would happen were I to reply: the slightest conventional phrase would be taken to imply interest, and Digby would go about everywhere declaring: "My remedy fascinates William Harvey, he has written to tell me so." In Paris, so I have been told, he has become a friend of the illustrious René Descartes, a man who does not always reason as correctly as he believes he does, but who nevertheless quite often has lucid ideas. If Descartes is really a friend of Sir Kenelm, I hope he will be able to straighten out his ideas for him. People should be taught that what are called the occult sciences can in no way be immixed with the natural sciences: the first stem from fantasy, the second from experience. But the more fantastic an idea, the more it takes hold of the man who proclaims it, and once he has set it down in writing it is useless to hope to make him change his mind. The opposite is true of a man like me. For I am prepared without the slightest bitterness to change my conclusions the moment a verifiable contrary proof is put before me. In a few years' time, no doubt, people will ridicule our century, which still permits an ambiguous borderline between two such opposing attitudes of mind.

The task of the philosopher should be to distinguish true science from the false, magical, so-called sciences. I would wish philosophy to be the art of forging a suit of armour against credulity. Alas, the philosophers of today are themselves entangled in confusion and esotericism; they seem to be afraid of expressing themselves clearly and being universally understood, they seem incapable of simplicity, one could sometimes swear that they take a delight in being unintelligible. They seem to hope that genius will be attributed to them through their very obscurity. Fortunately, they are not all like that.

One of the joys of my life has been my friendship with a philosopher of a very different persuasion. This one does not seek the recondite. Credulity is not his strength. He even refuses to be influenced by others and endeavours to be totally free in his quest for the truth. He has the kind of qualities that fascinate the naturalist in me. He also fascinates me because he is one of those men who, throughout their lives, concentrate their every effort on one single subject: for him, a reflection upon the world. In order to devote himself more completely to this purpose, he even decided to remain a bachelor. Thomas Hobbes is ten years younger than I, but he surpasses me in mathematics, in classical culture, in politics, and in many other subjects. And yet he never parades his knowledge, he knows how to listen before speaking, he has a kind, indulgent gaze. My friendship for him is of a rare order, and is vivified by admiration. My sole regret is that I see

him only occasionally; I miss him, he travels continually outside
England. He is now in France, and I fear he may remain there
until our Civil War is ended. Never, however, has there been a
moment in our history when his political reflections would have
been of greater aid.

It was of politics that we spoke, the last time I saw him. He
told me:

"I have already told you of my great design, which is to deduce from natural philosophy the principles of a natural politics. The plan of the work I am now engaged on is in the form of
a triptych; the first volume of which will treat of the mechanics
of bodies, the second of human nature, and the last of the citizen. I wish these three parts to follow on the one from the other,
because the rules all citizens and governments must obey derive
ultimately from the natural laws which are obeyed by both inert
matter and living matter. But the present situation in England
alarms me to such a degree that, against all logic, I am going to
try to have the third volume published first, and I shall endeavour to introduce into it all the political wisdom we need."

"Do you mean that the political tradition of England dis-
pleases you?" I asked him. (At the time of this conversation, I
could not envisage any rebellion threatening King Charles. Royalty suited me, and it seemed to me that our King suited
England.) "I believed you to be an out-and-out Royalist, as I
believe you to be a Christian and an Anglican."

"That is more or less the case," Thomas replied. "The aim is
to achieve the perfect regulation of the machinery of the State
and of the people, whereas the passions of the citizen, his frus-
trations, his spiteful actions, tend to create total disorder. What
is necessary, therefore, is rational government, and this supreme
function can only be achieved by the absolute power of the sovereign. But if the monarch is incapable of being identified with
this supreme function, if for example he does not adequately
defend the life of the citizen, even though the protection of life
is the most important of the natural laws, then I recognise that
every man has an unqualified right to resistance."

While he was thus evoking the image of a King whose mission
it is to see that order and reason circulate among his subjects, I

do not know why another image was superimposed in my mind, that of a heart whose mission it is to circulate throughout the body the blood that bears the necessary spirits.

"As to calling me a Christian and an Anglican," Thomas added, "that is quite correct. There again, it is a way of seeking order."

"Christian because of a liking for order?"

"For me, religion has no other foundation than the laws of the country, which is ultimately to say the will of the Prince and of the people."

"I understand now how it is that certain ill-wishers accuse you of concealing a seditionmonger under your apparent defence of the King, and furthermore of being a votary of that accursed race they call atheists. Forgive me Thomas—I was jesting. But allow me to put to you the secret question I cannot wait to ask: Do you believe in God?"

"Do you?" Hobbes asked.

"Most certainly. Medicine monopolises me too much to allow me to devote time to metaphysical reflection, and I have not enough natural rebellion to cast doubt on what the majority of apparently sensible men believe. I deliberately lack any critical spirit in either religion or politics, and that is why I so appreciate the fact that men like you undertake that task for men like me."

Hobbes nodded. I admired his intelligent, massive, leonine face. He smoothed his moustache and scratched the little tip of a beard he has under his lip.

"I am no more interested than you," he finally said, "in the question of the existence of God. That is not my problem. I have already extricated myself from that business: I have written that I entirely follow the teaching of the Bible in so far as the origin of man is concerned. The object of my work is elsewhere. My problem begins after the world was created. I find in it a society made up of bizarre individuals, who are afraid of death, who seek every possible way to remain alive, who feel alone and miserable, and who greatly mistrust other men. My problem is to understand what part all this plays in the law of Nature, and to deduce therefrom the rules that would permit us to master such an intolerable situation. Whether or not God be the inventor of the system, he is not the centre of my preoccupations."

I told him that I had difficulty in following him. As a doctor, I had seen my unfortunate patients grappling with too violent a desire for God to be able to reduce him to the mere creator of a system. I saw man as being seized by a necessity for warmth, a need for protection, a need to flee the irrelevance of his life, a need to be relieved at all costs from the heavy weight of anguish. If he were to be refused God, that would still not remove his urgent desire to escape elsewhere, to believe in other dreams. It would leave him defenceless, in a position to be subjugated body and soul by the most aberrant temptations.

"The anguish of the fear of death," said Hobbes. "I remember watching you open the chest and belly of a stag that had just died. The heart was about to stop beating, though the intestines were still contracting in irregular peristaltic movements. When at last everything had become completely still, it seemed to me that I had just seen a beautiful machine come to a halt. That was what death was—that and nothing else. It takes men's imagination to build so many dreams about this reality, and anguish is their punishment. And you, my friend, who have so often encountered death and its agony, are you tormented by it?"

"I refuse to be. A certain underlying vein of cowardice is of great use to me when I am tempted to question myself about the end of life. I deliberately thrust the question aside. I leave it out of the field of my thought. It is my good fortune to have my time more fully occupied by my profession, which is the preservation of life and the attenuation of suffering."

"Perhaps I should have been a physician," said Thomas Hobbes.

11 May 1647

I can see nothing but fascination in combining medicine and philosophy, in mixing science with reflections upon the world. But the mind is continually going astray through giving way to fascination. I admire Plato and revere Aristotle, but if they are sometimes mistaken it is always because they claimed reality for ideas that were unsupported by fact. What do our present-day philosophers offer us, those whom I respect, such as Hobbes and Descartes, and those whom I like not at all, such as the man with the viper's eye, Sir Francis Bacon? Ideas, nothing but ideas, not the slightest fact. It may well be that nothing will remain of their philosophy if they do not base it on new observation. I let them reason, but I take seriously only those who reason from natural events properly observed. Facts first, ideas later. Original and reliable observations—they alone have any chance of surviving the death of the man who has discovered them. *William Harvey revealed to the world a reality of which the world was in ignorance, viz., that the blood circulates.* (This passage should be omitted from my memoirs, for it would make me appear pretentious and self-satisfied, which I am not. I am proud, which is very different.)

Aristotle is great. But, in his *Historia animalium,* he declares: "If one blows into the trachea, the air goes directly into the heart." He had read this in Hippocrates. Now it is known that Hippocrates never dissected a corpse: everything, therefore, came from his imagination. And yet Aristotle does not even take the trouble to verify whether the air really passes from the lungs into the heart. Everyone who came after him reasons according to the same image, and of course reasons erroneously, because the image is erroneous. As for Galen, he performed the experiment and saw with his own eyes that the heart does not receive air, it contains only blood. I have verified this many times. Aristotle's *a priori* idea has vanished; Galen's *a posteriori* affirmation will remain true for all time.

The imagination, then, is both the god and devil of the mind. The god, since one observes, verifies and discovers only after one has imagined. The eye takes notice only after preliminary interrogation; the physician experiments only after having asked himself questions. But the imagination is also the devil, and the demoniacal ruses of temptation: how can one resist the admirable construct of one's own mind, how can one not wish that what one has constructed should at all costs be true, how can one remain unbiased at the moment of the clash between one's own so comfortable idea and the stupid obstinacy of the facts?

There is no science that does not derive from an *a priori* idea, but there is no solid and reliable knowledge that does not have its origin in the senses.

The power of the ideas contained in classical dissertations is sometimes so great that it can continue for centuries to make anatomists see things that do not exist. Hence everyone today teaches that there are orifices in the heart that cause the right ventricle and the left ventricle to communicate, and by dint of testifying to these orifices, one finally perceives them. I believe that the Fleming Vesalius, a century ago, has already exposed this illusion. But these imaginary perforations in the wall that separates the two ventricles must be extremely agreeable, since no demonstration has yet managed to remove them from the teaching of the majority of anatomists. And yet the cardiac septum is thick and compact. No pores penetrate it. Good God! There are no pores! I have myself very frequently verified this. From my first lectures, in 1616, I demonstrated this on the open heart of a corpse to all those around me.

There is something even stranger: the anatomists who finally allow themselves to be convinced that there are no orifices still remain so firmly attached to the idea of the passage of the blood through this septum that they imagine invisible pores or

mysterious transfers through the dividing wall. The theory sur-
vives the proof of its stupidity. Now that I understand how the
heart functions, now that I know that the right ventricle pushes
the blood towards the lungs and that the left ventricle directs it
to the rest of the body, it is obvious to me that any flow of blood
from one to the other of these two circulations would be both
quaint and damaging. But I also know that men's reasoning is
distorted. The time has not yet come when demonstration and
truth are seen as identical. Alas, it is easy to understand why I
have not managed to convince all those who read me or listen to
me, and why so many dogs continue to bark.

Correct reasoning is as important as knowledge. I fixed this
rule firmly in my head as a basis for my teaching, convinced that
future physicians must be trained, not just instructed. Every one
of my lectures was secretly divided into two phases; first I described and demonstrated, next I went on to more general comments. I remember my first amphitheatre, on Tuesday, April
16th, 1616, in the new premises at Amen Corner into which the
College had just moved. Two criminals, hanged the preceding
Friday, served me as corpses (we were entitled to six bodies each
year). I had been appointed in the previous August to give this
series of lectures and I had spent several months in preparing the
ceremonial, which I intended should be strict, not to say solemn.
The body of the dead man was, out of decency, hidden by a
curtain, which my stewards opened at the appropriate moment.
I was aided by two masters of anatomy and two stewards. I insisted that their apparel should be of perfect cleanliness. They
attired me in a great apron falling from my shoulders to my feet,
and in a pair of white linen sleeves that covered my arms, then
they put a bonnet on my head. They had within reach the silver-
tipped, whalebone wand which I would use to point to the organs of the corpse to which I desired to draw attention. There
was also a candle, to illuminate the parts dissected. On the floor,
in one corner, was a painted wooden coffin in which the body
would be respectfully placed at the end of the three lectures. For
the demonstration lasted three days; the first was devoted to the
abdomen, the second to the thorax, and the third to what I had
decided to name the divine banquet of the brain. The lectures
lasted from five to six, and when they were over I took off my

apron, sleeves and bonnet, put on my professor's robe and invited to dinner all those who had honoured me with their presence at the lecture.

On the occasion I began by defining what I meant by *anatomy*. I said that I should not confine myself to a description of the anatomical organs and regions, for the geography of the body is only an introduction to the comprehension of the life of the body, in the same way as the physical geography of a land is only an immobile, lifeless vision. Anatomy, for me, was the art of understanding the functioning of the human machine in movement, and not solely of describing its forms. When, in the third lecture, I had finished my dissertation on the open brain of that unfortunate criminal, I questioned myself out loud on the subject of this so remarkable organ, so well developed in man, so well protected by the solid skull.

"The brain," I said, "is a great honour to man. All animals have one most perfect part, and in man this is assuredly the brain. And so we may say that the head is the richest member of the body. Aristotle wrote that the brain is the centre of sensation, and Avicenna declared that the nerves are like slips of the brain growing out into the organs of sensation. I also believe this. The brain itself neither sees, nor hears, nor tastes, and yet it does all these things by reason of the sensations which are brought back to it from the eyes, the ears, the palate. And, having thus received a thousand continuous pieces of information, it combines them, shakes them, subdivides them, and works on them in such a way as to extract from them a world of thoughts.

"In a mechanism of such subtlety, it is not surprising that direct routes and tortuous paths should adjoin. The direct routes are those of reason, modesty and truth. The tortuous paths lead to illusion, conceit and error. The first are of the greatest beauty, the second render man vile, lead him astray, divert him from his marvellous power of knowledge and reflection."

I was aware that, speaking in this way, I was simplifying matters to the point of deforming them. All the sombre side of human unreason that I was denouncing is in fact just as natural to man as is his reason, and perhaps even more so. When the unfortunate man whose skull I was dissecting had committed the theft for which he was hanged, he had done no more than demonstrate the weakness of his brain. "I see another law in my members," writes Saint Paul in his epistle to the Romans, "warring against the law of my mind, and bringing me into captivity to the law of sin." In my discourse, I maintained to my audience that the path of reason is beautiful, but I hid the fact that it is the most arduous, and that human nature is not spontaneously inclined towards that arduous path.

I am quite wrong to allow myself to be angered by witches, charlatans and false savants. They merely follow a natural tendency which has a far greater declivity than the austere research of reason. Man thirsts after the marvellous, he cares little if what he is offered are false marvels composed of artifices. And yet it would suffice to show him the truth, Nature, life, the human body. These things are far more marvellous than any fictitious marvel. This is precisely what I have never stopped teaching. I have tried to show that a heart, a liver, a brain, are infinitely more prodigious than any imaginable things. We move in a world that deserves our constant wonder, science shows it to us in a more surprising light every day, yet we refuse to see it. Our very life is an eternally renewed miracle. This is a fact that should give our existence a kind of amazed joy. It should appease some of the anguish felt by the man who wonders what he has come to this earth to do.

A week after my first lecture, on the following Tuesday, the death occurred of a poet for whom I had conceived a certain admiration. Lord Carew, his neighbour at Stratford, who sometimes called me for a consultation, had introduced me to his works. I had seen several of his plays, in which he also acted. In my opinion, he expressed with great vigour something of our anguish of living. His name was William Shakespeare, and there are today some Englishmen who share my admiration for him, even if he shocks a greater number. In 1605 I saw at the Globe Theatre a performance of *Macbeth,* the tragedy of blood and death. And I remember that the King, in the last act, says of life that it is a tale told by an idiot, full of sound and fury, signifying nothing.

I grant that many men seek a meaning to life, and that this quest makes them unhappy. By good fortune, they often find the answer in the Bible and from the clergy. But to those who doubt whether God himself revealed to men the reason why he created them, I should like to answer that the question about the meaning of life is a bad question, perhaps even the stupid question of a narrow-minded man, a question such as that of wondering why we are born English, and at the worst, a question that is none of our business. I would like to say that inner peace is only to be gained at the cost of voluntarily abandoning this question. I would like to see this question trampled underfoot, as being artificial and contemptible. I would like us, finally, once we have expunged it from our minds, to allow these minds full rein to enjoy what we have been given: the very great beauty of a surprising adventure, of an admirable body and of a natural environment that we marvel at more and more, the better we come to know it.

12 May 1647

I spent a restless, anxious night; my right foot was painful and I got up several times to plunge it into cold water. I have just re-read, with some alarm, the notes I made yesterday, but on reflection I do not take back anything I wrote. Yes, the man who seeks a meaning to life asks a question that is futile if he does not believe in God, and indiscreet if he does believe in him (which, naturally, is my case, for I am not one of those who wish to stand out from the crowd). In both of these circumstances the question is presumptuous, as it implies that the meaning of the world is within the measure of man's understanding. This human quest for meaning undoubtedly has no meaning.

To reject this bad question about the meaning of life, however, does not refuse a man the right to give meaning to *his own life*. A more modest pretention, but more within our grasp, and more efficacious. I have given a meaning to my life by trying to achieve a better understanding of the human mechanism. It was, and still is, a kind of combat against the adversaries who unceasingly try to discourage me. To produce original work is the surest way to make enemies for oneself and to stimulate them to the attack, in the same way as bright colours excite the bull. To do nothing and to think nothing is the only way to have no enemies. And yet everyone should endow his life with a goal, offer his life the warmth of a goal.

I have many enemies, and of the most passionate nature. Personal hostility becomes mixed with scientific criticism as water mixes with wine; one can only guess at its presence by tasting the mixture. But what poisonous insect can have bitten that man Leichner, who has recently published a book whose very title wounds me: *Anti-Harveian Studies*? What have I done to Primrose, Parisanus, Severinus and company that they never stop harassing me with bitter criticism? They adopt the vilest methods with which to flay me.

There was the incredible plot about the serpent of blood. The whole business began eight years ago, when a pamphlet appeared, written by a Physician Extraordinary to the Queen, Edward May, and entitled *A Most Certain and True Relation of a Strange Monster or Serpent Found in the Left Ventricle of the Heart of John Pennant, Gentleman, of the Age of 21 Years*. The work was in the form of a letter addressed to the most eminent of the King's physicians, Sir Theodore de Mayerne. May related that at the autopsy of one of his young patients he had discovered in one of the ventricles of the heart a sort of great worm of monstrous aspect. That such an animal was able to lodge itself in the heart was clearly, so he wrote, irrefutable proof that the blood only circulates in the imagination of Doctor Harvey. The alleged circulation of the blood is to be put away in the storehouse of fables and illusions.

When I became acquainted with this senseless diatribe I saw at once the cause of the physician's mistake. I had myself more than once observed a similar elongated formation in an open heart: it was quite simply a blood clot, formed after death. This pitfall is known to all good anatomists.

But May's pamphlet continued on its way. Shortly afterwards, the Professor of Anatomy at Naples, Marcus Aurelius Severinus, echoed it. Although writing on a remote subject, in his book *On the Nature of Abscesses* he quotes the story of the monster in the heart, pretends to believe it, and approves the author in taking it as proof of the fact that I should be given little credit. Severinus was not sincere. It was impossible for him to believe what he wrote. Before publishing his book he had written to a friend in London, John Houghton, asking for more details about the mysterious serpent. Now Houghton had shown me his letter, and I had explained Doctor May's error to him. I know that he passed on my comments to Severinus who, as an experienced anatomist, could do no other than agree with my way of interpreting the monster. But it was too good an opportunity for the Neapolitan not to lash out at my work. People will stop at nothing to strike a blow at a man of whom they are jealous. Calumny has no need of truth. It prospers far more in lies and in the imagination than in sincerity. Its contagion is communicated through passion, not through reason.

From Naples, the contagion reached Paris. Riolan received Severinus's letter, found a new argument against me therein, and no doubt derived an unwholesome pleasure therefrom. For I believe that the Paris anatomist hates me, under cover of great courtesy. It is not a hate *ad hominem,* it is rather a horror of everything that violates the classical traditions, the fear that the immobile edifice of our knowledge and our convictions might collapse.

It is also envy and jealousy, contemptible attitudes, mirrors of baseness. I have always thought that the most precious of all virtues was enthusiasm for the effort of others, and that the most pernicious of vices was its opposite, which is envy. This is the natural disease of the mediocre man. He refuses to allow that another should be more talented or fortunate than himself, seeing this as unacceptable inequality, detestable injustice. But justice does not consist in reducing everyone to the lowest level. The truth is that envy is only the corruption of the desire for justice. And this corruption is extremely widespread in the body of scholars and savants. I have suffered from it all my life. May the jealous man be punished for his vice by the suffering he endures. Ovid, depicting the monster of envy, wrote that it is tortured at the same time as it tortures, that it is its own executioner:

> *Carpitque et carpitur una,*
> *Supplicium suum est.*

May the fires of Hell consume all those jealous men who, through envy, seek to destroy my work.

It is perhaps my last night's attack of gout and my state of exhaustion that today incite me to bitterness and anger. The disorders of the body have the power of causing pain to the spirit.

It is easier for me to despise attacks on my work when my health is good and my forces intact. Although I am perhaps wrong to despise them. They may lead to serious consequences. And not only by delaying the manifestation of the truth, but also by compromising my safety. I believe that people in this country still respect the men of the Art who, like me, have brought about Progress in science and medicine. I believe that this respect has protected me up to the present. If it disintegrates under the attacks of aggressive censors, if the seriousness of my work is doubted, if I am taken for one of those braggarts whom England hates, if the acrimony of the King's enemies is one day no longer restrained, I may well find myself their victim. I fear that they would then not hesitate to seize my person.

20 May 1647

Yesterday an emissary from Paris brought me a letter from Hobbes. I have always felt a slightly puerile emotion on receiving a letter; a real letter, I mean, in which my correspondent was all the time thinking about me as he wrote, in which he has given form to some part of himself and dedicated it to me. A letter is proof that one exists somewhere other than in oneself. Yesterday my joy was even greater: the message brought me, in my present anxious retirement, a little of the fresh air of the Continent.

Hobbes begins by expressing anxiety on my behalf. He asks whether I do not desire to go to Paris to join the numerous Englishmen who have taken refuge there while awaiting the end of the Civil War. But I am too old to desert England. The dear man must imagine the country put to fire and sword, and think me even more threatened and ill at ease than I am in reality. The only purpose in writing is to comfort me. He tries to keep up my courage by speaking of my admirers.

"Last week," he writes, "I saw Sir Kenelm Digby, who is living in great style in Paris. His private library of more than ten thousand volumes is much appreciated by his visitors, to whom he speaks of a powder of his invention which attracts mercury and which, he claims, is the admiration of the Court. Charlatan that he is, he can also show sound judgement, for he is a passionate admirer of your work on the circulation of the blood. He will not tolerate anyone expressing the slightest reservation about it. He showed me one of his books, published in Rotterdam, which contains three letters from Descartes on the circulation; Descartes accepts and speaks highly of your views on the subject, but refuses to believe that, as you have demonstrated, the heart is the motive force behind the movements of the blood. This criticism has enraged our Digby, who replies to it sharply in a book of which he has made me a present and whose title, as ambitious as the man himself, is: *Two Treatises on the Nature of Bodies and the Nature of Man's Soul*. I shall try to send you a copy for your amusement, unless you prefer to come to Paris to consult mine. For my part, I find myself less and less willing to suffer the pretentious Descartes, and I am pleased that he should be thus snubbed when he dares, without proof, to doubt your observations."

Hobbes's long letter brings many other agreeable pieces of news about life in Paris. At the request of the Marquis of Newcastle, tutor to the Prince of Wales, he agreed to teach mathematics to His Royal Highness: he is doing so, but from time to time, between two geometrical theorems, he insinuates a modicum of political ideas which may turn out to be useful if the prince one day accedes to the throne of England. He also tells me about the young John Evelyn, who has more than once served as a messenger between King Charles and our Ambassador to France, Sir Richard Browne, and who has just married the latter's daughter. He also believes that our Queen Henrietta Maria, who is in her third year of Parisian exile, is now in the greatest financial difficulties; her sister-in-law, the Regent, received her with great pomp at first, but today she protects her only feebly against the avarice of Cardinal Mazarin, who is the true master of the Kingdom. In short, Hobbes sends me the latest gossip from Paris, which is not at all his custom. He tells me that from his windows one has the best possible view of all the royal manifestations and official processions, and that he has many friends because of the location of his residence.

Hobbes's message ends without his breathing a word about his philosophical work. Nothing about the progress of the great book he was planning which he intended to call *Leviathan,* after the biblical monster. Since his *De cive*, which appeared five years ago, I have not read a single printed line of his.

After I had read Hobbes's letter, I began to dream. Of course

I would not go to Paris. But for a moment I could not prevent myself from toying with the idea. The images of my journey through France in 1630 came back to my mind. The King had commanded me to accompany his cousin James Stewart, Duke of Lennox, a young man of eighteen who was being sent to the Continent for three years in the hope of broadening his mind, which was less developed than his kindly heart. The Duke had left for France at the beginning of August 1630, with the Dean of Lincoln and some ten servants. I only joined him in December of the same year. I started my journey on a rowing boat by the Tower of London, two days later I continued it in a stage-coach from Sittingbourne, the next day I arrived in Dover, whence I embarked for Calais. Within twelve days I reached Paris.

It was a town that was both magnificent and repugnant. Magnificent, because of the triumph of its white stone, which for me was such a contrast to the brick and wood of which London houses are constructed. Repugnant, because of the filth and congestion of its streets. The fact is that Paris is even more crowded than London; they say the city contains more than four hundred thousand souls! That is a far cry from our villages with their human dimensions, or even from the Folkestone of my childhood, with its few thousand inhabitants.

I understand the temptation to build these great cities. They dazzle the visitor and encourage trade. But I do not know whether it is reasonable to crowd four hundred thousand people into one place. Villages have their harmless idiot. Cities engender malefactors, vagabonds, cutpurses and procuresses. When I was in Paris, I remember that assaults were a daily occurrence at certain street corners; the efforts of the constables of the watch and of the *bourgeois* militia made no difference. My life in London had already given me some warning of the dangers of too dense a population. In a mass, man loses some part of his soul. I do not like crowds. It is as if those who find themselves submerged therein suffer a metamorphosis which amputates the best of themselves. They become at the same time less lucid and less charitable. And weeds grow more freely in congested districts. Yet it is one of my failings that I have a blind love for London, and I found many attractions in the Paris of the thirties. Even if some of those attractions were perverse.

In Paris I was warmly received by the English residents. There was a great ferment at the end of the year 1630. The residents, who followed French political affairs with close attention and almost every day sent long despatches to London, tried to explain to me the torments suffered by Louis XIII. But I had no talent for understanding their explanations. I gathered that, during the month preceding my arrival, the Court had been shaken by an extraordinary reversal. Marie de' Medici, the King's mother, had woven a skilful plot, worthy of her Florentine birth. She wanted her son to dismiss Cardinal Richelieu, whose growing influence was becoming unacceptable. And yet it was the Queen Mother who had made the Cardinal's fortune, but now she hated him. She had stirred up all possible acrimony against him. She had even prepared his succession. There would be many positions to be filled, and this was already causing no little agitation. The residents had declared it probable that her enterprise would succeed and the Cardinal be disgraced. Now, at the very moment when Richelieu had thought himself lost, the King had decided that he would not go. The price the Queen Mother paid for her plot was exile to Compiègne, and most of her fellow conspirators were arrested or forced to reside at a distance from Paris. The English spoke of nothing but this *coup de théâtre,* and were forever passing on all the gossip that enlivened those memorable days. I was greatly bored by all the details, but I was captivated by the character of the Cardinal as described by my compatriots.

I never saw Richelieu at close quarters. But I was told so much about him that even today, seventeen years later, I feel as if I had known him. His good looks were legendary. Everyone who came near him agreed that it was difficult to resist the fascination of his great height and his noble countenance. A fine presence is probably an important political advantage (although my judgement on this point may well be that of a man who has always suffered from his lack of stature and whose visage is not to his liking). Another characteristic of the Cardinal was his lively intelligence; even those who did not like him were subjugated by it. But these exceptional gifts went hand in hand with a strange susceptibility; for a trifle, he was capable of breaking into sobs, and it was said that he wept copiously when he

thought himself lost through the machinations of Marie de'
Medici. At other moments, on the contrary, he could be iras-
cible, authoritarian, merciless. And all this was at the service of
extreme deceit and ruthless ambition. Persons of this stamp
change the course of history single-handed. On them depend
war or peace; the wretchedness or prosperity of the people; liberty or slavery. The hazards of their own lives operate upon the
hazards of the nation, as chance, or mischance decides whether
a town will succumb to an epidemic of the Plague or be spared.
I am well aware that these ambitious men of politics believe their
personal battle to be in the service of the nation. When one is
convinced that one is acting for the common weal, when one
believes oneself to be the only man capable of orienting history
in the right direction, when one is certain of being equal to the
needs of one's country, then the question of personal success is
transformed into an affair of State, ambition loses all vileness
and becomes the gift of oneself, taking on the colours of heroism
and devotion to duty. It was easy for Richelieu to tell himself
that he was fighting for the greater good of the Kingdom. Perhaps Cromwell, even though more vulgar, today follows a similar reasoning. In order not to be ashamed of what they are doing
through self-interest, in their own eyes they envelop it under the
mantle of a generous, noble design, as the Cardinal enveloped
his body, which was said to be sickly, within the stiffened folds
of his red robe. Great men of politics are often monsters.

During my stay in Paris, those who defended Richelieu were
rare. He was admired, he was feared, but he was not liked, he
was judged egotistical and cruel, even if he did occasionally
make a generous gesture. There were some, however, who
praised his government, and while I listened to them I gave rein
to my insatiable desire to understand the reasons that urge a
man to act. Clearly, the image the Cardinal had of his battle was
that of a strong and independent France: his struggle against
the Queen Mother became confused with the struggle against
the power of Spain and the Holy Roman Empire, both then
guilty of hostile encirclement. That was why he was urging
Louis XIII to make war. For centuries the greatness of France
had been an affair of victories and conquests: he was continuing
the tradition. The fascination Richelieu exerted over the King

was composed of military victories, such as that just won by the Royal Army in taking Pignerol, the key fortress of the Duchy of Savoy. But this military prestige was dearly bought. The English residents asserted that a third of the French were in the grip of famine, and that the poverty of the small towns had spread to the countryside. Wherein lies the true greatness of a country?

I accompanied the Duke of Lennox and his suite to Touraine, and saw the misery of France at close quarters. Blois was suffering from an outbreak of the Plague. The disease had come from the south. It had struck the north of Italy with great force, and then overrun the city of Lyon. From there it moved up into the regions of Tours and Blois. I advised the Duke to abandon his projected journey to Venezia, and even to leave Blois without delay. The French physicians knew the Plague better than we, they have suffered many epidemics in their country. Even so, I am not sure that they do not confuse different diseases under a single name. In Ambroise Paré's *Discours sur la peste,* a copy of which is in the possession of the College of Physicians of London, the famous surgeon writes that the Plague is not always of the same kind, and is sometimes named miliary fever, sometimes anthrax, sometimes pertussis and sometimes purpura. The plague that prevailed in Blois was very similar to dysentery. At all events, what I saw finally convinced me that the disease is infectious, even if poverty and dirt play a part in it. I did not understand those who denied its contagion. This was also the opinion of a French doctor from Lyon, Gaspard Chevalier, who had just published a pamphlet on the rules for effective protection against the Plague.

It was at Blois that I discovered the full horror of the epidemic. The cases of Plague I had seen in London had had the mildness of a fairly common disease. They were feared, but the authorities made light of them. The renewed outbreaks of 1625 and 1629 killed a few poor creatures, but there was no panic among the people. In Blois, terror reigned. The town was dead, fear kept the people within doors and emptied the streets. Barricades cut off all approach to the infected houses, whose doors were marked with great white crosses. The dying could be heard from afar, yelling for help. Pitch and turpentine were burnt outside the houses in the vain hope of destroying the miasmas.

Their unpleasant smell and suffocating smoke did not suffice to mask the stench of the rotting corpses waiting to be removed. I saw the heavy carts carrying the dead go past, pushed by men dressed in long Morocco-leather robes and wearing terrifying protective masks. They were on their way to bury their load in all haste in the common grave for Plague victims. A courageous priest followed, mumbling prayers. The rare passers-by, catching sight of the *cortège,* fled as fast as their legs could carry them. I was told that dead and dying were probably lumped together, and that some people were no doubt buried alive.

From the conversations I had with the inhabitants, in my inadequate French, I concluded that they were overwhelmed by terror and discouragement. The epidemic appeared to them to be some sort of natural scourge, like a flood or earthquake, striking men from too elevated a height for them to be able to do anything but pray. In Antiquity, in Greece and Phoenicia, epidemics were seen as a manifestation of the anger of the gods, and oblations and sacrifices were thought to be the only way to appease the divine wrath. On occasion the living were immolated, in the hope of preserving others. Even Christianity did not sweep away these superstitions, and present-day men still consider an epidemic a fatality for which there is no remedy. I have a horror of this passivity. A disease is fatal only so long as our ignorance renders us incapable of averting it. That is the meaning we must give to the medicine of today. The road will be long, but we must set to work, and reject more forcefully than our ancestors the image of disease as the equivalent of divine fury, of disease as punishment for our sins, of disease as inexorable fate. Men are mortal, and we may not deny death. But we may, if we are sufficiently skilful, reject disease and suffering: such a rejection represents the greatness of medicine, and perhaps of man. *This* war is authentic, and it has already been declared. We are already in a position to suggest certain ways of fighting against the Plague if we accept the fact, which I believe to be the case, that it is contagion that creates an epidemic. I longed to get back to London to work, even though my research is concerned with very different subjects from these. But that is of no importance, for the knowledge of the human body, of the whole human body, is the only possible basis for our fight against disease.

Ours is a singular destiny. Those corpses in Blois fired my imagination. I told myself that on the day we discover how to cure the Plague we shall be acting on equal terms with God, we shall be committing the sin of pride, we shall even perhaps have to pay the price of that sin, but man will have obeyed Christ's commandment to love and succour his neighbour.

We returned to Paris. There I found an invitation from Father Mersenne to visit him in his convent of the Order of Minims in the Place Royale. Hobbes had already spoken to me of him; he knew him well. A priest whose passionate interest in the science equalled or surpassed his passion for theology, he had published *La Vérité des sciences contre les sceptiques et les pyrrhoniens.* He was visited in his monastic cell by every illustrious scientist and scholar to be found in Europe. I went there on the appointed day. It was a memorable encounter.

Mersenne introduced me to another priest whom he had also invited and who, he told me, was one of his greatest friends. His name was Gassendi. The two men slightly resembled one another, with their regular features, their small stature, and their frail bodies. Mersenne had a long, thin face and black eyes, he spoke in monotonous tones, and there was a certain lack of vigour in his deportment. Gassendi seemed far less ascetic, more lively, his countenance was frequently illuminated by a mocking smile. Both men knew my *De motu cordis,* which had been published three years before. Mersenne told me that he had sent it to Descartes, in Holland, and Gassendi had sent it to Fabri de Peiresc, in Aix. What pleased them was that I had dared to contradict Aristotle. They both judged that our century, which as they said has produced many great minds, has an absolute duty to add many things to the teaching of the Greeks and is assuredly capable of so doing. It was necessary to see farther than our predecessors. Since we are mounted on their shoulders, we shall easily manage this; my work on the circulation was an example.

I perceived that these men's ideas of modern science were identical to my own. But their thought extended to branches that were less familiar to me than medicine: physics, chemistry, astronomy and even mathematics. In place of outdated Scholasticism, all of whose knowledge is taken from tradition,

they propose a method that would no longer be based on theology but would more modestly limit itself to the study of the
mechanisms of Nature through observation and experiment.
They admire Galileo, Descartes, Hobbes and even—and this
pleased me less—Sir Francis Bacon. They violently reject astrol-
ogy, alchemy, magic, the Cabbala, the Rosicrucian fraternity and
the followers of the sect calling itself "The Soul of the World." I
glimpsed, in this young seventeenth century, a movement of the
mind that might liberate savants from the weights I knew only
too well. The two men I was with were part of a community
that was in the process of laying the foundations of a profound
change in men's thinking. Mersenne was also dreaming of bringing these savants together in a European academy. It might possibly give rise to a hitherto-unknown advance, a new clarity in
science.

But how came it that these two priests of the Catholic faith,
the religion whose intolerance to new ideas I had seen in Italy,
were able to approve this schism between science and religion?
Neither Gassendi nor, in particular, Mersenne, accepted that
there was in fact a schism. On the contrary, they believed this to
be the best way to preserve the purity of the Faith. The people
who violated the respect for sacred things were the "Deists,"
those who attribute a soul to the world and who wish to inter-
rogate this soul about the whys and wherefores of things. They
do not see that it is not our business to know the reasons for the
Creation. God has not revealed them to us, and science must
have the humility to restrict itself to the observation of natural
phenomena, without committing the sin of pride and trying to
understand their reasons. Thus re-defined, this is the only kind
of science that is not impious. Mersenne made me a gift of a
work he had written several years before: *L'Impiété des déistes*.
Both Gassendi and he mistrusted everything that associates science with metaphysics and, while declaring themselves fervent
admirers of Descartes, seemed to suspect him of not seeing
clearly the dangers of such a confusion. When I left the two
priests I was filled with wonder and admiration.

I saw the Abbé Mersenne again at the house of the Dupuy
brothers, who every day in the late afternoon convened an assembly of erudite men in the splendid library of the Mansion of

the President de Thou, in the rue des Poitevins. Many extremely distinguished visitors were present there that day, but most people were surrounding a personage who seemed to be the man of the moment. I was told that he was a physician called Renaudot. His success was derived from an original idea he had had: the creation of a *Gazette*, whose first number had just been printed and which he proposed to publish regularly. The object was passed from hand to hand: no more than four pages, but handsomely presented, with legends in italic type in the margin, indicating the provenance of the news. More than a thousand copies would be printed each week and sold by pedlars in the streets of Paris. I knew of nothing of the sort in England, or in any other country. It seemed to me that, if this kind of gazette became widespread, it would represent a revolution in the propagation of events and ideas. Richelieu, so they said, was already interested in this enterprise; he might perhaps seek therein a method of disseminating what he thought wise to make known. Men already have trouble enough in thinking for themselves: what would happen if people began to fill their heads with ready-made thoughts? And yet it is a marvellous idea to make men better informed, it could help them to clear their minds of confusion. Information, no doubt, potentially contains both the worst and the best: the worst for tranquillity, and the best for exchange and progress. But the latter is more important than the former for everyone who hates a dreary, insipid life. Decidedly, this epoch is creative. Everything will progress very quickly from now on. Our time is beginning. I should like to live for many centuries, to know the outcome. Man's life is too short; he sees the beginning of the game, but he is always deprived of its end.

25 May 1647

My pretty niece, Mary, who last year married Heneage Finch, has just given birth to a stillborn child. I heard of this quite casually, as being the most ordinary of events, for the death of a child is extremely commonplace today. Mary's father, my brother Daniel, made his wife pregnant ten times, and six times the children died in infancy. My brother Eliab had eight children: four alone survived. My brother Thomas lost two children out of three. Such deaths are so frequent that no one is upset by them. The dangers of pregnancy do not spare the mothers, either, and I know they fear childbed as one fears single combat. If they come out of it unharmed, and if the child is well and truly alive, they say that this is by grace of God. They consider failure and death to be natural. Mrs Thornton told me that her sister, who was dying of exhaustion at the age of thirty after having brought sixteen children into the world, six of them stillborn, seemed happy that the Lord was finally good enough to call her back to himself. These things seem to be greeted with total indifference; they are a law of Nature, the norm established by God, they must be accepted with submission.

Such resignation revolts me. It is an error and a sin. Too many births come to grief for the simple reason that the mechanisms of delivery are misunderstood: medicine has a duty to reject this fatality. I have seen giddy young midwives pervert the whole business through unseemly haste. The woman in travail cries out in pain and calls for help. The midwife, lest she should seem unskilful at her trade, mightily bestirs herself, daubs her hands with oils, distends the parts of the uterus, administers medicinal potions to provoke its expulsive faculties, and finally retards a birth that would have been without complications if left to Nature. Not only does she endanger the life of the child, she also exposes the mother to injuries such as I have frequently encountered, some parts of the placenta and the membranes being retained in the womb, putrefying and becoming gangrenous, thus causing death.

One of my patients, of noble birth, suffered a severe fever after her labour, the usual lochia did not flow, her genitals were inflamed and swollen. I saw that the orifice of her uterus was hard and closed. I opened it gently with the aid of an appropriate instrument, and made an injection by means of a little syringe. Immediately, I saw a great quantity of black, coagulated, fetid blood flow out. Relief was instantaneous and my patient recovered. I have observed many analogous cases, and I have also seen other women die because, after an unskilfully conducted childbirth, portions of the placenta, pus and other sanious matters had been left to accumulate in the uterus.

The mistake usually made is to try to hasten the normal course of events by unseemly impatience. It is the old, old story of man attempting to force Nature. That he should endeavour to correct her errors is a good and noble aim, but he must never brutally maltreat her. The midwife must employ the same gentleness, the same delicacy, as is employed by the physician in his fight against disease. The task is to persuade and master Nature, never to violate her.

The College of Physicians has more than once had a bone to pick with midwives. Unfortunately for us, there is a stupid popular tradition that forbids the presence of any person of the masculine sex in the room of a woman in childbirth. When the physician has to intervene, it is not seemly for him to uncover the abdomen, he must perform his manipulations under the bedclothes without seeing what he is doing. These customs of a bygone age annoy me. My friend Percival Willughby told me of his procedure when his daughter, who is a midwife, calls him to aid her with a difficult delivery: he creeps into the room on hands and knees so that the woman giving birth shall not see him, and it is in this ridiculous position that he operates. Is that reasonable?

In England, the art of the midwife is not taught by physicians, it is not even taught at all. They learn their trade as apprentices to older women, their knowledge is not tested by any examination, and they are licensed to practise by the local Bishop, just as in the old days physicians too were licensed by the Archbishop of Canterbury. Our country, which is reputed to be dependable, is sometimes far less so than people imagine.

A textbook on the science of childbirth should be published. I have already gathered together some notes which could serve as its first draft. The mysteries surrounding our birth have always fascinated me. In the first place, is it the mother who expels the child, or the child who makes the effort to come out? That the maternal uterus has an expulsive effect seems to me to be undoubted. My master, Fabricius of Aquapendente, even writes that the uterus is assisted in the work of parturition by the muscles of the abdomen and by the diaphragm. And I would go farther than he: I believe that the whole body participates in the movement, just as the whole body is involved in a sneeze. I have seen a similar involvement of the entire body in the birth pain of bitches, ewes and mares. But I am convinced that the foetus contributes to its own birth. Fabricius says that it does so by its weight, which is clearly not the case, since it emerges horizontally both in an animal standing upright on its four feet and a woman lying in her bed. No, I believe that the foetus really does use its own efforts to reach the light. Do I need to recall the fact that chicks emerge from the egg by breaking the shell, with no assistance from their mothers? At the time of birth, the young of flies, moths and butterflies tear the fine membrane that surrounds them. In the same way, young vipers are able to emerge from the egg on their own, sometimes in the mother's womb, sometimes even on the second or third day after they have left it. In women, several observations cause us to think that the foetus is not inactive. I know of one woman who died one evening before giving birth, her corpse was left alone in her room during the night, and the following morning there was found between her thighs an infant who had procured its own release by its own effort. Gregorius Nymannus has collected together a number of analogous examples in his *De vita in utero dissertatio*.

The skill of the foetus is illustrated in other situations. I knew of a woman whose vagina had been lacerated and excoriated as a result of a first difficult labour. The damaged vagina coalesced and afforded no passage for anything, neither her husband's member nor a fine probe, nor even her menstrual fluxes. She nevertheless became pregnant again. When the time for her delivery drew near, the unfortunate woman was lamentably tormented at the idea that passage was forbidden to the infant. Laying aside all hope of ever ridding herself of her burden, she ordered her affairs, made her will, and took leave of her friends. Then suddenly, contrary to all expectation, the foetus forced open the passage and delivery occurred. He had saved his mother's life, and she quickly regained her former health. Another example seemed to me no less remarkable. The Queen had a white mare of very pure race and extraordinary beauty. As is the custom, the groom infibulated her genitalia with iron rings, lest by the serving of stallions she might lose her beauty. I do not know how, but despite this precaution she became pregnant, she foaled in the night, and the next morning her foal was found lying by her side. As soon as they told me of it I went immediately to the stable: the rings were still in place and the vulva hermetically sealed. The foal had made its way out through a yawning gap it had opened in its mother's croup, destroying this very strong part of the mare's body and proving how great may be the vigour of a mature foetus.

Another astonishing phenomenon in parturition is that the cervix, normally so hard and tightly closed, softens at the end of pregnancy in order to allow of its dilation. And immediately after delivery it regains its normal firmness. What is more, the junctions of the bones of the pelvis also become distended at the appropriate moment. I do not know how this comes about. But it is clear that these events that coincide with birth are not the result of chance. The whole forms so complex and so coherent a system that its harmony cannot be fortuitous. This is what is truly amazing when one goes more thoroughly into the mechanisms of birth. For what the study of parturition demonstrates here is to be found elsewhere in all the events of life. Everything seems to be ordered in a quasi-miraculous disposition. Even did we not believe in God (which God forbid), we physicians would have no difficulty in knowing what it is we fight for, since we know that life is an admirable thing.

In Sparta and some of the other Greek States, infants born deformed were put to death. It was the responsibility of the midwife to judge, immediately after the delivery, whether the child she had just brought into the world deserved to live, or whether it had no chance of becoming beautiful and vigorous. In the latter case, she handed it over to the executioner, who got rid of it for the State. The Spartan had some resemblance to the Puritan of today: an image of the world that professes to be severe but is in fact cruel. And if I seek the source of this cruelty that assails the soul of certain groups and certain peoples at some moment in their history, I believe I can find it in a kind of blindness: these men and women do not respect human life because they do not see that there is something prodigious about it. The miracle of the existence of a deformed child as well as of an Adonis. People may say that the life of plants and animals is equally admirable but that we do not hesitate to pick a rose, that is to say to kill it, or to flush a hare and slaughter it. But human birth is the birth of a thought, and it is this addition that makes all the difference. Theologians would expound on this subject much better than I, but I do not need to be a theologian to know that this difference places me, a physician, on the side of the child whose body is malformed.

I would wish that English schoolchildren might be taught the mechanisms of human life, the wonder it inspires when one achieves insight into its processes, and the infinitely precious object which, from that moment, it represents.

28 May 1647

An important piece of news has reached me today. The King, still a semi-prisoner at Holdenby House, received a petition last month from the Army. An officer went to give it to him in person. The Army expressed the wish that the King should place himself under its protection: his honour, his crown and his dignity would be restored. What marvellous news! It could save both England and the King. I know from a reliable source that the Army is now far from being the slave of the London Parliament. It obeyed it so long as it was well respected and well paid. But after the Battle of Naseby, Parliament believed Charles to be definitively beaten and the Civil War to be at an end. Far from showing gratitude, it thought only to disband an army that had become useless, troublesome and costly. Their pay was withheld, at the same time as the soldiers were being encouraged to find other engagements, against the Irish Papists, for example. The Army's fury is understandable.

I rejoice at these events. The London Parliament will get its just reward. I ardently hope the King will agree, as the petition requests, to place himself under the protection of the Army. Its commanding general, Sir Thomas Fairfax, is not one of the King's fanatical enemies. I respect Fairfax as an upright, straightforward man as much as I fear Cromwell's double-dealing. If, as I hope, it is Fairfax who has inspired this petition, I am sure that he will keep his word and protect the King. The disreputable London Parliament has been stupid enough to alienate its own army; may it please the heavens that the King agree to take advantage of this.

But once again, I am afraid that Charles will hesitate. He knows that the people love him, he heard the cheers and the bells ringing out all the way along the road leading him to Holdenby. He retains the illusion that England's attachment to his person will finally prevail over all his enemies' manoeuvres. His conception of royalty will probably not permit him to march on London with an army of rebels. He would like London to beg him to return, like prodigal sons demanding their father.

And then, the army that is appealing to him today was yesterday the enemy. How could he not still have bitter memories of past and lost battles? I was with him when his army confronted that of the Parliament for the first time. This was the beginning of the Civil War, five years ago.

On August 10th, 1641, I left London with His Majesty's retinue en route for Edinburgh. We reached the Scottish capital after a journey lasting five days. We were sumptuously received. The city of Aberdeen, through which we passed, elected me a free burgess and entertained me to a splendid banquet. But when we returned to London in November, a Parliamentarian named John Pym had organized a kind of plot in the absence of the King. By a narrow majority the House of Commons passed the Grand Remonstrance, which condemned the King's policies in violent terms. The authors of this Remonstrance were accused of High Treason by the Attorney-General in the House of Lords, but an attempt to arrest them failed. Civil War seemed inevitable. The King decided to leave London and began to travel from town to town to try to raise a Royalist army under his standard. Eight thousand foot and two thousand five hundred horse formed an impressive troop. I followed the King in these difficult peregrinations, which by the middle of October 1642 led us to Warwickshire. It so happened that the rebel army raised by Parliament was, unknown to us, quartered within a few leagues of our own. We were apprised of this on October 22nd. The King immediately decided to attack on the following day. He entrusted me with the care of the two of his sons who were with us: Charles, Prince of Wales, who was twelve years old, and his brother the Duke of York, who was nine. The two children were filled with joy at the idea of being present at a real battle and refused to allow themselves to be escorted to the rear. Men claim that they venerate peace; children confess that they like war. The young prince brandished the short sword he had been given and cried loudly: "I fear them not." I have often seen children playing at soldiers in the streets of London; I believe that they are possessed from birth by a secret urge to fight. They grow, the Bible and their mothers teach them the marvels of peace, they make an effort to learn the lesson, they may even end by believing in the blessings of peaceful behaviour, but the temptation of war, never hidden very deep, is always ready to surface at the slightest pretext and, as in Aristophanes' comedy, to imprison peace in a cave. War and peace—this is a subject about which the human race shows the greatest hypocrisy. Peace is everywhere extolled, but men never cease making war. The phenomenon seems so firmly entrenched in the nature of human societies that I see no possible remedy, unless it be a great, passionate, universal movement that would fire new mental forces, forces as yet unknown, forces capable of checking a propensity that I assuredly judge to be natural. But the Church herself does not believe that we can instill a compelling desire for peace into all minds: rather than make the attempt, she has invented Holy Wars. Perhaps it is as difficult to prevent men killing one another as it would be to forbid them to drink, to eat, or to couple.

I stayed with the two children, then, not far from Edgehill, where the King's army had taken up its position. On the morning of Sunday, October 23rd, I heard that battle was about to commence. At mid-day the preparations were still not completed. At three in the afternoon the light began to fail, they wondered whether it would not be wiser to postpone everything until the morrow. But would not the enemy thus have time to receive reinforcements? They decided to delay no longer the encounter of the two armies. The King's soldiers charged down the hill, a confused battle was joined, whose din I heard without being able to watch its progress. I was told later of the various episodes in the combat, of how our cavalry passed through the enemy lines and pursued their charge so far that our infantry was abandoned to the thrust of an enemy disposing of superior numbers; how an entire regiment of the rebels swore allegiance to the King; how both armies after the battle declared themselves victorious; how we lost two hundred men, but the enemy far more.

At the height of the battle, while I was reading aloud to divert the Prince of Wales and his brother, a cannon ball fell not far from us. I was extremely alarmed and made haste to remove the boys from that place. The fear of death has never particularly tormented me. Having seen it at close quarters throughout a long life as a physician, it has become as familiar to me as a travelling companion. And yet it still retains all its strangeness for me. How can a cannon ball, or the miasmas of an epidemic, lay low at one stroke the incomparable edifice that is the body of a man or an animal? Were I to see the Tower of London or any other masterpiece of architecture suddenly disintegrate and crumble into dust, I would not be more astonished. But this astonishment is a sin against the spirit, for it is our duty to observe, and keep silent. Death is no more surprising than everything which surrounds us, and which we do not understand any better. If the surprise is greater and the emotion more lively, it is because this particular event destroys our desires and our loves, including our personal desire to live, and our love of ourselves. A physician's *sang-froid* does not protect him from the innermost emotions to which the image of death gives rise. For a long time now I have kept in my study a preparation of opium, which, when the time comes, will release me from my pain. But all men cannot avail themselves of opium. And opium is no protection against the unendurable loss of a mother or of a beloved wife. It is evident that the only way to render this singular destiny tolerable is to surround it with the comfort of sublime images. There is comfort in the conviction that our soul does not die when our body decays, for we have more esteem for our soul than for our body—to which, furthermore, we offer the hope of resurrection. So the men who govern us are right to forbid any form of atheism. And yet I have seen sincere Christians suffer from the idea of death as one suffers from a scandal.

The military condition must also reduce the fear of death to some extent, by surrounding it with the excitements of martial ardour. At the Battle of Edgehill, I saw our unfortunate General ride to his death in apparent transport of exaltation and joy. Even the humble Royal Guards, who could have remained in safety with the King, begged for and obtained permission to fight in the front line. All such men obliterate death by assigning it a role in the meaning they give to their life.

The King expressed his gratitude for the care I had taken of the Prince of Wales, although I had no other merit than that of having read to him and kept him company. As a memento I was presented with a portrait of the Prince painted by Dobson, which represents him against a battle scene with, lying on the ground in the lower left-hand part of the picture, a Medusa-head symbolising the discord of war.

8 June 1647

As I feared, the King has rejected the Army's petition. But the Army does not consider itself beaten. A few days ago—I have only just learned this—a detachment of cavalry, commanded by a Cornet, went to Holdenby House to remove the King and take him to Army Headquarters.

It was a somewhat strange abduction, for the King, so I am told, seemed both hesitant and charmed. The Cornet, with incredible audacity, woke him at midnight by making a great noise and then forced his door, his hat in one hand and a pistol in the other. He declared, with extreme courtesy, that the officers had got wind of a plot hatched against the person of His Majesty and had charged him to conduct the King to a place of safety where he would be under the protection of the Army. "Have you nothing in writing from the General-in-Chief, Sir Thomas Fairfax?" the King is reported to have said. "Tell me what Commission you have?" Pointing to his troopers behind him, the Cornet is said to have replied: "Here is my Commission!" But this response which, if it be true, seems to me of the greatest impertinence, was delivered with such grace, so many protestations of fidelity, and the assurance that the Army's only concern was to defend the King, that His Majesty allowed himself to be persuaded. My feelings for him do not prevent me from perceiving that he always shows a great deal of credulity when he is treated with flattery. If the events really occurred as they were recounted to me, they are of a composition that no more than half-pleases me. I do not understand why General Fairfax did not address a personal message of allegiance and explanation to the King. But I am no doubt wrong to dismiss the pleasure I feel: Charles by the side of Fairfax, removed from the ferocities of the Parliament, protected by a hitherto-victorious army—this is assuredly a happy reversal of a situation that was worsening day by day. I cannot wait to know more.

Ancient history is full of Kings, Emperors and Generals who had to make an instantaneous decision that might prove expedient or fatal. Quintilius Varus, a Roman legate, receives in his camp his enemy Arminius, who makes him solemn protestations of fidelity and offers to put at his disposal the army he commands. The Roman has to choose: shall he take Arminius prisoner, or shall he let him go free so that he can fulfill his promise? He hesitates, decides to trust the German, allows him to leave, and soon pays for it with his life. If I remembered more of what I was taught at Cambridge I should be able to cite other examples. To command, to reign, is to have to decide without always knowing the proper weight of the pros and cons.

But is not this obligation to choose, and often to choose blindly, the lot of all men? The physician, who holds lives in his hands, knows this well. How many times, in my practice, have I not experienced this agonising hesitation between two possible paths. Only one of the paths leads to recovery, the other may lead to death, and yet science does not enable us to make any infallible prediction. The patient expects certainty, the physician must give it to him without possessing it himself.

I have often encountered this doubt when I have had to decide between two opposing opinions, one advising surgery, the other advising against it. In 1642 I was consulted by the wife of Doctor Thomas Bennet. Binnes wished to operate but Fleete was against it. The poor woman had already been treated for two years for painful swellings on her face, which nothing could relieve. Binnes had at first thought that two rotten teeth were responsible. The teeth had been pulled, but the swelling had only increased. King Charles agreed to touch the patient, according to the belief that a disease may be cured by the touch of the King's hand. This time the result was piteous, and shortly afterwards I saw Mrs Bennet afflicted with an enormous deformation of the face; there was a hard, swollen mass upon her temple and upper jaw. This mass resembled an enormous, sinister-looking abscess. Binnes wished to open it; Fleete, another surgeon called in by the Bennets to give a second opinion, disagreed. Binnes is an excellent surgeon, attached to our hospital, and I inclined towards his point of view. But I was far from sure that I was right. In the end they operated, the patient recovered, and I thanked Heaven for having inspired us correctly.

There was also the case of Sir William Smith, one of the most difficult of all. For many years this elderly man had suffered from a huge stone in the bladder. He was in great physical distress and had already sought many opinions. Not only was he in pain, which affected the whole of his lower abdomen, he also complained of sleepless nights during which his incessant desire to urinate forced him to get up at least ten times, only to pass a few drops of reddish urine. It was, I believe, towards the end of 1619 that he came to ask my advice. His face was drawn, his complexion yellow, his gaze anxious. The man was desperate. Certain physicians were urging him to find a good surgical specialist who would finally rid him of the accursed stone. But surgery terrified him. He had heard that I possessed a secret remedy against the stone. Could I help him to avoid the operation?

On rectal palpation of his bladder I could not feel the calculus, although I was able to do so during a second examination a few days later. The stone seemed enormous, it was clear that no remedy would be capable of dispersing it, and that the only way to deal with it would be to cut it surgically. But for this tired, worn-out man, whose heart demanded to be spared after a too long and too painful life, cutting would almost certainly have been fatal. I have advised other patients to be cut, and the result has sometimes been successful. But it is still a terrible act, which kills more men than it cures. I recognise the progress surgery has made since the far-off time when Hippocrates demanded that the future physician should swear an oath never to have recourse to it. But it still remains a fearsome deed. I find it difficult to credit that even today itinerant surgeons go from town to town and cut poor unfortunate people who, although given temporary relief, will die a few days later. Even the cuts performed by the best specialist in our hospital leave me with an agonizing mental picture. The method, which is fairly recent, is that of the so-called "Greater Apparatus." The poor man is tied on to the sloping table, firmly held by four robust young men. One grasps his head, the second half-lies over his abdomen to keep the scrotum and penis elevated, the last two hold his legs, but in the position of a man about to be quartered. Then, between his legs, the surgeon goes to work, armed with his lancet and strange instruments, skilfully searching the wound he has made between the anus and the scrotum, and triumphantly extracting the stone, when the operation succeeds. And yet pain, fever, blood and pus are further ordeals for the days that follow. I was almost certain that William Smith would not come out of an operation alive.

But which is the better fate? To live in perpetual suffering, or to risk death in order to cease to suffer? It seemed to me that I must at first try to assuage the pain, although I was not sure that I would be able to attenuate it sufficiently for it to become tolerable. If I could manage this I would no longer have any scruple in refusing the hazards of the operation: Sir William's life would be painful, but acceptable. If, on the other hand, his suffering was not alleviated, there would still be time for the more dangerous action.

Where is the frontier between an intolerable existence and one that is painful, yet still ardently desired? The will not to die is of such great force in man's mind that it allows of incredible acceptances. Life becomes a struggle between the desire to live and the weariness of living. To arrive at a correct decision, the physician has at every moment to be aware of what point in this struggle has been reached by the patient who puts himself in his hands. I did not know Sir William well enough, I could still not clearly divine his underlying philosophy, which it was my duty to respect if I were to give him correct advice. I decided to see him frequently, and suggested that I should no longer receive a fee for each visit but that he should pay me an annual sum of fifty pounds for an unlimited number of consultations. I knew that some of my colleagues in the College of Physicians adopted this practice, although I had never previously had recourse to it. He agreed. I prescribed opium, which dulls pain better than any other remedy; furthermore, I gave him a preparation to disperse his stone, a secret empirical mixture much praised by certain

Italian physicians. In reality I had great doubts about this remedy, but I was anxious to give Sir William the unequalled consolation that is the hope of recovery.

My decision to procrastinate was of no avail. The months passed and Sir William's martyrdom became more and more unbearable. At length he himself demanded to be cut; he preferred to die rather than continue to endure such suffering. I gave in. The operation took place at the beginning of 1620. Two months later, Sir William was dead. The decision of a physician involves no more than the life of a sick person. Whereas the decision of Kings involves entire peoples. In both cases, however, the difficulty may be as acute; in both cases it is a man who decides, and his weakness is greater than his confidence, even when he is a King.

9 June 1647

I am irritated by the fascination exerted over the English by the image of the surgeon. They fear him, and yet they venerate him. There is something of a demi-god about a man who dares open bodies. They do not perceive the ignorance hidden behind the skill. No barber-surgeon has any knowledge of medicine. English law is right to place them under the tutelage of the physicians.

What, after all, is a barber-surgeon? A man who is sufficiently dexterous to wield the razor when he cuts a beard or opens an abscess. A person who is skilful with his hands, no more. A performer. As soon as the act extends to the inner organs, such as the bladder, instructions and control can come only from the physician. I had had no great difficulty in getting this rule accepted by the four surgeons placed under my orders at St Bartholomew's Hospital until the day when one of them retired and was replaced by Mr John Woodall.

There was no doubt that he was an excellent surgeon. Some sixty years of age, he already had a long career behind him. Woodall had first practised his art in France, Poland and Holland. Then he had been appointed first Surgeon-General to the East India Company. He had been Master of the Barber-Surgeons' Company. At about the time of his arrival at St Bartholomew's he published a manual of the surgical art, *The Surgeon's Mate,* which was a great success. The moment I saw him I realised that he would not be an easy subordinate. I was not wrong.

Of Herculean stature, with chiselled features, slow movements and an obstinate forehead, John Woodall was an honest man who had skilful fingers and a narrow mind. Like others of his kind he took offence the moment one tried to reason with him. He would not accept guidance. Having been a naval Surgeon-General, he had no intention of taking orders from a London physician. He despised academic instruction in medicine, saying that it could never be as valuable as the years of experience he had gained in his itinerant life. Anything taught in books, he had learnt far better from practical experience. He had seen actual cases of scurvy, and asserted that they could be cured by lemon juice, a remedy not mentioned in any book. He would be capable of teaching any young whipper-snapper of a graduate a trick or two. It was ludicrous for him to be forbidden to treat as he thought best the patients on whom he was asked to operate.

I showed myself as obstinate as he. But first I paid him a compliment. I was convinced of his ability, his dexterity amazed me, the movements of his hands were so admirable that I was ashamed of my own awkwardness. In point of fact, the law was not made for men like him. But he had to understand that the barber-surgeons of London were quite a different race. Almost all were former barbers, who for many years had known no more than how to shave a beard and cut hair. They had then become so bold as to use their razors to open an abscess. They had learnt to bandage a wound or use a cautery; a few had some slight knowledge of how to reduce a dislocated bone. But none of this manipulation made them competent to recognise diseases or prescribe their remedies. I told him of the horrors I had witnessed when I was one of the Censors of the College of Physicians. We had had to judge Stephen Bredwell, who was secretly fabricating pills containing bizarre and dangerous ingredients. The case of Edward Clarke was even more disturbing: he had killed several patients by prescribing mercury pills and other purges and sudorifics, not knowing the harm he was doing. There were also those barber-surgeons who employed magical practices, such as Robert Booker, who anointed his patients' bodies with a mysterious oil while pronouncing these cabalistic words:

> Three biters have bit him, heart, tongue and eye,
>   Three better shall help him presently,
>   God the Father, God the Son, and God the Holy Spirit.

What was there in common between these men and John Woodall? Did he not understand the peril that threatened honest, deluded citizens?

My remarks had not the slightest effect on the old naval surgeon. Some time later, I heard that he had called a secret meeting of three of my St Bartholomew's surgeons and eight other London barber-surgeons. They had prepared a petition to the House of Commons, in which they vilified the College of Physicians. They complained that the College had a strangle-hold on the surgeons, and prevented them from treating their patients in the correct manner. The College, they alleged, enjoyed an exorbitant privilege of which the patients operated on were the first victims. From their long experience, the surgeons knew the potions and other remedies most necessary for the cure of their patients. Through the tyranny of a corporation jealous of its monopoly, the physicians were raising an obstacle to this cure.

At a meeting of the College Comitia in 1621, consideration was given to what action should be taken against the surgeons' petition to Parliament. Something had to be done to prevent the naive Parliamentarians' agreeing to the barbers' request. It was later decided that the Fellows should be asked to explain to all the burgesses of Parliament of their acquaintance the dangers to which the population would be exposed if the privilege accorded to the College by the King were to be abolished. I was asked to visit the two members for Cambridge University, Dr. Goche and Sir Robert Naunton.

I was given a somewhat cold reception by these two gentlemen. Sir Robert, who had recently been promoted to the office of Secretary of State, declared that he had complaints to raise against the College. We admitted, said he, many more doctors from other universities than from Cambridge. Our selection was unfair and our examinations "unworthy of doctors." I tried in vain to prove the contrary. As is the case with many men of politics, it was clear that he would assist us only if there were a *quid pro quo* of which he could take advantage for the benefit of the university he represented.

We discussed the matter at length at the College in secret session. The general opinion was that no sacrifice was too great if it resulted in our quelling the senseless claims of the barber-surgeons and thus protecting our patients. It was decided that for the future, only candidates from Oxford and Cambridge should be admitted to the College. Furthermore, it was decided that a copy of the College's new Royal Charter should be taken to the university representatives. The result of all these efforts was excellent, and the barber-surgeons' petition was adjourned *sine die*. The College may have shown a certain cowardice in the face of the exigences of the Parliamentarians, but any form of cowardice is justified when the higher interests of the country and the health of its inhabitants are at stake.

John Woodall was not angry with me; quite the opposite. It seemed to me that he respected me more for not having yielded to him. But I was fairly sure that this deference and obedience were reserved for me alone. As my service to the King obliged me to be away from my hospital duties more and more frequently, I judged that the physician replacing me during my absence would have to deal with a John Woodall who had once again become recalcitrant. I spoke of this to the administrators of Saint Bartholomew's, and we agreed that the time had come to draw up a new set of rules in which the rights and duties of everyone would be clearly defined. I prepared a list of sixteen articles, which the Governors approved. It was laid down that the Physician to the Hospital should have sole power of decision over everything concerning the admission of patients, the treatment they were to receive, the date of their discharge, and in general over the whole administration of the hospital. No surgeon was to be permitted to open a body, trepan a head or perform any other operation without the approbation of the physician. No surgeon was to prescribe any remedy that had not first been approved by the physician. The apothecary was to make up the physician's prescriptions but was not to disclose to anyone the content of the prescribed remedies. The physician, on the other hand, was to be kept informed of everything, and the Matron and Sister were to be obliged to report to him every detail of the activities of all patients, apothecaries and surgeons.

Some years have passed since then, and I do not think I should be so severe today. But I remain certain that no community can live and act unless it has a leader who judges and decides. Animal communities seem harmonious because they have no knowledge of controversy: each follows the rules with blind obedience. Men, fortunately, are not animals, either in this respect or in others. But they pay dearly for their unceasing inclination to contest the order of things. I know well that this contestation reflects credit on man; to be a physician is to contest disease and death. But where the mania not to cede to the opinion of others exceeds all reasonable measure, the human group becomes inoperative and nothing good can result. So it is the happy mean that we should seek. At one extreme lies tyranny; the subordinate revolts, his wings have been clipped, his achievements lose all excitement for him, the crew let the galley drift and no longer propel it. At the other extreme, the contested leader can no longer guide the ship, anarchy ruins the assemblage, the community disintegrates.

The leader, then, must inspire not fear but respect. He must be followed for the joy of following him, and not passively obeyed. To succeed in such a design is perhaps the most difficult and important task, for a London hospital as well as for many other human groups. It seemed to me, in the course of those long years, that I was gradually discovering its secret. In the first place, the leader must manage to make others understand and share his pride in belonging to a community whose task is unique, noble and difficult. Every member of the community must feel the same pride, the same commitment. Not all can command, but all must have their share in the effort recognised, their share in the glory affirmed. There is something more. The leader must be more knowledgeable than those who surround him. If he is not, another must take his place. If I finally managed to gain the allegiance of my rebellious surgeons it was because my knowledge, my experience, my reading, my journeys, had given me an understanding that they did not possess, and because it was possible for me to offer them repeated proof of this.

31 August 1647

Ashburnham was in London for two days. I could not resist the desire to meet him. He had come from Hampton Court, where the King is being guarded by the Army. Ashburnham is the only man capable of informing me of the developments in the struggle between the Army and Parliament, and I was impatient to be in a better position to weigh up hopes and fears.

I have known him for many years. The King has complete confidence in him. He is a courtier, in the good old meaning of the word: a loyal, faithful servant, as blindly devoted to Charles as Eumaeus was to Ulysses, refusing to hold a different opinion from that of his King on any subject whatsoever. He had accompanied the Queen in her exile to Paris, but as soon as the King was once again in a position to receive his friends, towards mid-July, he hastened to return to England.

Ashburnham says that Charles is full of suspicion. He doubts the real intentions of the Army, in whose midst the subversive complaints of the formidable Agitators are daily more loudly heard. General Oliver Cromwell and his son-in-law Ireton rule the Council of War, but the Agitators are in the majority in the Army Council. Moreover, the King doubts Cromwell, also. Two months ago he was charmed when the General claimed to be his defender; it was he who, in June, allowed the King's chaplains and friends free access to him; it was thanks to him that the King was installed at Hampton Court, in the splendid old palace which Charles has always loved and where the royal hunts, to which I was occasionally invited, used to take place. It was Cromwell, finally, who at the beginning of August declared to Ashburnham, with tears in his eyes, that he was ashamed of having been mistaken about the person of the King, and that from then on God would read nothing in his heart other than total sincerity in the service of His Majesty. But he is one of those men whose sincerity vanishes when interest commands. Ashburnham believes that Cromwell is torn between two opposing sentiments. If the King—and his followers—could be persuaded onto its side, the Army could be certain of having the power to reduce Parliament to its mercy. But if Cromwell were to declare himself a Royalist he would become suspect in the eyes of the Agitators, and a traitor in the eyes of Parliament. Ashburnham thinks that Cromwell is still vacillating. He has prepared a treaty and submitted it to the King: this may equally well be a sincere act or a masterpiece of hypocrisy. In it, the Army and the King are turn and turn about adulated, but no one is given supreme command except, of course, God and England.

The King hesitates to sign this treaty. He says that it would be to sign his submission to the will of the Army and Cromwell, whereas it is his destiny to be a free arbiter between the Army and Parliament. He knows that if he chooses one of the two camps he will be bringing it the promise of victory. He senses the vulgar bargaining underlying all these transactions. He chooses to be above such malfeasance.

I have no difficulty in imagining Charles shrinking, once again, from all compromise. And yet, once again, this news disturbs me. If he continues in his refusals I fear that he will end by wearying those who still attach respect and political value to his person. He alienated Scotland and the Parliament in London merely for the honour of defending his Bishops; he is in danger of alienating the Army through the mistrust inspired in him by the vulgar mind and the ambition of Oliver Cromwell. This mixture of intransigency and scruple no doubt exists in many men. In Kings, it is called a sense of honour; in simple mortals like physicians, it is called *amour-propre*. *Amour-propre* is probably the source of more irritation than is a sense of honour, but it is more easy to subdue.

But who would dare to give advice to the King, in these

critical circumstances? Certainly not Ashburnham; he is too respectful and courteous. No one, in truth, and the King is assuredly more alone now than he ever was. I seem to see him in
the marvellous flowered paths that make the gardens of Hampton Court so enchanting, trying to decide what a sovereign worthy of the name ought to decide in the circumstances. He
implores God to enlighten him. All around him, the great palace
and the vast park remind him of the grandeur of the reigns preceding his own. A few years ago, in the same park, I sometimes
came across Charles of England as happy as a child, even forgetting that he was King.

Hampton Court is a rich harvest of memories for me. It was
there that part of my experimental work took place. Some time
in the 1630s the King, who used to go stag-hunting in the nearby
forest, spoke to me of my work. I told him that I was leaving
aside the mysteries of the heart and the circulation for another
enigma, the enigma of a phenomenon that is no doubt Nature's
greatest miracle, and yet a daily occurrence: the conception and
creation of a new being. A man penetrates a woman, he impreg-
nates her with his sperm and by some inexplicable means a new
human being will be born. In man, as in all animals, everyone is
agreed that both the male and the female have a necessary function in the genesis of the progeny. But no one has yet established
how it is that the sperm of the male renders the female fertile.
Our knowledge of this extraordinary phenomenon has not pro-
gressed for centuries, for lack of methodical observation. Tor-
rents of words have been pronounced, but no one has adduced
the slightest definite fact. I explained to the King that our century would reverse this scientific procedure: observation of Nature would come first, and reasoning afterwards. Charles was
passionately interested in these things. It was as if the study of
the phenomena of life were to him as a new toy is to a child. Not
only did he allow me to dissect whatever animals I chose from
those he killed in the hunt, he also wished to follow personally
the progress of my observations.

I liked to study the uteruses of pregnant hinds and does, because only with large animals was I able to see with the naked
eye the changes that take place in the first days of fertilisation.
The first thing to be determined was what became of the male

semen in the body of the female. Did it immediately evaporate? Did it penetrate into the uterus? I opened the uteruses of hinds killed during the days following coitus but could find no visible semen in them. I simply observed what I already knew, that in the rutting season—September—the uterus of the hind does not have its usual appearance: its interior is lined with a kind of slimy, viscid substance and seems to have lost its normal asperities. But it contains no semen. I showed these wombs to the King and told him that in order to learn more, it would be necessary to examine the cavity of the womb at regular intervals between the moment of coitus and the development of the foetus. The King consented, and gave orders that a dozen does were to be segregated in an enclosure immediately after they had been mounted by the bucks at the beginning of October; they could thus be sacrificed at increasingly longer periods of time after their separation from the male that had impregnated them.

A surprise awaited me: I dissected several wombs, and in none of them did I find the slightest trace of semen, nor the slightest apparent rudiment of a foetus. And yet all the does that I had not dissected later fawned at their appointed time. The keepers and huntsmen could not believe their eyes. It is impossible, they said, that the womb should be empty after conception. And yet the fact remained: after impregnation by the male, there was an interval during which nothing appeared in the uterus; it was only a little later that the foetus of the fawn began to develop.

The strangest suppositions came to my mind. It might be that the sperm is no sooner introduced into the vagina than it becomes transformed into an impalpable substance capable of giving the necessary instructions to the female organism from a distance, in the same way as the brain gives an architect immaterial instructions to enable him to construct a building. But I have to admit that I did think the fabrication of an embryo by distant command extremely conjectural. Aristotle and the Ancients so frequently invoked so-called subtle and invisible spirits to explain what they did not understand that I am on my guard against such constructs of thought. They can see nothing to link cause and effect so, being unable to tolerate this void, they invent something to fill it and rely on suppositions which, by their

very essence, will never be able to be proved. When confronted
with an incomprehensible phenomenon, man's reason has every
right to build hypotheses: this insatiable research into the unknown is even one of the most natural and marvellous passions
of the human spirit. But the procedure is not the same for the
scientist and the majority of men. The average man may indulge
in whatever divagation he pleases, but the man of science must
choose only those conjectures that can be proved by experiment;
he must leave the unverifiable to other activities in which science
has no place. And, if he cannot find an hypothesis that it is possible—at least provisionally—to verify, he must have the specific
courage of the scientist: he must confess his ignorance. To say *I
do not know* is not a defeat, it is a victory over oneself, it is a
door left open for the men who will follow us and whose understanding will be different, an encouragement to research. I do
not know, I still do not know, how the sperm of the male fertilises the female and gives rise to new lives.

1 September 1647

Ki ng Charles has always been interested in medicine. And anyway, Kings and gods have from the beginning of time kept a close eye, whether fascinated or hostile, on our discipline. Zeus entrusted it to his son Apollo. Apollo took the matter sufficiently seriously to delegate all power in the art of healing to his son Aesculapius. But on the day when Aesculapius took it into his head to resuscitate Tyndareus, husband of the beautiful Leda for whom Jupiter felt great affection, his grandfather flew into a rage and struck the imprudent healer with a thunderbolt. Thus, from time immemorial, physicians have learnt to their cost that political power can wantonly mete out to them either its wrath or its favours.

I remember the business about tobacco which was debated in the College of Physicians in October 1628. The King had asked us for a report on the tobacco plants grown in England and Ireland, their value, and their effect on health: an apparently inoffensive question but which in reality concealed an affair of State.

Its secret was confided to me in the course of a private conversation with a member of the King's Privy Council. What the King wanted from us was a condemnation of the tobacco grown on English soil, because it was in competition with Virginian tobacco: the King had good reason to oppose everything that might be injurious to the Virginian weed.

Virginia had always been a difficult English colony. It was a long time since the Indians from the River Chickahominy had been on terms of mutual friendship with the British colonists and had become proud subjects of His Gracious Majesty King James. Powhatan, their great chief, had given his favourite daughter, Pocahontas, in marriage to John Rolfe, an English Captain, and she had been received at the English Court in a manner befitting the most beautiful of all foreign princesses. Powhatan died, and his successor declared the most cruel and bloody war on our Virginian compatriots. The British colony was overwhelmed by misfortune, famine and discouragement. James, and after his death Charles, decided to take things firmly in hand. In 1627 Charles sent Virginia a Governor well known for his severity, energy and arrogance, a man who although he is no relation of mine bears the same name: John Harvey. His mission was to keep the colonists within bounds, to intimate to them that they were in the pay of the King of England, that they did not have the right to sell their tobacco to any other buyers than the King's representatives, and that they must understand once and for all that the entire profits must be passed on to the Crown. I should add that they were refused all the civil rights enjoyed by citizens living in the motherland. A revolt was only to be expected.

The crux of the matter, then, was a question of competition. If the English and Irish were allowed to grow the precious weed, the source of such great profits, on our soil, that would be so much hard, solid gold that would escape the King's coffers. Moreover, rumours of a possible rebellion among the Virginian colonists were beginning to reach London. Tobacco constituted the entire wealth of Virginia; it was grown everywhere, even in the streets of Jamestown. If the colony were no longer able to sell the magic plant it would be ruined at one stroke, and attempts at revolt would be more difficult to contain. It was therefore necessary to forbid tobacco to be grown in England, but as ours is a country that does not take kindly to such prohibitions, the College of Physicians was required to declare that only Virginian tobacco was acceptable for the health of English citizens.

And above all, the College was not to write that tobacco was unwholesome in itself. At the beginning of this century King James published a pamphlet against the habit of smoking, a copy of which is in my library. He adjured his compatriots not to follow the barbaric and atheistic Indians in this bestial habit.

The Indians, he wrote, had spread the idea that tobacco was good for the smallpox: this was not true! And at all events, was it not these primitive peoples who had given the smallpox to Christianity? Is it not indecent to see civilised men, like savages, sending the stinking vapour into their noses, and from there into their brains? The tobacco habit is repugnant to the eye, detestable to the nose, dangerous to the lungs, deleterious to the brain. It is against Nature, it has the smell of the fumes of Hell.

There are also, in James's pamphlet, many medical considerations which I will not transcribe here, because while they may perhaps be of a certain literary felicity they have little scientific foundation. But that is not the important point. If the College of Physicians had really been required to produce a work that would be useful to the population, it should have been asked for a study of the detriments and benefits of tobacco in general, not for a comparative study of the Virginian and English plants. But the art of government is certainly not the art of protecting the citizens, as the naive might suppose.

The meeting at the College was animated by divergent opinions. Everyone now knew what the King expected of us. All wished to accede to his desires, but none wanted to give a shameful answer. We were being asked to make a declaration that bordered on mendacity, and we would not agree to lie. Our text had to contain sufficient ambiguities to be to the King's taste without causing us to lose our innocence and our attachment to the truth. After interminable discussion it became apparent that we could not draw up so difficult a report in committee. One of us, in the silence of his study, must first produce a draft plan. There then occurred what I had feared: I was nominated for this impossible task by the fifteen or so members present, and there was no way I could avoid it.

I wrote that the tobacco grown in our country had not yet proved itself innocuous. I wrote that we should not expect it to gain the perfection of other tobaccos grown under meridional skies. I wrote that in southern climes, those other tobaccos had their natural maturity, vigour and efficiency. My report did not contain a single untruth. The College adopted it without a single alteration.

Once again I had experienced the bad conscience stemming

from hypocritical words and the impossibility of never having recourse to them. This need for purity that possesses every one of us is perpetually clashing with the obligation to dissimulate. It is fairly easy to be an upright man in the eyes of others, more difficult to be one in our own eyes. The perfection of the English tongue has now placed hypocrisy within every man's reach. I think I use our language as well as any other man, but it often leaves me with a bitter taste, which is not reasonable. The passion for truth has been my sole mistress throughout my life, yet I have often been constrained to be unfaithful to her, while each time feeling this as a blemish on the image I have of myself. Perhaps that is what pride is? Man is so made that he seeks to avoid every inner contradiction, but he never manages to do so. He believes that serenity demands that he be completely at peace with himself, but he perceives that this peace is impossible. And in this way we go through life. With luck, we appear to others as an upright, harmonious, balanced person, whereas in our solitude we every day encounter the flaws in our apparent limpidity.

CROYDON
4 September 1647

The Army is approaching London by easy stages. I have been advised to leave, and to be forgotten for a time. If by ill-fortune events were to turn against the King, the rancour of his enemies might be sufficiently virulent for them to call for my imprisonment. My brother Daniel has offered me hospitality in his house near Croydon. It will be hard for me to be exiled from London, no doubt, although I am not afraid of a retreat in the country. I shall be closer to the trees, flowers, insects and birds, objects which are in keeping with my meditative mood and which may even lead to new experiments.

Daniel's house is called Little Valley. It is a vast, beautiful residence, entirely covered with ivy and surrounded by a park whose vivid green lawns, multi-coloured flowers and sturdy trees make life pleasant to Nature lovers. My brother Daniel is often away from home. His business keeps him in London. But his son, also called Daniel, lives here, and I spend some part of each day with him. The mother and daughters leave us on our own, our conversations bore them. At sixteen, my nephew has already acquired a gravity that enchants me. I speak to him of life and death, of the sap that rises in the tree trunks, of the blood that circulates in us, of Nature whose daily miracle in the long run we forget. I try to show him the secret links that unite all living beings and are even harmoniously inscribed within inanimate beings. The peace in this garden, far from London, has revived my enthusiasm for the observation of Nature. The image of Adam in a verdant Paradise is renewed in my eyes when I see that handsome adolescent, who resembles a Greek ephebus, walking lithely by my side along the flower-lined paths. In truth, man has the setting he deserves, unless it is the setting that deserves to be inhabited by men, so that they shall marvel at it. Daniel appears to be touched by my meditations on Nature, and his emotion pleases me, for in the England of today young men of his age seem to me to have lost the curiosity and enthusiasm that fired my youth and which remain, for the old man I have become, my only reason for loving life.

My nephew had heard his parents allude to my work on the circulation of the blood; they had told him that it was an important and admirable discovery but that some jealous doctors had declared it to be fallacious. I explained to Daniel what I had demonstrated. I told him how the traditional teaching was that the heart and arteries are filled with air, whereas in fact they contain nothing but blood. People had formerly imagined that the blood ebbed and flowed, but I had proved that it follows a closed pathway of its own, circulating from the left ventricle of the heart down to the extremities of the limbs, then rising to the right ventricle, going from there to the lungs, closing the circuit in the left side of the heart, and so on. This great idea of the perpetual *circulation* of the fluid that is the most essential to our life had been the mainstay of my existence. It was true that many embittered men had refused to believe in it, simply because of their blind attachment to the teaching of the Ancients. But I, and some others, had fostered a new spirit in science which refused to submit to the authority of ancient texts when they were contradicted by more precise observation. I had as much pride in my contribution to this new method, to this revolution in thought, as I had joy in my discovery of the circulation. But—and why should I hide it—this discovery had filled me with satisfaction. Not only was I sure that it was true and that the present-day hesitations would disappear in the future, but I found the image of a circular flux pleasing, because it took its place in a customary law of Nature. I saw it, when I allowed myself to dream, as linked to the circular movement of the heavenly bodies, to the eternal re-birth of the seasons, the perpetual cycle of water which evaporates from the sea to the sky, then falls as rain, before once again evaporating. To discover one of Nature's secrets, however small, is always a joy, but to discover a secret that appears to be in harmony with universal laws is pure delight. Daniel seemed to be drinking in every one of my words. The story of the heart and the blood captivated him. His eyes shone like those of a child hearing the thrilling tale of the adventures of Robin Hood for the first time.

We walked on, side by side. There is a difference of nearly half a century between my age and his. For a moment I had been speaking to him as to a friend, a man had been exchanging his thoughts with another man, the half-century had been obliterated, the chain of the generations had taken on the misleading appearance of an equal understanding between travelling companions. But the gulf that separates the man who has his life behind him and the one who is only starting his can never really be bridged. You make signs of recognition from one bank to the other, affection is exchanged, the mature man brandishes the torch that the other will soon have to hold in his stead, the same youthfulness possesses both for a moment. And then the years separate them once again; the one makes his way towards life, the other towards death. I write these lines without bitterness, for a naturalist does not rebel against the death of man. Death brings him nearer to all his fellow living beings who, without exception, obey this same law: all the links in the chain must disappear after having engendered those that will follow; no link, however proud, signifies very much in itself; it is only the chain that counts.

5 September 1647

I find the image of a chain of men pleasing: I, like many others, am a careful but uneasy observer of that chain. Each successive generation enriches the adventure. But how many obstacles, how many reversals there are. The history of Athens and Rome was an attempt to conquer a new dignity. A morality and an art of living were born on the shores of the Mediterranean. At the same time, the knowledge of numbers and of Nature made immense Progress, endowing man with an increasing power of mastery over the elements. The path seemed to be leading slowly upwards. Then came Christ, who announced that this path had a meaning. From then on there was an abundance of nourishment for the soul, as for the intellect and for action. True, some people consider that the whole movement consists of artifices that men have forged to conceal the *signifying nothing* of the Tragedy of Macbeth, in the same way as an unguent conceals a wound. But even such soured minds do not deny that our destiny has a pace and a progression. The passengers that we all are thus put their shoulders to the wheel of a cart which they may believe is travelling towards successful accomplishments.

Meanwhile, ever since Antiquity, these images of hope, this confidence in the future, these efforts, have coincided with decadence and degradation. Athens has fallen asleep, Rome is no more than the shadow of an empire that once taught the world, and we, who have taken over from them, shall tomorrow perhaps see our own foundations shake in their turn. The barbarism of men and groups is perpetually undermining the path.

And yet human existence becomes intolerable if we can no longer encompass it within a work that surpasses it. I want to believe until my dying day that my work continues that of Aristotle and Galen, and that it will lead to the work done in the centuries to come. This too is a circulation, but this time one which started with the men who lived before us and will be perpetuated to the time of those who are not yet born. The continuity of the intellect is superimposed on the continuity of Nature, such as I have encountered it in all my studies of generation.

I have already spoken in this diary of the generation of the Cervidae that I observed at Hampton Court. I have spent even more of my life in trying to understand how the egg is born from the bird, and how the bird is then born from that same egg.

Once again, my predecessors were marvellous; if they were grossly mistaken it was because they allowed full rein to their imagination without going to the trouble of careful observation. Aristotle certainly lighted the way. I know that he opened hens' eggs, trying to understand the generation of the chick. Yet he reached wrong conclusions. He probably followed preconceived ideas rather than strict, rigorous observations. At the beginning of my research, I decided that my master Fabricius, who is one of the best anatomists I ever knew, would be my guide. But soon I discovered he had made great mistakes in his *De formatione ovi et pulli*. The reason is that he relies on the assertions of those who came before him instead of himself looking into the egg. He writes that the chick is created out of the white of the egg, by the chalazae, that is, those twisted membranous appendages of the white that go from both ends of the egg to the yolk and serve only, as I have demonstrated, to suspend the yolk as if by ropes. Ulysses Androvani even advances the entirely imaginary supposition that the chalazae are the seed of the cock. These errors do not prevent me from highly respecting these great men. A discovery always owes its basis to the work of predecessors, even if their work was fallacious. I sometimes contradict Aristotle, but in my opinion he remains the great founder of what we know about living creatures. Yet I believe that we must stick more closely than our predecessors to controlled facts and experiments. If I was fortunate enough to detect the past errors, it is because I decided to open hens' eggs each day, after the mother hen had begun to sit on them to in- cubate them. I saw that the creation of the chick is begun not in the white, but in a very small spot that grows on the coat of the yolk which was erroneously named a cicatricula (for it is not a cicatrix) by my master Fabricius. I have seen this spot grow from hour to hour. I saw it glisten, turn red, and pulsate from the fourth day on, and through close observation I saw that the ver- milion point pulsating in its centre was a heart. Towards the end of the third day I was even able, with the aid of a magnifying lens in a bright light, to see the purplish, palpitating rudiment.

That the heart of a bird is created in three days, and innumer- able similar hearts in innumerable eggs of innumerable clutches, that all these hearts are placed in the correct part of the body of innumerable chicks that are incredibly identical to their par- ents—this is a great miracle that will still astonish me when I draw my last breath.

This miracle of the egg, which by successive metamorphoses ends by creating the perfection of the fully developed being, is not confined to birds. I imagine that all living beings, or almost all, have their origin in an egg, even though I have not yet been able to discover with certainty the egg that generates man. But the new light that my observations have thrown on the bird's egg merely sharpens my curiosity. As always, the discovery of new facts makes me more aware of the gaps in our knowledge. How does the egg manage to reproduce so exactly the forms of its progenitors, thus assuring the immortality of the species? How is it that the egg, which is obviously fabricated by the fe- male, is fertilised by the male through a kind of contagion anal- ogous to that which generates the pox, leprosy or phthisis in the body of a healthy individual, through contact with a sufferer from these diseases? I shall die before men have understood the final secret of this essential mystery. But I shall have clearly per- ceived the web of the destiny of our bodies: a male, a female, fertilised eggs, other males, other females, and both the human species and the animal species perpetuated in this fashion, while the individuals disappear one after the other. For them, a short life; for the species, limitless time. And for them, therefore, the obligation to melt into the species and derive pleasure there- from, in order that there should be no bitterness in their cer- tainty of being no more than a passing link.

10 September 1647

My brother Daniel died this morning. He came back from London yesterday and complained of lassitude and pains in the chest. I watched over him all night long. He was bled, but it did not the slightest good. We closed his eyes at dawn.

20 November 1647

I have just learnt of a most unexpected event. The news came to me in a letter from John Ashburnham, one of the King's faithful companions. He knows of my retreat in Croydon, where I had asked him to keep me informed. Today's news is momentous: Charles has escaped from Hampton Court.

I prefer to transcribe Ashburnham's letter in his own terms here, for fear of betraying so extraordinary a narrative by inaccurate notes.

"There was a rumour that some Agitators had determined to assassinate the King. His Majesty was anxious. The projected treaty with the Army, which I mentioned to you, had been rejected by Charles, and after this refusal General Cromwell's visits had abruptly ceased. The King then wrote him a flattering letter in an attempt to appease him. Berkeley and I were charged to deliver this letter to the General in person, but he did not even receive us.

"At the same time, the Army were doing nothing to hide the rumours of the assassination plot; it was as if they wished to provoke him to flight. His Majesty called Berkeley and me to him in secret, and told us to wait for him with only a small escort at the edge of the forest. He joined us during the night. He guided us through the forest, with whose paths he was more familiar than any of the party. Strange to say, we met no Army sentinels. The King told us that he had left a letter to the Houses of Parliament on his table in which he announced that he thought himself bound, both by natural and political obligations, to retire for some time from the public view of both his friends and enemies. I observed that he also left behind him his favourite greyhound Gipsey, a dog he loves even better than he loves us: this detail shows the measure of his distress.

"Once out of the forest, our party stopped in order to decide on which road to take. It was only then that I realized what an extraordinary situation we were in: the King did not know where to go. He spoke of making for Southampton and taking ship for Jersey. But there had been no time to prepare a vessel; it was a mad venture. I suggested the Isle of Wight, as being much easier to reach. It would always be possible to find another boat there. Moreover, I knew that there were very few soldiers on the island, that the inhabitants had remained loyal, that Sir John Oglander's house would provide a safe retreat, and finally that the Governor of the island, Robert Hammond, could probably be won over to the King's cause. Hammond is the nephew of the King's favourite chaplain. It is true that he is also the nephew of an old officer who is extremely hostile to the Monarchy, and that he is himself a Colonel in the Parliamentary Army. The King remembered him, for his chaplain uncle had brought him to Court in former days. We decided on the Isle of Wight.

"When we had reached the coast facing the Isle of Wight the King decided to wait at the Earl of Southampton's house at Titchfield, and to send Berkeley and me on alone to ask Hammond whether he would give him sanctuary. We were to tell him that the King's design was not to flee the Army, but to put himself out of the reach of a small group of corrupt men who had sworn to assassinate him. He had chosen to take refuge with Hammond because he knew his birth and his sense of honour.

"We were apprehensive. Berkeley, always ironic, told me that he foresaw very clearly 'the image of the gallows' awaiting him. Before we left the King we begged him not to await our return too long but, if we were not back within twenty-four hours, to assume we had been taken and make plans to escape on his own.

"When we found ourselves face to face with the Governor I deputed Berkeley to address him, but he began in a most unskilful fashion. We had agreed not to reveal the fact that the King had left Hampton Court, but with his first words Berkeley idiotically gave away our secret: 'Who do you think, Governor, is near you?' Colonel Hammond understood immediately and turned deathly pale. He exclaimed passionately that we had put him in an impossible situation. If the King had not already left Hampton Court, he begged us to leave him there. If he was on his way, he, the Governor, would have to choose between his duty to His Majesty and the observance of his trust to the Army. Gradually, however, Hammond recovered his sense and invited us to dinner and a conference. Finally, he told us his decision; he would come with us to the King, to show that he was prepared to perform whatever should be expected from a person of honour and honesty.

"Hammond asked the Captain of the Castle to come with us. We all four left for Titchfield, where we had left the King. I asked the others to wait below and went in alone to the King. When he heard that we had brought Hammond with us the King became vastly agitated; never in my life have I seen him thus. I believe that for a moment he actually thought himself betrayed. He told me that in our absence he had thought of a sure way to procure a vessel, but that now, through our fault, everything was in jeopardy. How could we have made the fatal mistake of bringing a Colonel of the Parliamentary Army to him before being assured of his total fidelity? I was so heartbroken to see His Majesty in such a state that I suffered a momentary aberration. Trembling, I asked him whether he wished us to dispatch the Governor and the Captain who were waiting below, unarmed. Luckily, the King replied that one did not assassinate two innocent men, even to save a crown. You, dear Doctor Harvey, who know men's weaknesses, I hope you will forgive me this minute of madness during which I considered becoming a murderer. I shall never forgive myself for it.

"In a hollow voice, the King said that since his hand had been forced, he now had no choice; all he could do was leave the issue to God. The Governor of the Isle of Wight was introduced and made humble and respectful protestations to the King, which appeared to restore His Majesty's peace of mind. Hammond seemed sincere. He conducted the King to Carisbrooke Castle and assured him that he would be in perfect security. May that be the truth!

"God keep you. Do not forget the King in your prayers.

"Your obedient servant,

John Ashburnham"

I am grateful to John for having related the events to me in detail. No doubt he felt the need to put all vicissitudes in writing. I have read and re-read his letter in order to try to find more hope than irritation in it. I cannot prevent myself from thinking that an escape, to be propitious, should be better prepared. Alas, Kings are often maladroit in such circumstances. The best of them have learnt to reign, but not to flee. In that they are less skilful than simple citizens. Since the time when Pompey fled to Egypt in order to save his life, although death awaited him there, many men of State, many sovereigns, have made the most fatal usage of their flight.

25 November 1647

How unjust the English sometimes are to those who govern them! Peoples do not make the same use of their reason as individuals do. Considered separately, men seem wisely egotistic, they know how to weigh up their advantages, they act to defend them. Gathered together in a nation, the same men seem to lose their sight. They become deaf to their own interests. It is sufficient to offer them a few skilfully coloured images to disturb their humour and their judgement, they become fired with enthusiasm for a man, a party, a certainty, or even a construct of their minds, they dream of an imaginary society in which everyone would be King and, animated by these uncertain dreams, they destroy a reality whose value they have forgotten.

When I compare the wealth and good fortune of England with the misery and misfortune of the countries I have visited on the Continent, I feel bitter about the folly of the ruinous Civil War that is tearing us apart today. I know no country that has been so well protected from famine as England. In truth, the diet of the English is often too rich, both in the country and in the towns. I have encountered country repasts that fill the purses of the physicians and gravediggers. I have lived in London for more than forty years, and observed its increasing opulence right up to the beginning of the recent troubles. One has only to walk in the heart of the City, at the Stock Exchange, to see merchandise from the four corners of the globe, and crowds of buyers jostling one another in the shops. The streets are constantly enlivened by splendid equipages. Quite recently, carriages that may be hired by the hour or by the month have begun to compete with the boatmen's small craft in which for a small sum one may travel up and down our waterway, the Thames. If one enters a tavern such as the *Mermaid,* or the *Crown and Harp,* one sees my compatriots stuffing themselves with poultry, ham, venison, sturgeon or various choice pies, and drinking gin or sherry to the point of intoxication. The oxen in Smithfield Market are all big and fat. In London, the theatres are full every evening, the churches and palaces display great treasures, the parks and gardens offer visitors the agreeable sight of flowers, fruit and vegetables, or even, as at Lambeth, the rare plants collected by John Tradescant, our King's gardener. Another thing I like about England is that there is no barrier between the nobility, the *bourgeoisie* and the world of commerce. I like the fact that at the establishment they call *The Ship,* where woollens, satins and velvets may be bought, the shopkeepers are the sons of Sir George Hunt. I like the fact that the most eminent personages frequently resort to their local tavern to drink with their cobbler or their fishmonger.

If the English had seen what I have seen across the Channel, they would recognise their good fortune, and they might very well not lend themselves to a Civil War which only serves the interests of a few ambitious men. During my visit to France in 1630, I was struck by the misery of the countryside in Normandy and Touraine. I was even more affected by the distress of Germany in the course of the long continental journey on which I accompanied the Earl of Arundel in 1636. Tomorrow I shall try to note down in this diary my recollections of that journey.

26 November 1647

Lord Arundel had been sent to Germany by King Charles on a mission to the Habsburg Emperor Ferdinand II. This was on the eve of the Diet of Ratisbon that was to choose the future Elector Palatine. Charles considered that the title belonged as of right to his nephew Prince Charles Louis, but the latter had a formidable rival in Maximilian von Wittelsbach, Duke of Bavaria, who had already been occupying the Palatinate for some years and who, moreover, had just married Emperor Ferdinand's daughter. Arundel's was a difficult mission. He had to prevail upon the father-in-law to abandon his son-in-law, using only the force of persuasion, for our King rejected all thought of going to war to secure the Palatinate: it was an almost hopeless task.

Lord Arundel had asked for a very large retinue and much ostentatious pomp. The Emperor had to be impressed. This was also necessary as a protection against possible unfortunate encounters on a route infested with the troops of an interminable war into which, for the previous eighteen years, all the countries of Europe had been dragged.

The King ordered me to accompany this embassy. I was glad of the opportunity, for I could see in it the possibility of meeting distinguished anatomists and physicians with whom I was not so far acquainted. The King's ship *Happy Entrance* landed us on the shores of Holland on April 10th. We travelled to The Hague, and thence to Arnhem. There, a battle was in progress, and the Spaniards refused to let us pass. But the next day the Dutch commander had regained the advantage, and he allowed us to continue on our way. We soon left the United Provinces behind us and entered Germany. Sailing up the Rhine, we decided to sleep in the boats, for there was a virulent epidemic of the Plague in the region. We were told that dozens of people died from the disease every day. At last we reached Cologne, which the epidemic had spared. There I visited the church of Saint Ursula, where it is said that the Saint is interred with eleven thousand virgins. Our barge, pulled by nine horses, reached Koblenz, where once again a battle was raging. Hearing who we were, however, both sides most obligingly suspended the fighting and allowed us to pass.

The farther we advanced up the river, the more desolate was the sight that met our eyes. The towns and villages on both sides had been ravaged. The state of the survivors was pitiable. Food no longer got through, and famine completed the effects of the war and the pillage. The inhabitants were reduced to eating grass, dogs and rats. Despite their lassitude, their gaunt faces and their ragged clothing, they remained smiling and accepted with dignity the money and provisions distributed to them on Lord Arundel's behalf. Men are astonishingly capable of enduring the most unendurable situations. According to whim, we call this either courage or resignation.

But why that immense misery extending, like leprosy, over lands that seemed made for man's delight? Why have men, once again, lost this Paradise? Why so many undernourished people here, while others, elsewhere, gorge themselves and waste so much? Why do we not know how to avert these great ills? Men pray to Heaven and build cathedrals, but should they not first take their affairs in hand themselves? It was the denial of disease that gave rise to medicine, but is not the misery of the world another disease, which requires other studies and other doctors? At the origin of their misery is war, which men say they do not like, but for a naturalist observing them this is obviously not true. If it were, they would not indulge in it. War brings in its wake poverty, famine and epidemics, in the same way as a disease is followed by complications and sequelae. Alas, this century is still disposed to believe in the fatality of war and misfortune. And then, the fact that the population of all these regions is increasing provides more fertile ground for the birth of hatred, for killers who no longer know their victims, for indifference to the fate of other people. It may be that men were created to live in small, rather isolated groups, where individual aversions would counter-balance individual loves without too much disturbance. Respect may be found between two individuals, but not between two multitudes. We need to make a clean sweep of all pre-conceived ideas and, as if we were dealing with a question of anatomy, make a list of the errors committed by our ancestors that we are still not knowledgeable enough to correct.

Continuing on our way through those desolate regions, we reached Nuremberg on May 11th and stayed there for eleven days. This lively, joyous town afforded us some respite from the malaise from which we had suffered while traversing those wretched lands. I knew that Professor Caspar Hofmann lived at Nuremberg, or rather Altdorf, not far away. He was a distinguished anatomist of whom I had heard much and who, I had been told, was violently opposed to my conclusions on the circulation of the blood. Here I had a chance to convince him.

Seven days after we arrived I gave a public demonstration in the largest amphitheatre in the whole of Germany, the anatomy theatre at the University of Altdorf. Only one of the many auditors interested me: Caspar Hofmann. My sole design was to prove to him the truth of what I had written eight years earlier in my *De motu cordis*. When the demonstration was over, Hofmann promised to let me know his thoughts on the subject the very next day. I was looking forward to hearing from him; the truth was so dazzling that it could not fail to be obvious to the eyes of the Altdorf anatomist.

The very next day, in fact, I received the following letter:

"Your unbelievable kindness, my Harvey, makes me not only like you but love you. Hence you have more readily obtained from me my fulfillment today of what I promised you yesterday, namely my opinion of your circulation. I hope, moreover, that you will accept it in the spirit in which I give it to you, with no malice to vex you . . . but simply and frankly . . .

"I will first deal with you here rhetorically.

"I. You appear to accuse Nature of folly in that she went astray in a work of almost prime importance, namely the making and distribution of food. Once that is admitted, what degree of confusion will not follow in other works which depend on the blood?

"II. You appear to disapprove of that which you praise in word, namely the universally accepted view of Nature, that she is not lacking in the essentials but does not, however, abound in unnecessary things . . .

"Fare you well, my Harvey, and walk well with your most illustrious Count, my most gracious Lord, whose hands I humbly kiss.

"Written at Altdorf the 19th May 1636,
Caspar Hofmann"

I felt extremely bitter when I read this missive. It seemed, then, that eminent personages, widely esteemed and respected, were capable of denying obvious facts by taking refuge behind so-called principles. By what means may we judge of the reason or folly of Nature? How can we have the conceit to decide that the circulation of the blood is unnecessary? I am in possession of a truth that is inherent in facts observed with humility, and not in principles asserted with arrogance: shall I always be faced with Caspar Hofmanns who try to stifle my discovery? I took up my pen and wrote that obstinate anatomist a very long letter which was in no way inferior to his in courtesy, but which firmly re-stated my proof. I even went so far as to tell him that his own work had helped me to clarify my ideas on the circulation, and that I had mentioned his name in *De motu cordis*. Some years later I heard that Hofmann was still mocking those whom he called the *circulators,* a word also used, I was told, for itinerant quacks. The particular characteristic of men like him—and they are legion—is a narrow-mindedness that is the product of the meeting of their intelligence and their pride. They are intelligent, and soon become aware of the fact. From it they derive pride, and begin to admire their own intellect to such a degree that they deny anyone else the right to encroach on their certainties.

28 November 1647

My recollections of my journey through Germany also bring back the memory of that noble lord, the Earl of Arundel. When he died in Padua, last year, I lost a protector and friend, and England lost its most eminent connoisseur of art. He had communicated his passion for painting to King Charles, and helped him bring two excellent contemporary Flemish painters to London, Rubens and Van Dyck. Nevertheless, the King's especial predilection was for the Italian canvasses of the last century, and he asked Arundel to bring back all the Raphaels, Correggios and Veroneses he could buy in the course of our travels.

I had known the Earl for more than twenty years. I had been in medical attendance on his family and had often seen him after that time. Everyone who knew him was struck by his great height, his strong features, his dark eyes, his aquiline nose, his natural elegance. A year before our mission to Germany the Earl had asked me to perform one of the strangest autopsies of my whole existence. It was on one Thomas Parr, an exceptional British subject because, first married at the age of eighty, he had done penance for adultery when he was a hundred and five, had re-married at a hundred and twelve, and died, so they said, at the age of one hundred and fifty-two. The Earl had brought him to London from distant Shropshire in order to show him to the King. But the journey and London life had been fatal, and Thomas Parr had died in Arundel's house. The autopsy revealed organs in as good condition as would have been expected of a subject who had lived half as long. I suspect that some men have the coquetry to add a few years to their real age, just as some women have the coquetry to subtract some from theirs.

I wrote a detailed report on my findings and gave it to the Earl. He thanked me at length, with the extreme affability he never abandoned no matter what the occasion. I wondered what had made him take an interest in this case of exceptional longevity. The answer was obvious: more than anything else, Lord Arundel was a *collector*. He had a passion for every rare object, he was prepared to pay the necessary price to have such treasures within reach, to be able to contemplate them, admire them, extract their secrets from them. He was a lover of curiosities. A man of over a hundred and fifty years was a curiosity just as likely to fire his imagination as the portrait of an ageless Erasmus, painted by Holbein the Younger, which Arundel had often mentioned. He told me that whenever he looked at this portrait he felt as if immobilised by some strange force: Erasmus's hollow cheeks, his thin, scornful lips, his sunken eyes whose gaze seemed to be directed beyond the real world—all this set the Earl dreaming, and his dream was peopled with supernatural figures which no doubt had some resemblance to the old man who had forgotten to die at the usual age.

Lord Arundel has had a profound influence on my present attitude to works of art. He taught me to look at them, to prepare myself for the particular joy offered by some of them. The galleries in Arundel Castle contain not only the most beautiful Holbeins in all Europe, but also many other treasures. The emotion distilled by certain canvasses is very different from the emotion inherent in scientific knowledge. The former strikes directly, not through any kind of logic but rather by emitting invisible signs, every one of which evokes the lost memory of a past emotion, but these signs and memories are being brought together for the first time. Scientific emotion, on the other hand, is derived from reason; it is an adjunct to a cold, logical operation of the mind, as beauty may arise out of a cold geometrical figure. In the past, the fact that there was no distinction between art and science was no doubt a source of confusion, to the detriment of science and without great profit to art. But art may be the repose of the scientist, as love affairs may be the repose of the warrior. For my part, I have not only found rare pleasure in art, but also the proof that man's works are not solely those of his intellect and observation. Half of our being eschews logical rules, and that half is as valuable as the other. And all the joy I have derived from art I owe, in the main, the Earl of Arundel.

In the gardens of his castle there were hundreds of statues, busts, carved stones, antique vases and other objects. During our journey up the Rhine, Lord Arundel told me of the way he had very gradually assembled these priceless collections. That was how I heard the extraordinary story of the Paros marbles.

The adventure had begun about a dozen years previously. The Earl had a permanent agent in Italy, whose only mission was to find him new masterpieces, and who excelled in this pursuit. This agent was the Reverend William Petty, and I made his acquaintance much later. Twelve years before our German excursion the Earl had decided to send Petty to the Levant, to bring back all the rare pieces he could discover. Petty heard that in the Aegean, on the Isle of Paros, a *chargé d'affaires* had found antique tablets inscribed with Greek characters and had bought them for fifty *louis*. Petty had been adroit enough to acquire these marbles and had brought them back to England. Lord Arundel immediately became tremendously enthusiastic about these admirable tablets, had them set into the walls of his castle and asked a famous scholar, an expert in ancient scripts, to try to decipher the mysterious inscriptions. Two years later the work was completed and the texts published in a Latin translation. That was when the Paros marbles revealed their secret. They consisted of nothing less than the Parian Chronicle which recounts, in chronological order, the chief events of ancient Greek history, from Cecrops, who founded Athens in the sixteenth century before the Christian Era, to the Archontes who governed the city more than two thousand years later. Everything is to be found there: the history of the foundation of Thebes; the arrival of the Egyptian colonies; the institution of the Panathenaea, of the Eleusinian mysteries, and the games in the forest of Nemea; the siege and fall of Troy; the invention of weights and measures by the Argive Pheidon; the birth of Comedy and Tragedy; the murder of Hipparchus; the Battle of Marathon. It speaks of Homer, Aeschylus, Euripides, Aristotle; and each time Arundel cited a famous name I trembled with emotion as the memory of my school years came back to me, for whenever I heard the epic stories of ancient Greece I was always in raptures. Strange correspondence across time: I, William Harvey, a citizen of a country as dissimilar as possible to the one in which Aristotle and Plato lived, convinced that we should not accept their teaching without first having submitted it to criticism; an Englishman above all, without a drop of Hellenic blood in me, I feel myself to be a son of this vanished Greece, which blew on the human heritage the most noble wind of intelligence and beauty that the world has so far known.

1 December 1647

I left Nuremberg with the Earl of Arundel and his party and we went on to Ratisbon, where the Diet was about to choose the future Elector Palatine, and where the Earl was to see the Emperor and plead the cause of His Majesty's nephew. The vicissitudes of Arundel's journey then took me on to Linz, Vienna and Baden. But it was my stay in Prague that left me the most vivid memory, for there I met one of the strangest men in the whole of Europe.

The town itself seemed to me to be as disturbing as it was admirable. Like one of those exceedingly rare black pearls that are sometimes to be found in sea shells and are said to be the sign of the Demon, Prague nestles in a kind of conch formed by seven hills, on both banks of the River Vltava. No sooner has one passed through the outer wall than one comes upon a bizarre jumble of narrow alleyways, tall houses, mansions, palaces, gardens, monasteries and churches, the whole dominated by a castle of theatrical aspect. The visitor already realises that he is no longer in the Europe of Hobbes or Descartes. Prague is the perfect setting for the diabolic art and for sorcery; it is a place where you expect to find persons under the spell of the supernatural. And on this point, the person I visited did not disappoint me.

His name is Joannes Marcus Marci of Kronland. He is the only Professor of Medicine in the University of Prague, and he has a considerable reputation. He is even known as far away as England, where some call him the Hippocrates of Prague. He was about forty at the time. He was a thinnish man, even rather sickly-looking, with prominent cheek-bones, and long hair which fell on either side of his face onto a very large round beard and moustache such as are not to be seen in England. At the time of my visit he had just had an important work published—magnificently—by the Episcopate of Prague, under a never-ending title that began with *Idearum operatricium idea.* He presented me with a copy, and told me that I should find in it the result of his meditations on the generation of living beings. Do I need to say that I was passionately interested in the subject? The book was written in Latin, like my *De motu cordis,* and we spoke Latin of course, as I do not understand the Bohemian language that is spoken in Prague, and the Bohemians do not understand English. Indeed, exchanges would be impossible between savants, doctors and philosophers if we had not agreed on a common language. I know some Englishmen who would like the whole world to speak English. They are wrong, for a common language necessarily becomes a bastard language—it is enough to think of what Latin has become, a language which used to be so beautiful and which is now in decline. The language of a country, and hence its thought, is preserved so long as it really belongs to its own country.

Marci took me first into his physical laboratory and I realised that his chosen fields were not only medicine and philosophy, but also physics. He showed me copper spheres of various sizes, and explained that he had formulated the mathematical laws governing the impact of spherical bodies. He pointed to a series of prisms on another table; he had discovered how the prism splits white light up into a multitude of coloured pencils of rays. All his physics seemed to me of sterling worth. It was obvious that Marci shared my concern with observation and experiment. He cited Aristotle several times with respect, but declared that he only accepted the views of the Ancients after having submitted them to personal verification. Alas, this was only the lucid side of this savant; I was soon to discover the obscure side, which imperceptibly confused the real with the imaginary.

He spoke of the phenomena of life. He gave me to understand at first that he tried to study them as if they belonged to the realm of physics. And this exordium delighted me. Next, he informed me of the substance of his work on the generation of living beings. As light is the source of all things, it is therefore the source of life. Hence it is the science of optics that should guide our steps in the study of the formation of embryos. In order to create the new being, the soul of the parents emits forces that I, Marci, name plastic forces. These forces obey the same destiny as rays of light and, like them, are subject to reflection in mirrors and decomposition in prisms. They explain the creation of living forms, which are eternally renewed. They may also explain the origin of monsters, giants, dwarfs and diseases. I have kept the astonishing work Marci gave me and I occasionally glance through it. God is present on every page, but the Devil is not far away.

My host continued his fabulous discourse for many hours. He became more and more excited with every word he spoke. The austere, methodical scientist had gradually become metamorphosed and I had before me a thaumaturge engaged in reconstructing the world according to his own dreams. He entrusted me with its secrets; he felt himself possessed by the breath of Prometheus. Just like the city of Prague, where beauty rubs shoulders with the odours of Evil, this man combined the best and the worst, the rectitude of the savant and the blind exaltation of the mystic, in an incoherent mixture that fascinated me. He was the very image of this uncertain century, in which science has not rid itself of its old shell. It has been burdened for so many years by the weight of the traditions it has respected, by the appeal of the mysterious and the supernatural, that it will not be easy for it to purify itself. This will take time. And there will always be the diabolical temptation to allow the imagination full rein, and forgo the rigid discipline of methodical verification.

12 December 1647

I gave an account of my visit to the University to the Earl of Arundel. He listened with his customary smiling affability, but it was clear that he was indifferent to Marci's medical cogitations. His curiosity lay elsewhere: what interested him to the highest degree was the war ravaging Europe and the serious rifts dividing Christianity. He sought all possible information on the subject. He asked me to question Marci about the troubled hours Bohemia had been living through for the last twenty years.

I went to see Marci again, and he was only too eager to speak of those terrible years. Bohemia, according to him, has a longer history of religious agitation than any other country in Europe, and the University of Prague is its most ancient centre. The Rector of the University at the beginning of the fifteenth century was none other than Joannes Huss, an eloquent, seditious priest who declared war on Roman Catholicism and managed to convert not merely Queen Sophia, whose confessor he was, but all the nobility and common people of Bohemia. He was the father of Christian schism long before Luther or Calvin. Prague had known no peace since the day he was burnt alive and his ashes thrown into the Rhine. Many Bohemian churches went into mourning, and that was the beginning of the religious war that was to set all Europe alight. Today, Emperor Ferdinand II is trying to restore peace, a *Pax Romana* perhaps, but a Roman peace is better than war. It is true that excesses were committed in order to impose this peace. The rebel leaders were severely punished. But it must be said that these rebels had not hesitated to defenestrate two imperial officers. Violence begets violence.

"I think I am a good Catholic," Marci added, "and my dearest friend is the Archbishop of Prague, Ernst Albrecht von Harrach. I have joined the Catholic General Action party, whose leader he is. What we want is calm, serenity and tolerance. We fear the excess of zeal of certain people. We do not at all like the Society of Jesus, which demands intransigency and, furthermore, total control over our University. Even if the Roman Church has committed errors in the past, she is great enough to be able to reform herself without violence, contrary to what is asserted by those agitators who today are called Protestants." Marci suddenly remembered that England was no longer Papist, and declared that the Anglican Church was certainly close to his own way of thinking, and had his full approval.

I listened in silence to this most indulgent discourse, which smoothed over events as if to remove their painful thorns. But I knew the reality. I knew the terrible repression suffered by the Bohemian Protestants. I knew that twenty-seven of their leaders had been publicly decapitated, to the sound of drums, in the Old Town Square. I knew that their heads for a long time had been exposed to all comers. I knew that thousands of *bourgeois* had had all their property confiscated, and that thousands of peasants had been forcibly converted to Catholicism. It is true that violence begets violence. Wars of religion are like all other wars: they obey implacable physiological laws, as do the functions of the human body. In the beginning, there is a man, or there are a few men, motivated by passion. It matters little whether it be a sincere and generous passion or one of hate and selfish ambition. The main thing is that this man, Joannes Huss, for example, should know how to speak with eloquence and to contaminate the masses with his faith. The machine has been set in motion and the event has become irresistible. Other men, also either sincere or ambitious, will watch with disapproval as the strength of the group increases, and will attack them. One side or the other will win a first victory: nothing is more effective than a victory to aggravate the hatred of the conquered and, when the time comes, to tip the sinister scales in the other direction. Men should fear victories as they fear the Plague. Gradually, other fanatical individuals, other impassioned mobs, will join the conflict and keep the flame of the disputes eternally alight. When I was in Prague, this European war had already lasted for eighteen years and even now, ten years later, it is still not over. And when it *is* over, other wars will arise in exactly the same way. Men are caught up in their own system, like birds that cannot prevent themselves from flying into the mortal net.

It is true that we speak of *men* as if we were speaking of an individual who enjoys mastery over himself, who thinks for himself. In the eyes of the naturalist, nothing is more false. The moment there is a multitude, logic falters, contagion is exacerbated, the passions are no longer controllable, and the judgement of good and evil is not the same. A new multiple-being has been born who, to the unbiased observer, is somewhat monstrous. It may be that in the future a correct individual education will be able to protect men from this loss of soul with which they are threatened as soon as they gather together. But I am not even sure of this: will there not always be perverse educators?

Marci was still speaking. He spoke of the soul of the world. "I believe," he said, "that there are unknown powers hidden in the heart of Nature and of living beings. I prove the existence of the soul of the world by the mysterious power of certain animals, of certain herbs and certain stones; by the prophetic effect of enthusiasm; by the influence of the word on the cure of disease; and by the influence of the imagination on pregnant women."

Marci's philosophy is of the kind that plays with words which at first are devoid of reality but which end by giving the illusion of the real, providing one plays with them long enough. What did his *soul of the world* signify, if not the reflection of a comfortable construct of his mind, in permanent search of explanations? He also frequently used the expression *natural magic,* which certainly has not any more meaning. I have retained a fond memory of this man of Prague, but I cannot find myself in sympathy with those garrulous philosophers who juggle with words instead of becoming the servants of facts. The day will come when, like men of science, philosophers will no longer dare allow their speech to follow their flights of imagination for the sheer pleasure of indulging their fancies and of hoping to strike an answering chord in ours. For that sort of pleasure belongs to another domain: that of poets, theurgists and other fabricators of incantations.

13 December 1647

Yesterday I was scoffing at Marcus Marci of Kronland, but on reflection we have stranger characters here in England: I am thinking of Doctor Robert Fludd, the visionary.

He has been dead these ten years. And yet he was my elder by only very little. When one reaches my age, one gradually sees one's contemporaries disappearing as if down a trap: one has the feeling of moving through a forest of friends in which the trees are falling one by one.

Robert Fludd was one of those men who go astray in their search for truth, for *their own* truth. And of all such men, he was assuredly one of the strangest. In truth, like many of them, he had two faces: that of the good days, when his thoughts were sound and brilliant (he was one of the first to praise my discovery of the circulation of the blood), and that of the bad days, when he created imaginary worlds, was metamorphosed into an exalted mystic and believed himself a creator of miracles.

The first time I saw Robert Fludd was at the College of Physicians. I had just been made a Fellow; he was applying for the fourth time for a licence to practise. He had an Oxford medical degree and was not ignorant. But he had behaved tactlessly when the College Censors examined him: he had been called arrogant and insolent, had dared to speak disparagingly of Galen, and the President had forbidden him to practise.

A year later, in 1608, I believe, he applied once more for admission and I was for the first time one of the examiners. In those days the College was still in Knightrider Street, close to

Ludgate. The room was small and the furniture rudimentary. I was seated at the end of the table, and being the most recently elected Fellow of the College, it was my duty to take notes for the great register in which all the examinations of the candidates are recorded. The President invited the petitioner to express himself in Latin, but I considered Robert Fludd's Latin most imperfect.

Nevertheless, his discourse was marked by more modesty than on the preceding occasions. One of the Censors asked him to enumerate the divers kinds of temperaments. Another questioned him on the difference between a fever and a disease. A third requested him to give a list of the elements. Yet another questioned him on the urines of patients suffering from jaundice. Robert Fludd replied pertinently to most of these questions. The President then invited him to withdraw to an adjoining room, and the discussion began.

I heard for the first time the rumours current about our candidate. John Argent (who was one of my examiners in the previous years) declared that he had it on reliable authority that Robert Fludd was a member of the secret society, the Rosicrucians. When I asked for details, I was told that the Rosicrucian Brotherhood had been founded in Germany with the intention of reforming the world by uniting science to the wisdom of the Orient and to the Cabbala of the Rabbis. "They call themselves the *Invisible Ones,*" said Argent, "for they like to work in absolute secrecy. Yet, since he returned from his long continental journey, Robert Fludd has made no great mystery of his Rosicrucian membership. He even tries to make converts. It is a matter of the greatest indifference to me if these people indulge in occult practices. But they dabble in medicine. They quote Paracelsus and Agrippa of Nettesheim as their authority. What is more, they have singular principles; they take an oath to remain celibate and chaste, and to practise medicine gratuitously. Believe me, they are dangerous." Other Censors, however, defended Fludd. Our task was to judge candidates according to their medical knowledge, they said, and not on rumours about their mystical convictions. Someone testified that Fludd was a fervent Christian and convinced Anglican—and I discovered later that his statement was correct. As they recalled the lack of respect

Fludd had shown towards Galen on his previous appearances at the College, I suggested that a critical attitude towards the medicine of Antiquity did not necessarily imply disrespect. Finally, after a tumultuous debate, Fludd's cause prevailed and he received his licence. The following year he even became a Fellow of the College.

After that I saw him frequently. He had come to live in London, in Fenchurch Street, and he had a large practice. There was talk of the marvellous cures he effected by allying a magnetic medicine to the traditional remedies. I saw some of his patients: they were not far from regarding him as a witch-doctor who had supernatural powers. I began to feel somewhat suspicious of him. But my suspicion turned to irritation on the day I learned about his *weapon salve*.

I had been told that I would find all the details of this miraculous therapy in a work entitled *The Theatre of Anatomy,* which Fludd had had published by a Frankfurt bookseller. I procured a copy of this book, which I thought very handsomely produced. In the ninth chapter I discovered all the secrets of the mysterious salve. Fludd particularly recommended it for cut and thrust wounds made either by hand weapons, shafted weapons or missile weapons. A drop of blood must be taken from the wound, mixed with the salve (whose detailed formula Fludd provided), and applied, not to the wounded man but to the offending weapon or, in default of that, to an identical weapon. A sympathetic magnetism was then formed which could cure the wounded man from a distance, however far away he was from the operation. Everything took place as if, on contact with the spilled blood, the weapon were seized with remorse and sent a beneficial influx across space to repair the damage. Fludd had thus cured his brother-in-law, Sir Nicholas Gilborne, of a wound received in the service of His Majesty. This distant transmission of curative virtues reminds me of Sir Kenelm Digby's *powder of sympathy,* which was also said to be able to heal wounds at a distance. Need I say that these magical procedures greatly displeased me?

Shortly after my return from France in 1631, Robert Fludd attempted, for an entire day, to initiate and convince me. He invited me to the estate he had inherited from his parents,

Milgate House, near Maidstone, thirty miles from London and on the road to my native Folkestone. It was one of the loveliest manor-houses I have ever seen. The large garden was full of flowers, there were innumerable rose bushes and rare plants. Fludd told me that he grew the principal medical species of the pharmacopoeia there and that he himself prepared the remedies he gave his patients.

Next, he showed me the laboratory he had installed in a charming, foliaged summer-house at the bottom of his garden. Formerly, it had probably been used as a little folly to accommodate gallant rendezvous in the days of the Fludds' splendour. (Robert's father had been a great personage. He was Treasurer of the Cinque Ports in the days of Queen Elizabeth, by whom he was knighted.) But inside, I found indescribable disorder. There was a jumble of tables, stools, work-benches, trestles, stoves, retorts and other bizarre apparatus. Fludd had a passion for making little machines. He showed me an automaton that imitated bird song, a boiler that whistled, a lyre that played music by itself, a thermometer that predicted the weather. I complimented him on all these ingenious inventions. In this room, fires were burning under vases filled with water, and clouds of steam wafted through the air.

Afterwards, we went back to the house and my host took me to a study in which there was a profusion of books piled one on top of the other in what appeared to be great disorder. He invited me to sit by his side at a table on which papers and parchments were heaped up.

"To begin with," said Fludd, "I would like to make you a gift of a little treatise I have just written in reply to Parson Foster, who has made the most serious accusations against me in a malicious pamphlet with the contentious title *A Sponge to Wipe Away the Weapon-Salve.*"

He handed me a quarto volume of some forty pages, entitled *Dr Fludd's Answer unto Mr Foster; or, The Squeezing of Parson Foster's Sponge.*

"They accuse me of magic," he said. "They should know that magic is nothing other than wisdom; both terms come from the same Persian word which means at the same time wisdom and magic. Magic is the wisdom of the mages, and it is of divine origin."

The oblique light coming through the window illuminated the little man from the side and accentuated the contours of his face. With his bald temples, the dark rings round his eyes, his luxuriant moustache and his beard cut to a dagger-sharp point, he reminded me of one of those anchorites whose minds abstinence and private prayer have excited to the point of frenzy.

"Medicine is nothing," Fludd continued, "unless we place it within the framework of a general knowledge of the world. And knowledge of the world is the only way to save men. Not many are capable of carrying out this great plan. An illumination is necessary, which God reserves for the chosen few. It is a question of re-discovering the keys to knowledge which were given to the Son by the Father and which Adam, the first man, no doubt possessed. After his Fall we were left with only scraps. The task I have allotted to myself is the conquest of this lost enlightenment. It is no easy task, for we have been placed in the centre of an incessant struggle between Light and Darkness, and the darkness is ceaselessly maintained by the Demon and his innumerable messengers. Lucifer, who became Satan, the Ancient Serpent, the Great Dragon, is the master of the four noxious winds. He transforms Evil from potentiality into actuality. He created Death, which existed only *in posse*. The Evil One's army has not infiltrated into men's blood. It is the real cause of disease."

Fludd spoke at great length, continually waving his slender hands about. He was possessed by a kind of inner fire that contrasted with his impassive face. He never stopped uttering one absurdity after another. How was it still possible, in the seventeenth century, to attribute diseases to the work of little devils? What overweening vanity had driven this little man to believe himself chosen by God to receive what he called supreme knowledge? I imagine that the sect he belonged to encouraged its adepts in their secret dream of living an out-of-the-ordinary spiritual adventure.

"You have just come back from Paris," said Fludd. "Do you know that two of my fiercest enemies, Mersenne and Gassendi, live there? Mersenne attacked me personally, in his *Quaestiones celeberrimae*. He called me an insane heretic. He dared to ask King James why he gave me free rein to publish works of sorcery. It is he who has caused me all the troubles you have heard of."

Fludd had, indeed, been asked by the King, to whom sorcery was no laughing matter, to exculpate himself from these accusations. He had been obliged to write a long memoir in his defence.

"I replied sharply to Mersenne in my book *The Struggle of Wisdom and Morality*. The work Gassendi published last year on my philosophy is less savage; his volume opens with a letter from Mersenne accusing me of blasphemy on six counts, but the rest of the text is courteous, and sometimes even benevolent. What lies behind all these diatribes is jealousy. If anyone should be accused of blasphemy and mendacity it is Mersenne. He denies God the power to illuminate certain souls. He rejects all divination. According to him, I wrote that God is nothing other than the world, whereas I simply demonstrated that the world is the reflection of God. Mersenne reproaches me for saying that the origin of evil is to be found in demons: let him re-read Saint Matthew, the Book of Revelation, Zechariah or Job, and he will become acquainted with Satan. For my part, everyone knows that I am without the slightest reservation a faithful member of the Church of my country, and no one can doubt my piety or my faith in God. In truth, it is he who inspires me, it is he who chose me to share in the efforts of the Rosicrucians, the sole possessors of the true philosophy and the secrets of universal medicine."

He continued talking for a long time, and showed me strange drawings representing the world, God, light, darkness, the macrocosm of the universe and the human microcosm. In his drawings as in his discourse he seemed haunted by circular symbols. When he wrote that my *De motu cordis* deserved the highest praise, it may simply have been because he wished to turn the image of the circulation of the blood to the advantage of his obsession with the circle.

"Reflect on my philosophy," Fludd continued. "For the mystery of disease can never be solved unless it is accepted that everything in the universe is double. There is the light, which is male, and the darkness, which is female, just as there is the full and the empty, the yes and the no. And hot and cold, sympathy and antipathy . . . But in the celestial hierarchy, to each demon an angel is opposed: good may triumph over evil.

On my way back, after I left Milgate House, I was still possessed by the day's images. A man of great culture, then, an erudite doctor, learned in science and physics, an ingenious inventor, and furthermore English by birth and education, was at certain moments capable of taking refuge in the most alarming divagations. It might even have been his erudition that made his extravagant projects so ambitious. All men, even the most humble, are in need of spiritual and transcendent evasion, but they express this need within the limit of their attainments, which is to say with only modest pretensions. The man of great learning is exposed to far graver risks, unless he allows reason and common sense to hold him back. He dreams of new systems, of dazzling creations, he demands to be elevated above the crowd. Hence, he indulges in grandiose and obscure dreams. If he belongs to a sect, he will have the joy of sharing his dreams with people of like mind. I feel myself so remote from such men that I am tempted to believe they suffer from a disease of the reasoning, as others suffer from a disease of the body. But I am wrong: they are simply possessed by the metaphysical itch that is natural to human beings. It is only with a great effort that the savant can acquire the necessary humility and reserve.

I was back in London by night-time. I was exhausted, I threw myself down on my bed and fell asleep immediately, dreaming of devils with cloven hooves and of fiery hells.

20 December 1647

To re-awaken dormant memories is, they say, a good way to forget one's worries of the moment. Alas, I am too much attached to the present time, the passing moment is too precious, for me to be satisfied by images from the past. Indeed, I should find nothing painful in the present time were it not saddened by my anxieties regarding the fate of the King. My brother's garden, however, is conducive to tranquillity. I feel closer than ever to what my man from Prague called the soul of the world, and my Milgate House Rosicrucian called the reflection of God. My long walks with my nephew, the impression he gives me of being pleased to hear the story of my past enthusiasms, his precocious skill in the art of listening, are a solace in my retreat and half-console me for my painful nights.

This morning I received news that my fervent young friend George Ent will come to see me at Christmas. I am delighted: he too brings back happy memories. I saw him for the first time during my journey with the Earl of Arundel. The Earl, whose diplomatic mission retained him in Ratisbon, was growing impatient at being obliged to delay the quest for works of art with which the King had entrusted him. He wrote nearly every day to the Reverend William Petty who, as I have already mentioned in this diary, was his permanent agent in Italy, and a man skilled in discovering and buying valuable objects. Lord Arundel insisted on his trying to find works by Leonardo da Vinci, Raphael and Correggio to enrich the royal collection. He was afraid that Petty might be somewhat indolent, and asked me if I would agree to go and spur him on. I accepted with joy, delighted at the idea of once again seeing the Italy I had known as a young man.

After an eventful journey, which I will perhaps describe one day, I reached Rome in October, and the Reverend William Petty joined me there. I dined one day in the refectory of the English Jesuit College, which was a meeting place for English travellers. It was at this dinner that I got to know George Ent.

I learned later that he was of Dutch origin. His father, a Rotterdam merchant, had taken refuge in England to escape the persecution of the Spanish Governor of Flanders, Fernando Alvarez de Toledo, the famous organiser of the "Council of Blood" which executed thousands of men in the Low Countries in the last century. George Ent had begun his studies at Cambridge and then, as I had done thirty years earlier, had gone to study medicine in Padua. He had just taken his Doctor's degree and was still full of memories of the five years he had spent in the University that was so dear to my heart.

My imagination has always been greatly stimulated by every new encounter with a young Doctor. I want to weigh him up, I try to guess his future, and perhaps, without ever admitting it to myself, I feel I am engaged in the search for someone who will continue my work and my thought.

George knew my work, which flattered me. In my turn, I tried to interest him. I spoke little of medicine, but more of Italian painting. I told him of the quest for works of art with which the Reverend William Petty and I had been entrusted, and the very next day he accompanied me on my visits to the collections. We saw two famous galleries owned by dealers, and also several monasteries, churches and palaces where nothing was for sale but in which admirable paintings from that astonishing Italian period, the *quattrocento,* were to be seen. I still remember the Raphael rooms, to which we were allowed access thanks to the good offices of Petty, who obtained special permission for us from Pope Urban VI, for these rooms have been closed ever since they were damaged during the Sack of Rome by the troops of Charles V of Spain. They are full of treasures. We stopped in front of the immense *Triumph of Religion,* and I showed my new friend the astonishing rhythm of Raphael's painting, the way the semi-circle of the sky balanced the human masses below, symmetrically grouped around an altar. I also remember the fresco on the wall opposite this *Triumph,* which represents the history of philosophy. On the left, Plato, his raised arm pointing towards the heavens, is surrounded by the cohort of thinkers whose knowledge of the world is derived solely from their imagination. On the right is Aristotle, his hand outstretched as a sign of moderation, accompanied by those who, like him, were concerned to subordinate their intelligence to the observation of reality. I explained to George Ent how important this opposition was, in my eyes. Art translated what the evolution of science today demonstrates with dazzling clarity. The Platonists, despising the real, had turned their minds towards imaginary universes. They may perhaps have revealed the forms of our inner world, but it was certain that they in no way helped us to a knowledge of the real. They led bad savants into bad habits. Aristotle, on the other hand, showed the way, even if he was sometimes mistaken. His errors were of little consequence; the essential lay in his Principles. One should start from a basis of concrete experience and go back to that basis a hundred times along the way. Man got outside himself, he began to have a real relationship with the world, he merged with it, it was the birth of a new plan for humanity. It is to this plan that I shall have dedicated my life.

Petty told us that Raphael had painted Plato with the features of Leonardo da Vinci. If that is true, the painter made a mistake. Leonardo is in the other camp, that of Aristotle and the science of today, the camp in which the imagination defers to the facts of Nature and does not twist their meaning. And besides, Leonardo was a physicist, an engineer, a constructor, a geometer, an instrument-maker, and even an observer of men and beasts, as much as he was an artist. I know that he made dissections. In Spain, Lord Arundel acquired a volume compiled by Pompeo Leoni which contained more than two hundred folios and included many anatomical drawings. I remember Leonardo's perfect drawing of a human embryo in its mother's womb and, all around, the illegible scrawl of his left-handed mirror writing. Lord Arundel also possessed a copy of another work by Leonardo, reconstituted by the same Pompeo Leoni, entitled the Codex Atlanticus: it contains a hymn to Experiment, mother of

Truth. No, Leonardo da Vinci is not a Platonist. I see him as one of the inventors of the spirit by which science is today animated.

But at the same time: what art, what beauty! I understand why Arundel tried to acquire the least little drawing by Leonardo. Those he had already collected in London seemed admirable to me, through a combination of freedom, audacity and, at the same time, rigour. I saw in them the symbol of the possible union of art and science, and I even feared I might succumb to the temptation of the idea of that union. For a man of science who allowed himself to be guided by the desire for beauty would run the risk of confusing the beautiful with the true, whereas the true may have the outward appearance of ugliness, and the beautiful may be imaginary. It is my belief that the naturalist must conduct his studies with a total lack of emotion. But emotion is essential to works of art. The naturalist must never allow himself to be affected by beauty until his work is complete; only then has he the right to admire the splendours of the secrets revealed by observation and experiment. These, however, must be carried out with cold objectivity; it is only later that passion may be permitted. This idea is very obvious, our century is putting it into practice on all sides and it seems to hold out the promise of extraordinary advances in science, and yet a Leonardo da Vinci nearly obscured it in my mind through an inextricable mixture of witchcraft and truth. But the mixture is accidental, it is merely the encounter in one and the same man of two dazzling geniuses, the one inspired by a luminous intelligence, the other by an extraordinary sense of beauty. It may be that embryos of both these universes exist in other men, but they are on such a minor scale that it remains possible for them to coexist without seriously encroaching on each other's territory. In Leonardo, they overrun one another with such force that it is no longer possible to distinguish them.

George Ent seemed to find these reflections to his liking, and that was the beginning of a great friendship. William Petty advised me to continue my journey as far as Naples, so I asked Ent to accompany me. During our journey we spoke at length of the circulation of the blood. George had heard my work criticised at Padua more than once. He told me that during his last year there an old physician from Venice, Emilio Parisanus, had published lengthy extracts from my *De motu cordis* with, on the opposite page, acerbic criticism, paragraph by paragraph, of everything I assert and demonstrate. He goes so far as to write that the sounds of the heart exist only in my imagination: this Parisanus must truly be hard of hearing. George declared that these venomous denigrations must be refuted, and that he would willingly undertake the task. He kept his word: five years later he published his *Apologia pro circulatione sanguinis, qua respondetur Aemilio Parisano, medico Veneto*—a work more precious to me than many others.

Naples was an enchanting town, even though the people seemed to be suffering under Spanish rule; we were told that they were crushed by taxes. I saw no works of art for sale that might have interested Arundel and the King. But the dozens of churches, castles, palaces and fortresses grouped in a semi-circle around a magnificent bay gave grandeur to the city where Virgil went to die. The Viceroys of Naples, the representatives of the Spanish Crown, had just had a palace built with its back to the sea. We also visited the Cathedral, which shortly before had been embellished by a wonderful chapel. This chapel, I remember, was dedicated to the Patron Saint of Naples, San Gennaro, and owed its existence to a recent epidemic of the Plague. The inhabitants had made a vow: those who escaped death would collect enough money to offer the saint this testimony of their gratitude. They collected an enormous sum, nearly a million ducats. I have never seen so rich a chapel. Between clouded-marble columns, its walls are covered with treasures, many of which are paintings representing miraculous cures. One of these pictures is by Domenichino and shows a young man saved from a mortal disease; I considered it the very image of the aims of medicine.

It was in this chapel that George and I were shown the famous ampullae containing San Gennaro's blood. Above the altar, in a little bronze tabernacle with silver doors, two long-necked, broad-bellied flasks containing a few drops of clotted blood. Twice a year, in May and September, the blood of the saint suddenly liquefies. For everything to go well in Naples, this miracle is essential. If it does not take place, the people become worried; the greatest calamities may strike the town. And if the miracle is delayed, an enormous crowd gathers around the chapel, shouting: *San Gennaro, fa dunque presto*—hurry up, San Gennaro, hurry up. I discovered that George could on occasion be rather mischievous, for he explained that a mixture of spermaceti and alkanet produces a very acceptable red jelly which melts, and even begins to boil, as soon as the warmth of the hand takes the chill off the vase containing the mixture. George claimed that a strange story was told in Padua, in licentious circles, about the miracle of San Gennaro's blood. When Charles V of Spain inherited the Kingdom of Naples from his mother Joanna the Mad, the miracle no longer occurred, and the people saw this as a clear sign that God was opposed to the accession of the new King. Thereupon a Captain in the young sovereign's army informed the clergy of the cathedral where the relics were housed that some of the priests would be imprisoned if the miracle did not take place forthwith. A few minutes sufficed for the blood of San Gennaro to liquefy, and joy returned to the people. I answered George that such slander in no way affected me, it merely proved that Joanna's son was an unbeliever, and in any case Heaven had severely punished him, because I rather thought he had had troubles all his life.

George asked me whether I believed in miracles. I told him that I found the question shameless, and that it was not in my nature to cast doubt on the religious verities. He retorted that he had no need of miracles to feel himself an honest Christian. Indeed, I replied, the little miracles that liquefy clotted blood are merely contemptible if we compare them with the great daily miracle observed by the members of our profession. For my part, every drop of blood that I have seen circulate, every heartbeat that propelled this blood, have always inspired me with far more wonder than any petty occasional miracle.

28 December 1647

George Ent came to Croydon on Christmas morning. First he complimented me on how well I was looking: this is what young men feel obliged to say to old men because they imagine that old age is intolerable and deserves some consoling viaticum. I told him that I found it difficult to be altogether happy in a Kingdom so full of disturbances, where I was myself caught up in the turmoil. I should have little desire for a longer life were I not still so attached to my studies of Nature and to the meditations resulting from them. Ent immediately seized on this innocent remark and replied that, as it happened, my reflections on Nature were of great value to the philosophy of our time. Should I not take advantage of my leisure to prepare a manuscript and allow others to benefit from my observations?

"It is true," I told him, "that I have accumulated some notes on the generation of animals. But I have no intention of publishing them. Have you forgotten the trouble I was caused by the publication of *De motu cordis*? Have you forgotten the pack of dishonest detractors who are still harrying me even today? Must one really write for other people, who are not in the least grateful?—may one not simply write for oneself, merely for the solitary, splendid pleasure of committing to paper the new knowledge one possesses? There are some writers who hide their manuscripts at the back of a drawer, knowing that they will never be read by anyone. I imagine they derive secret delectation from this dissimulation. They will have been the only ones to know their masterpieces. No one will ever make the slightest criticism of them. Nothing will tarnish their joy. On the other hand, however, those who publish their writings are selling their most intimate truths, and they are selling them to readers who are on the watch for their weaknesses on every page, like robbers skulking in a wood, watching for their victims."

"You do not think anything of the sort," George replied. "A doctor cannot think in that way, let alone the greatest doctor in England. In choosing our profession we chose to serve other people, to forget our own gratification, and to despise critics when we have done our work honestly. And the way for you to serve other people is to communicate the greatest possible amount of knowledge to them. You once told me that you had never examined the body of a living person without unexpectedly learning something new. Your honour and your duty require you to transmit this extra knowledge to other people."

"It is true that the dissection of the body of an animal has always been a delight to me. I believe that it does not merely provide us with information about the vital functions, it may be that it also enables us in a modest way to approach the great secret of the Creation."

From this moment, I knew that I was going to give in, and show George my manuscripts. But I acted the part of the man who does not wish to be too easily persuaded and who, without admitting it to himself, is seeking an honourable way of changing his decision without changing his mind. I added:

"The writings you are about to see do not constitute a complete work on the generation of animals: it lacks my notes on the generation of insects which, as you know, were stolen when my lodgings at Whitehall were plundered."

Nevertheless, George had already seized my voluminous manuscript and he exclaimed: "It is incredible that you should have managed to produce such a monument in the tumultuous years you have just lived through. Please let me have it. I will collate these precious sheets and take upon myself whatever care is required in the oversight of the printing."

He continued at length in this vein, uttering words full of enthusiasm, declaring that he felt like a second Jason enriched with the Golden Fleece. Why did I allow myself to be persuaded? Perhaps it had something to do with George's blandishments; how could I remain proof against them? George is a skilful tempter because he pays his compliments with a calm, handsome expression, without the grimaces of the professional flatterer. But what I most appreciate in him, what convinces me, is his quality of enthusiasm. That is a quality to which I attach considerable value: nothing great or beautiful can be created without it. In Greek, *enthusiasmos* means possessed by a god, inspired. The Athenian athletes used to say that in enthusiasm, the god was within them—for there is in the word the root *theos,* which means god. When this fire abandons a people, when the youth of such a people grow lukewarm, when censure triumphs over enthusiasm and substitutes criticism of weaknesses for admiration of successful achievement, then decadence is not far away. I have been imbued with this idea for so long, I have worked so hard to convince young Englishmen of the truth of it, that it is not difficult for the warm enthusiasm of a George Ent to become more than a match for me.

And yet I am very clearly aware of the imperfections of the manuscript. Whereas my *De motu cordis* was written with great concision and rigour—concision effortlessly follows on from rigour—*De generatione,* taken as a whole, is looser, less firm, because my ideas on the mysteries of generation are less clear than my ideas on the circulation of the blood. There are some fields—and generation is one of them—where it is necessary to make an immense leap between the observed facts and the secrets they conceal.

After the mid-day meal I began to explain to George how I had classified my manuscript, which I had divided into seventy-two Exercises.

First, I had written a long introduction dedicated to Aristotle and Galen. I wanted to express in the strongest terms my enormous admiration for these great men. Too often have I been reproached for disrespect to the Ancients. And yet the reverence they inspire in me is completely sincere: the more I have disputed their assertions and exposed their errors, the more my admiration for them has grown. The monuments they built are models of an extraordinary ambition to gain universal knowledge. What does it matter if some components of the ensemble need to be replaced? I see great marvels in them: the audacity of wishing to observe everything, to understand everything; the human will to grasp the world and life. They are among those who set in train the movement of the adventure of mankind, a movement which, as I have said before, only lack of admiration and enthusiasm would be able to kill, as it can kill all enterprise and all progress. The united chorus of stupid censors may well drown the disunited chorus of constructors: I refuse to be one of the censors. Almost two millennia after Aristotle, I consider myself his respectful disciple and I only modify his work in order to ameliorate it. This is what I had tried to write in my introduction, before going on to show, however, that the methods I myself employed in the study of generation in no way resembled those of the Peripatetic school.

The first thirteen Exercises are devoted to the comparative anatomy of the reproductive organs of the hen, the goose, the duck, the pigeon; frogs, serpents, fish, crustaceans, molluscs; bees, wasps, butterflies, silkworms; sheep, goats, dogs, cats, the Bovidae and, of course, the most perfect of all the animals, man. Anyone who wishes to understand Nature's intention is obliged to make the comparison between these so very diverse species. And it must be confessed that it makes the naturalist wonder. Why such a great variety of species? And why such a similarity of structure from one species to another? Everywhere, males and females. Everywhere, proximity of the sexual organs and the orifices through which urine and faeces issue. Everywhere, except in man, a mating season. Everywhere, in that season, a certain upheaval in habits and disposition. Everywhere, the female charged with making the egg and the male charged with exercising on this egg a strange power that will generate the new being. And is it not remarkable that this new being will inevitably belong to the species of its progenitors?—since we cannot cross a serpent with a fish, a duck with a frog. It is only artists who have drawn these chimaeras that they have seen in their dreams. Although the ordinary man is capable of imagining them, the naturalist knows that they do not exist, and this non-existence becomes a problem he has to solve.

The next thirteen Exercises describe the development of the

chick in the egg. I have already written in this diary of the wonder I felt when I discovered that the creation of the heart of a
chick is accomplished after only three days of incubation. What
I have not yet mentioned is the patience the hen's egg demanded
of me. It needed dozens and dozens of hours of study. I had to
note down without error the exact moment when each incubation began; next, to determine the length of time that elapsed
before the opening of each successive egg; to render myself free
without fail at each of these times and, the egg once open,
to give proof of infinite delicacy and patience in order to discover and note the slightest discrepancy between it and the preceding egg.

Patience is not my strong point. I am by nature impatient. But
with this business of the eggs, what happened was that my extreme impatience to know more became the source of my patience. And I realised that this was the secret that enables some
men to make progress in the knowledge of Nature. Science originated from an intense curiosity, an impatience to know and to
understand. This impatience is perhaps innate in man; at all
events, it acts as a spur to the scientist, it is the basic motive
behind all his activities. But from the very beginning of his observations he discovers unexpected difficulties, he has doubts, he
makes blunders, the slowness of his progress discourages his impatience. And yet this impatience continues to keep him on the
alert, it will not allow him to abandon the quest, it is as obsess-
ing as a budding love, it will produce the miracle of rendering
him patient. The presiding genius of discovery, no doubt, is this
impatient patience.

It is also, I believe, one of the secrets of the genius of the artist.
And on this point science and art, for once, meet. A French pot-
ter, Bernard Palissy, has written some fine pages on the subject.
The book is in the library of Lord Arundel, who gave it to me to
read after showing me some of this artist's rustic figulines in his
collection, enamelled terra-cottas decorated with plants, fruits
and little animals in relief. Bernard Palissy's book is entitled
something like *Admirable Discourses on the Waters and Fountains, Metals, Salts, Stones, Earths, Fire and Enamels*. He writes
in it that those who labour impatiently at the art of fashioning

earth run the risk of losing everything through their impatience. This artist, who discovered the secret of transparent enamelling, was probably also one of those men who are seething with the desire to create but who are nevertheless capable of transmuting their ardour into infinite patience.

From the twenty-sixth to the sixty-first Exercise, I tried to assemble the various theories of generation, showing the beauties and the errors in the work of Aristotle and Galen. And I entitled the sixty-second Exercise "That an egg is the common original of all animals." To tell the truth, I did not have the complete demonstration of this. I had proceeded more by intuition than by certainty. In the quest for truth there are auspicious instants in which, having accumulated observations and experiments, one begins to wonder whether the significance of the facts one has discovered does not go beyond the bounds of the limits envisaged. One has started from the hen's egg, gone on to the fish's egg, from there to the eggs of insects and, perceiving that in extremely diverse species every individual issues from an egg, the temptation arises to make a generalisation that encompasses the whole living universe. In animals where the egg is not easy to see, such as the human animal, one imagines that this structure is perhaps simply very small and that magnifying instruments, now being invented, will be necessary to provide evidence that every living creature is born from an egg. To generalise in this manner is certainly to make a wager on an uncertain future. But such a method is probably essential to science, on condition that one is not deceived by the process, that one does not assert that which remains problematical, that one confines oneself to asking: "Is it not thus that things occur?" thereby giving rise to future studies which will reply: "Yes, you guessed correctly." Or, on the other hand: "No, you must look elsewhere. The generalisation was an honest possibility, but experiment shows that it must be returned to the domain of unreal dreams, it does not belong in the domain of truth." I shall have no regrets if I am one day proved to have been mistaken in supposing that an egg is the original of every living creature.

When George Ent had left I experienced a strange feeling: of joy and of anxiety at the same time. I imagined a parturient woman giving birth to an imperfectly formed child and then entrusting it to another woman, for her to perfect it. The manuscript I had given to my friend still needed some finishing touches, and I had agreed that someone else should assume this responsibility. Twenty years previously, it seemed to me, I should not have consented.

29 December 1647

Was it because George took my *De generatione* away with him? I dreamed last night of Bass Rock, the island of thousands of birds' eggs.

Bass Rock brings back memories of 1633. Charles, King of England, went to be crowned King of Scotland, and I was fortunate enough to be one of those in attendance on him. Charles has always had an affection for Scotland, where he was born. He was two years old when he left it, and he had never seen his native land since. He had been promising himself for a long time that he would go there, but the project had constantly been postponed. In 1633, however, the King realised that this journey had become urgent. The old hereditary hostility between Scotland and England had come to the surface once again. The pretext was that eternal cause of contention: religious disagreement. Scotland is at heart Presbyterian, she resents the attempts of the Anglican Church to impose its rites and its Bishops on her. Furthermore, the Scottish people were subjected to the tyrannical pressure of an aristocracy that had arrogated to itself a good part of the powers of the locally vacant throne. Charles therefore decided to journey to Scotland with all the pomp necessary to make it clear to all that he was the one and only sovereign.

This was, indeed, the most sumptuous journey our country had ever seen. We did not merely constitute a simple group of travellers, but a huge retinue, an immense cavalcade, a procession. There must have been four or five thousand of us. Behind the Chief Herald and the Garter King of Arms, who were accompanied by other heralds wearing their tabards and crying "Make way for the King," came His Majesty's magnificent carriage, drawn by twelve horses superbly caparisoned in gold and silver. The Lord Chamberlain and his gentlemen followed, well mounted on parade horses led by hand; then the Master of the Horse, the Earl Marshal of England, the Earls of Northumberland, Southampton, Salisbury and others I have forgotten, each with dozens of retainers and horses; the Under-Secretary of State for England and the Secretary of State for Scotland; the Lord Treasurer; the Comptroller and Master of the Household; the Sergeant in Mounted Arms; the principal private secretaries; the gentlemen ushers; the grooms of the bedchamber; the major-domos; the four public esquires trenchant; the four private esquires trenchant; and hundreds of cooks, musicians, chaplains, apothecaries, barbers, pages, trumpeters, guards, in addition to many fine equipages the names of whose noble occupants I no longer remember. I myself was on horseback, riding with a Scottish physician, and I had good horses and diligent menservants. We followed the Great North Road, a less bumpy thoroughfare than many in England; very few carts, coaches or carriages were overturned. We covered the 330-odd miles in eighteen stages, and having left at the beginning of May we arrived at the end of June. It must be said that at almost every halt extraordinary receptions and magnificent entertainments awaited us. It seemed that the English lords wished to show that they were as capable as the Scots of welcoming the King to their castles in appropriate fashion.

The most splendid entertainment, I think, was that given by the Earl of Newcastle at Welbeck Abbey, half-way between Newark and Doncaster. Notwithstanding the magnificence of his palatial residence, the Earl was not able to accommodate us all, and Lord Portland and I were offered hospitality by the Earl of Arundel in nearby Worksop Manor. At Welbeck Abbey the Earl of Newcastle had organised an almost uninterrupted series of festivities. There were masques, ballets, concerts, fireworks and other diversions of all sorts. A crowd of elegant ladies, and lords and gentlemen glittering in their rich clothes, filled the gardens and lofty halls of the Abbey. All seemed to be enjoying themselves and thinking of nothing but gallantry and frolics. I myself was not so charmed as they by this ostentation. I felt a kind of malaise. Leisure activities and frivolous pastimes do not suit me. While I appreciate a good play that stirs my imagination and provokes me to thought, and a good book that allows me to hold a silent conversation with the author, I am quite indifferent to these meaningless ballets and masques. Their plots are no more than a vague pretext for curiously disguised characters, who represent nothing real, to move in time with the music. They have no knot, no situation, no *dénouement*. I felt very much alone in this noisy disorder; I felt chilled by the exuberance and liveliness of the others. The only real pleasure I had was one afternoon when, in a setting by Inigo Jones, with admirable mechanisms, they gave us Ben Jonson's comedy *Volpone,* which I had already seen in London in my youth.

I had met Ben Jonson in person at the Friday Street Club which met at the Mermaid Tavern, where my friend Selden had taken me one evening in 1620 or 1621. Donne, Chapman and Fletcher were there, with a few other poets. Ben Jonson presided. Many Englishmen today consider Jonson superior to Shakespeare as a man of the theatre. But his youth was really that of an adventurer. After schooling at Westminster he worked as a bricklayer, then joined the British Army in Flanders, became an actor, killed a fellow-actor in a duel but escaped death by benefit of clergy. After his release from prison he wrote *Every Man in His Humour,* which was performed by The Lord Chamberlain's Men and through which he achieved fame. When I was at the Court of King James the King commissioned several masques from him; these were entertainments rather than true theatre, and in my opinion he wasted a great deal of time on such frolics. He wrote no more than five or six comedies that deserve to be remembered, but they are exceedingly well made. When he was forty-two he suffered a paralytic stroke, from which he never quite recovered. He was my near-contemporary, but he died ten years ago.

Back at the Earl of Arundel's house after the performance of *Volpone,* Lord Portland had a terrible attack of lithiasis, with a fever and severe pains. I calmed him as best I could, thanks to the remedies I had in my bag, and I advised rest. Lord Arundel informed the Royal Comptroller that we would not be able to continue the journey with the royal procession the next day. We joined the King a few days later, just as he was arriving in Scotland.

Our Scottish reception was extremely sumptuous, and the coronation was a splendid occasion. At a banquet in Edinburgh the Freedom of the City was conferred on me. The next day, at the Chapel Royal, I helped the King, who had agreed to "touch" the swellings of about a hundred people suffering from scrofula, the disease that is also called "The King's Evil." We stayed two weeks in Edinburgh and it was from there that I went to the little town of North Berwick and thence to Bass Rock, a tiny island off the coast.

I had heard that this island was a prodigious bird sanctuary with an abundance of nests. I had been told extravagant tales about the fruits of certain trees being turned into birds, or again that on falling into the sea these fruits gave birth to solan geese. Two fishermen in the port agreed for a small consideration to take me to visit the Rock, which is about two miles from the coast. Once there, I found nothing that resembled the fabulous tales of which I have spoken, but what I saw was quite extraordinary enough for a naturalist who is interested in the mysteries surrounding the birth and habits of birds.

The fishing boat taking me to the Rock advanced slowly. To the rhythm of their oars, the two men mumbled some old Scottish songs whose words were unfamiliar to me. Behind us, I could see the wide estuary of the Firth of Forth. But the houses in the port and the distant hills were shrouded in a blanket of fog; it floated round the boat, deadening the sounds, enveloping the swell in a blurred halo. I felt as if I were being transported out of the real world. There are some places in Scotland where the air seems to be filled with strange and almost disquieting spells. I was overcome by a kind of distress, as if some fabulous marine monster might at any moment suddenly loom up through the fog. The crossing was very short, but it seemed interminable.

All at once, lit up by the summer sun, the Rock appeared in front of us. It is no more than a mile in circumference, and rises to a height of three hundred feet above sea level. But it is no ordinary rock: as you approach it it shines with a white glazing and resembles a mountain of the purest chalk. This is because the ground is entirely plastered over with eggshells and the whitish excrement of the birds. The approach to the island is difficult, so steep are its cliffs. It is inaccessible save on the south-west side, and even there you can disembark only with the aid of ladders and ropes. You immediately come upon an incredible quantity of nests, eggs and chicks, while thousands of birds fly like a cloud overhead, making a great noise, meeting and passing, winging their way in all directions, pursuing their prey, diving into the sea, coming up, swimming, and then once again taking wing and surrounding you on all sides until your head spins. I saw that for the most part they were guillemots, those birds which resemble penguins, but that there were also many other species. I observed that there were large eggs that stood on end, as if by a miracle, no doubt being cemented to the ground by the excrement covering it, or perhaps because they are of a particular shape. Rowing round the island, I observed that the cliffs, all the escarpments, all the caves, and also a kind of natural gallery which seems to traverse the whole island, were inhabited by colonies of birds of different kinds and sizes.

The fishermen told me that these birds do not live on the island: they resort there in the spring, each year, to lay their eggs. In what far-distant sea do they originate? Who will ever find a way to follow their fantastic journeys? Perhaps sea-birds have different abodes, some for their residence, others for their pleasure ground, and still others for their love-making, like certain noble lords of my acquaintance who regularly migrate in the winter to sunnier climes, or who hide their affairs of the heart in the remote summer-houses of their castles.

I shall never be weary of admiring all that Nature offers to the observer, and I shall always marvel that so few men find joy therein.

5 January 1648

I should like to have been a universal man, and not to have been restricted to the study of living beings. I should like to have learnt mathematics and astronomy, to be an historian and a geographer, to be able to draw and paint, to explore far-distant seas and mountains, and also to excavate those lands and ruins which tell of the past of the earth and of men. But no one man today can combine in himself the knowledge of all the others. So many fields have already been conquered that no one can now be an expert in them all. The consequences are serious, for every man sees the world through what he himself knows and, starting from different images, two different individuals will be most unlikely to agree on the paths to be followed.

I am nevertheless one of those who have had the good fortune not to be narrowly confined within their own profession. Several times during my life I have left medicine (not really left it, one never leaves it) in order to practise zoology or botany, to take myself for a philosopher, to seek out objects of art for the collections of a King, or to become literary adviser to a writer or a poet. On one occasion I took part in an expedition entrusted by King James with the mission to study ancient stones to discover what they might reveal of the history of the past. This was in 1620. I was in attendance on the King when he visited the Earl of Pembroke at Wilton House, near Salisbury. Some seven miles away is the most astonishing ancient monument that can be found in the whole of England: Stonehenge. The King ordered his architect, Inigo Jones, to investigate the site with a view to discovering what no one yet knew: who had built Stonehenge. Jones took a small group of some twenty men. Thinking he might need a companion versed in the natural sciences, he requested me to accompany him.

Jones is five years my senior. I have known him for a long time. He was also famous for his knowledge of the arts of Antiquity, which he acquired during a long stay in Italy. He has played an important part in the formation of artistic taste in England. He was an adviser to King James, as he was later to be to King Charles, and he helped them to create their admirable collections. I believe it is to him that Lord Arundel owes part of his knowledge of the painting and sculpture of former centuries.

As we approached Stonehenge, even from a distance I found the sight extraordinary. An immense circle of standing stones about three hundred feet in diameter surrounds a second circle, in the centre of which is a monolith that seems to be the heart of the whole assembly. Each stone is some twenty feet or more in height. Some are far wider than the trunk of a big oak tree. There are more than one hundred enormous boulders, rising up towards the heavens like cathedrals. Some of them support prostrate slabs and, from close to, one can see that they are affixed by mortise and tenon. The site is completely silent and deserted, as dead as a graveyard, but I could not help imagining the great crowds who used to haunt it in former days. Those men had disappeared so totally that we did not even know what race they belonged to, or what they thought, what they feared, what they loved. But they had left witnesses more unalterable than their miserable bodies, and those standing stones silently proclaimed that the men of those days had, like us, their impulses, their ferments, their passions, their anxieties, and possibly their certainties. No doubt we underestimate the strength of the skill and artifice that enabled them to manipulate, raise and assemble those gigantic rocks, without any of the modern architectural methods we think we are the first to have invented. No doubt they built Stonehenge for themselves, and not as a message to be read after their death, in the same way as I am writing this diary for myself and not for the future. But ever since men have existed, they have probably been possessed by the strange desire not to disappear completely but to leave behind them some trace of what they have been. Perhaps, without realising it, I too am secretly tempted to imagine that someone will read these notes after my death, so that at least the inner world that inhabits my frail body may live for a brief moment in the mind of another.

On an order from Jones, our assistants began to dig carefully into the earth round the stones. At the end of three long days of work we finally extracted some bones and a few fragments of burnt coal and charcoal not far from the central monolith. I was naturally requested to pronounce on the nature of the bones. None of those which were brought to me could have belonged to a man. The were animal skulls that I had no difficulty in recognising: skulls of bulls and stags. Jones took that to be irrefutable proof that Stonehenge was of Roman origin. He even ventured to assign its date to the first century of our era, in the reign of Agricola. The animal species we had discovered, he said, were precisely those which were sacrificed in those days. I have always admired the skill of the experts who instinctively find an answer to the most difficult enigmas, even when they have very little evidence on which to base their judgement. I was to learn later that Jones was probably totally mistaken, even though it is still a moot point today whether Stonehenge should be seen as a Druidical monument or be attributed to the Danes, who would have used it as a ceremonial site where they elected their Kings and lit their sacred fire.

I am in no way competent to make a personal archaeological judgement. But I am sure that Stonehenge was an important religious shrine. The dimensions of the circles surrounding the sacrificial stone are sufficient evidence that when the people came here to pray to their gods it was a significant event—for the circle has always seemed to me the purest, most powerful geometrical figure, the one most charged with symbolism. It matters little to me whether the gods who were invoked here were Roman or Gallic, Gaelic or Nordic. All gods are alike. They are egoistic, domineering, cruel. They do not love men, they chastise them and punish them. I can imagine the crowds jostling one another at Stonehenge, suppliant and terrorised. Their fate depended on powers who were all the more redoubtable in that they remained invisible. Invisible, yet present at all times and in all places; to be certain of that it was sufficient to see the signs of their fury, thunder and lightning, calamities and diseases, men's misfortune. What sacrifice could be sure of appeasing the wrath of these hidden forces? Our ancestors could only feel they were in bondage, in chains, the slaves of an obscure destiny, and hence certain that they were in the hands of fearsome masters forever amusing themselves by pronouncing unpredictable judgements. I give thanks to Christianity, which revealed a benevolent God, a God who loves men. The genius of the Christian religion is to have offered us that love, in a Heaven where before there was only indifference and anger.

I know very well that there still remains a paradox, and it has sometimes embarrassed me: that of a benevolent God who allows us to lead a life full of suffering. But after all, it is enough to admit that our minds are incapable of understanding such things. The beauty of the adventure is well worth this little effort. And if our thirst for understanding torments us to excess, the beautiful, clear images of the Gospel are there to provide us with all the answers.

All things considered, I am glad I am not a pagan.

25 January 1648

Snow has fallen over the house and garden. I put on my warm boots, my seaman's thick woollen jacket from Folke-stone, pulled a fox fur cap well down over my ears, and went for a long walk as far as the neighbouring forest. The cold can do my gout no harm, as when I have an attack I treat it by plunging my foot into icy water. My nephew Daniel, who since his father's death has become the master of this estate, accompanied me. I spoke to him about medicine. It is my secret desire that he should be tempted to enter the profession. His intelligence and solicitude for others would do wonders in it.

I told him how I discovered the real function of the cardiac muscle, the motor organ of the circulation of the blood. The heart, in man and many animals, is in reality an assembly of two hearts that work in harmony at two different tasks. Each of these hearts is made up of a little cavity, an auricle, which re-ceives the blood and passes it on to another, larger, cavity, the ventricle. The right ventricle of the heart propels the blood towards the lungs, the left ventricle distributes it to the other organs and to the limbs. I picked up a dead branch and drew in the snow the two connected hearts.

I explained that it had for long been thought that the heart was a flaccid organ, passively tossed about by the blood, whereas on the contrary it has such powerful muscles that it can of its own accord propel the blood to the farthest extremities of the body. I had measured the weight of the blood expelled by the heart with each pulsation and, multiplying by the number of pulsations, I had calculated that it sends more than a hundred pounds of blood to the body every half-hour. In this way the left heart abundantly irrigates the whole organism with the precious nourishing liquid, while the right heart receives this liquid after it has been exhausted by a long journey, and directs it to the lungs for some sort of refreshment. And the movement is perpetually repeated. For this, the heart must contract with the regularity of clockwork, thirty, sixty, a hundred times a minute, according to the species (but always in a more or less definite rhythm for any given species): and this is what it does. The left and right hearts must send an equal weight of blood in the circulations they control, to avoid a mortal imbalance: this is what occurs. And finally, the mechanism must never stop, throughout a lifetime: that is what happens. All the other muscles become tired: the heart never does.

In truth, for me the heart is a masterwork, a king of organs.

We walked on in silence. On Daniel's handsome face I caught a glimpse of that grave, intense expression I knew so well, and it made me think I had won him over. But he asked me:

"In your opinion, Uncle, is the perfection of the heart proof of the existence of God?"

I was surprised, and even irritated, that a boy of sixteen should be seeking *proofs* of the existence of God. For my part, I have long since set on one side that kind of question. The quest for *proofs* belongs to the scientific study of a phenomenon, it has no place in matters of belief. I have put away my respect for the things of religion in the same drawer as my respect for traditions. I have such great respect for them both that I feel no need to buttress it with logical demonstrations. But I did not wish to appear indifferent to Daniel's thought. I encouraged him to tell me more about his religious misgivings.

"I have no misgivings," he declared after a moment. "It is simply that I do not understand why men are not more straightforward about these questions. If they believe in God, as they declare they do, they should forthwith make an effort to lead a life nearer to the precepts of the Gospels. And, despite my lack of experience, it seems to me that they do nothing of the sort."

I recognised in these words the intransigent rectitude characteristic of the youth of men of quality. I was still annoyed at the

turn our conversation had taken, but for some unknown reason
I remained under the influence of the charm of the young man. I
should have liked him to be my son. I decided to come straight
to the point:

"Does the study of medicine hold any attraction for you?"

Daniel did not reply immediately. I realised that he was afraid
of hurting me by too unequivocal a rejection, and his tact atten-
uated my chagrin. He declared that he had a desire identical to
the one that had motivated my life as a doctor—the desire to
choose a profession in which he could be of service to others.
But rather than care for their bodies, he wished to help to found
a better society. The devastation of England, the incessant wars,
the miseries and misfortunes of a people subjected to the ca-
prices and ambitions of a Cromwell and of a sick Parliament—
all this revolted him. Young men of his age had inherited an
intolerable society. They rejected this inheritance. He himself
wanted first to travel in foreign countries to see whether, somewhere or other, the rulers or the ruled had discovered a more
agreeable method of organisation.

"What I do not know," he said, "is what profession to choose
so that I too may contribute to changing the society of men."

"Changing the society of men," I thought, "what a Utopia! It
would be necessary to change men's souls, which are as deeply
rooted in them as their very nature." I asked Daniel whether he
did not believe that England's salvation might not lie in the res-
toration of the threatened Royal Power.

"Does your King deserve the confidence and fidelity he inspires in you, Uncle? I have been told that he is rash and indeci-
sive, touchy and credulous, violent and vulnerable. He believes
himself to be free and safe, on his Isle of Wight, but they say that
Cromwell will decide his fate as he wishes, when he wishes."

I said that I did not believe it. Charles is too beloved of the
English people for anyone to touch a hair of his head, even
Cromwell. But I had no wish for further debate. I assured Daniel
that his search for a profession that would be useful to the community had my entire approval. But who can influence the
march of events and ideas?

"I know," I said, "only two sorts of men who are under that

illusion: philosophers, who write, and politicians who orate. And I distrust them both.

"The philosophers who build models of happy societies are intelligent, generous, imaginative, and totally ignorant of what constitutes a man, such as the physician sees him day after day. Inventors of systems would like man to be reasonable and docile, but he is passionate and rebellious. They offer him a logic based on their calculations, but though man may admire mathematics he does not like it. They would like him to be enthusiastic about solutions intended to be of benefit to him, but he is interested only in his own initiatives. Their beautiful theoretical edifices clash with human reality. And if man resists them, it is he who is wrong, not their theory.

"Politicians sometimes claim kinship with philosophers. But they act differently. Politicians are cunning enough to realise that 'correct' reasoning does not suffice. It is better to play on sensitive chords that have stood the test of time: the lure of wealth and flattering rewards; the hatred of others (other races, other religions, other castes); the love of one's country or tribe; and even the obedience to God or the fidelity to some popular leader. I am well acquainted with their behaviour, because it is similar to that of the charlatans I have had to combat. The healer knows that it is incumbent on him to find the imaginary words and arguments that alone are capable of creating the emotion necessary to induce the subject to surrender. Not all politicians are of this stuff, of course. There are excellent and respectable men among them, such as those who see it as their duty to act as administrators, in the service of others. Thomas Harvey, your grandfather, was several times Mayor of Folkestone, and his only thought was the proper administration of the port. I myself have spent many an hour on the administration of the College of Physicians, as Censor, Elect and Treasurer, and I think that was good politics. Nothing to do with the games played by those men whose only aim is to achieve their personal ambition or to give free rein to their prejudices.

"Because, for both politicians and philosophers, these are indeed only games. But medicine is not a game. It sees man as he is, not as people would like to imagine him or to model him: the true man, the naked man. In suffering, in fear, at the approach of death, the inessential vanishes; only the essential matters." Daniel had been present with me at the last hours of his father. Had he not seen the real questions of our life manifest themselves? I described to him the death of a King.

King James had for some days been suffering from violent attacks of fever; they worried me as well as his other physicians. We sent a message to Monsignor John Williams, who was at the same time the King's spiritual and temporal adviser, being both a Bishop and Keeper of the Great Seal. He came immediately. There was a great stir around the sickroom. For some weeks the King had been profoundly affected by the trouble that had come between him and his favourite, Buckingham. Some vilifiers had been spreading the rumour that the Duke wished to hasten the King's death and had had poisoned plasters and malignant potions administered to him. There was no truth in these insinuations, as was demonstrated a few days later by the King's autopsy: his illness was caused by a kidney that had been irrevocably damaged by voluminous stones. Was James aware of these rumours? At all events his last night, at which I was present from one end to the other, was greatly tormented. He struggled, tried to get up, fell back on his bed, exhausted. Now he cried: "Are they trying to kill me?" Now he took the Bishop's hands and murmured: "I am in peace, help me to go to Jesus Christ, whose mercy I entreat and expect." King James was now no more than a poor man. He lived his death as we may all live our own. All the everyday artifices had disappeared.

I also remember those Plague-stricken men who escaped death after they had believed themselves lost. This was in London, during the 1629 epidemic. During the previous recrudescences of the disease, the College of Physicians had recruited, for hard cash, some practitioners whose special task it was to care for contaminated Londoners. But the results had been so bad that these mercenary physicians had had to be summarily dismissed. This time it was decided that we would ourselves take care of these unfortunate people, and I saw the Plague at close quarters. It was not the horror I was to find in France a year later. But the death of a Plague victim is very painful. Nevertheless, for the first time in my life I saw some cases of recovery. I am not sure that these providential outcomes were due to our poor medicines. I simply remember the survivors, with their hollow eyes and trembling hands, who could not even manage to smile when I told them that they were saved. They had glimpsed those terrifying shores where life hangs in the balance and where images appear that can never be effaced from the memory.

It is these visions that give the physician the certainty that in general there is a great confusion between what is, and what is not, important. Important—are miseries, anxieties, the difficulties of daily life, joys and sorrows, the untiring search for an impossible peace both with others and within oneself. Unimportant—are people who build societies on paper, and their theories; people who pronounce anathemas, and their war cries. It is my belief that physicians, and perhaps priests, help men more than politicians and philosophers.

"Are you not excessively severe," asked Daniel, "towards political philosophy? For my part, I still have a naive belief in the power of the ideas transmitted by those who meditate on man's fate. You yourself, Uncle—have you not taught me that the beauties of Nature, the marvels of animal life, the masterpiece that is a human body, are things that we can teach to others, and in so doing enrich their existence? Is it not a good thing to propagate ideas that give meaning to life? To promote the knowledge of art and the joys it can bring—is that not useful work? May we not hope that this particular kind of politics will successfully take men's minds off the difficult condition that life, alas, will always offer them? If I ever go into politics, I should like to devote all my efforts to ways of educating the young people of England. It may well be that if men are better educated they will find something other than war to amuse them."

Even though I considered these generous thoughts illusory, I was still pleased that Daniel should speak thus, and from the heart. I shall not forget this winter walk for a long time. There are some instants when one wishes one did not have to die. I should like to know what sort of man Daniel will have become in twenty-five years' time.

26 January 1648

I hate the fact that Daniel is attracted to politics. It appeals to him because it gives the illusion of having virtues it does not in fact possess. He sees it as a generous philosophy in action. Would to Heaven that this were true.

I have seen politicians trying to be philosophers at the same time. The two paths have always seemed to me to be opposed to one another. It is true that certain men of politics are so skilful at manipulating speech and writing that by inventing new images they make people believe they have discovered new concepts. I still have in mind the irresistible memory of my conversations with Francis Bacon, who had reached the highest echelons of the political hierarchy and at the same time managed to acquire the reputation of being England's premier philosopher. In Paris, Gassendi had told me of his admiration for the great man; he had been much affected by his recent death, he considered Bacon to be one of those men who opened out unknown paths towards a perfect system of thought. I refrained from answering, *Angleterre oblige,* and I said nothing of what I knew about the celebrated Lord Chancellor.

What do glory or obscurity depend on? Celebrity is understandable when it is merited, but how can it attain the same heights when it is usurped, as was the case with Francis Bacon? Renown is deserved by the man who presents the world with a new thought, an original discovery. But false renown brings just as much glory to the man who gives the illusion of having broken new ground. The preface to a work is a good intermediary

for this conjuring trick: no doubt many readers do not read further, even though they talk volubly about the work as a whole.
For this, they rely on hearsay. Life is short, and works are so
long.

It is true that I was myself taken in when I first met Francis
Bacon. He was not a very tall man but he was always dressed in
rich and gaudy clothes which, with his long, stiff face and steely
eyes, his vast ruff rising high behind his neck, his very ornate,
very tall hats, could give him considerable presence. He had
called me on account of his health, which he said was delicate,
although on close examination his puny body was seen to be of
great strength. The disorders he complained of were clearly
those of a man who is in no way ill, but of a hypochondriacal
and anxious temperament. He had just published his *Cogita et
visa de interpretatione naturae,* and been made Attorney-
General by King James. This was the beginning of a remarkable
rise towards the greatest honours, for he was soon to become
Keeper of the Great Seal, Lord Chancellor and a peer of the
realm. An eminent man of the law who is interested in science—
this was enough to captivate me. A man who could write "We
cannot command Nature except by obeying her" gave one food
for thought. A commentator on science who declared "The
understanding must not therefore be supplied with wings, but
rather hung with weights, to keep it from leaping and flying"—
this was a rare tribute to the scientists who observe patiently
before they begin to speculate. Alas, I was to change my tune
and feel first distrust, and then a kind of disgust, for England's
greatest politician-philosopher.

Before writing these lines I re-read his *Novum Organum
Scientiarium,* which is no doubt his principal scientific work. I
have emerged irritated from this reading, like a reader whose
appetite has been whetted by a promise that not only has not
been kept but that has been followed by its opposite. The promise, the words that attract me, are the affirmation on the very
first pages that the scientist must submit to the facts, his observation must be patient and his experimentation circumspect.
Francis Bacon, who never soiled his own hands in the examination of the facts of Nature, nevertheless lays down the whole
modus operandi necessary to avoid error. His use of words is

attractive, as for instance when he qualifies the sources of our errors as *idols*. By that he simply means the prejudices that falsify observation. But he gives them fine names, speaks of Idols of the Tribe, Idols of the Cave, Idols of the Market-place and Idols of the Theatre. I do not understand a word of these subtleties. Bacon goes so far as to suggest *tables* to help us poor blunderers in our task. If you observe, he writes, that when one phenomenon is present, another is; that when the first phenomenon is absent, the other is also absent; that if the first varies, the other varies in the same way—then you can conclude that the first is the cause of the second. These are extremely good intentions, and one feels like applauding.

After these excellent principles, however, everything deteriorates. In order to turn the results of experiment to the best advantage, Bacon has discovered a completely new secret, entirely invented by himself, never used before him. One must start with particular sensation and facts, says he, and from them extract propositions which will lead on in continuous and progressive fashion until they finally arrive at the most general possible affirmations. That is what he calls induction. This so-called new instrument of thought is in his opinion capable of reaching the goal he assigns to the scientist: to discover the cause, and the essence, of phenomena. For true science is the science of causes. This is what can render it fertile in both theory and practice. And what plays the role of cause in speculation will become a rule for practical action.

This is how, from an extremely sensible point of departure (like Bacon, I am convinced that facts should take precedence, and that obedience to this concept constitutes this century's great revolution in ideas) this drawing-room philosopher, who has never set foot in a laboratory, reaches the point of understanding nothing of the two-way game between experiment and speculation. He authorises speculation to take wing on its own the moment the laboratory notebook has been closed, whereas it must constantly return for further verification.

On the day my experiments and observations led me to think that the arteries start at the heart and send the blood into all parts of the body, I did not allow myself to be carried away by speculative induction into rash generalisations. On the contrary, my speculation led me to make new experiments; nothing else was capable of confirming what until then was only an hypothesis. Choosing a lean man, I tied a bandage round his arm and made it as tight as he could bear. I observed that, below the ligature, towards the hand, there was no arterial pulsation, whereas above the ligature the artery pulsated more strongly and swelled as if it were trying to burst through an impediment to its passage and continue on its way. Soon I saw the hand whiten and become cold; no particle of blood was then reaching it. I decreased the compression, and the hand immediately coloured and became warm again. Therefore, the artery did indeed send the blood into the extremities. The first observations gave rise to a hypothesis, the hypothesis instigated the experiment, and the experiment confirmed the hypothesis.

But this result in its turn led on to other speculations: if the blood goes to the extremities by way of the arteries, we may think that it returns to the heart by way of the veins. And here once again the scientist is led back from speculation to experiment. I had the idea of compressing the arm less strongly than in the previous test, so that the obstacle should be insufficient to stop the strong pulsation of the arterial blood. I then saw the veins swell below the ligature and become congested with the blood whose return up to the heart I was preventing. This was a repetition of the procedure with the garotte, which was demonstrated to us in Padua although its lesson was not understood. I had followed the same procedure, but this time it was inspired by a speculative hypothesis which had itself originated in other observations. And this is how we make Progress in the search for truth, not by following the Lord Chancellor's "new instrument." In the same way as the blood circulates in the body, the mind must let its thought circulate between facts and imaginings. The magic of that circle is the only true secret of science.

But the science Francis Bacon speaks of is no longer that of our age. He goes astray when he writes that the aim of science is to penetrate the essence of things, for it is really something more modest: to understand their mechanism. Descartes, in spite of his failings and contrary to what Gassendi told me, goes a great deal farther and is much sounder than he. Finally, despite his wish to be the greatest innovator, Bacon is still completely enmeshed in a decadent form of Scholasticism. He wants to be new, but he will not accept change. He mocks Copernicus and Galileo, and I once heard him declare that to imagine that the earth moves is completely absurd. What is absurd, what is the product of a narrow mind, is to criticise an idea in the name of a tradition, without even being prepared to hear the proofs adduced.

Perhaps I am unfair. It is probably because I cannot separate what I know of the man himself from what he wrote. They say that it is only the work that counts, and the moral conduct of an author should carry no weight in the judgement passed on his work. No doubt this becomes true some centuries later. But when one is a contemporary, and when one has seen at close quarters the stuff an individual is made of, is it possible to forget it? And with Francis Bacon, I did see it at close quarters.

Queen Elizabeth, who never agreed to confer on him any of the official functions his fierce ambition made him sue for, judged him correctly. Unable to impress the Queen, he managed to make an impression on her favourite, the Earl of Essex. I heard later how Essex brought all his influence with the Queen into play over a long period of time and finally succeeded in obtaining a position at Court for his *protégé*. All he was given, however, was a nominal title which had no real function. Lord Essex was so good to Bacon that to console him for this disappointment he presented him with an estate. In thanking him for this magnificent gift, Bacon is reported to have declared that he would owe allegiance to the Earl until his dying day; he would consider him second only to the Queen. But then Essex fell into disgrace. He was hatching some sort of a plot against the Queen, was apprehended with arms in his hand, accused of high treason before the House of Lords and committed to the Tower of London. A few days later he was taken for trial at Westminster Hall. There he found Bacon as his prosecutor, seated next to the Attorney-General. Bacon had agreed to represent the Queen in court and to bring about Essex's downfall. He compared him to Cain, to Pisistratus, to the Duke of Guise, so eloquently that the accused was condemned to death. The whole country also knows, I think, that after his execution Essex was still too popular, and the judgement was too controversial, so Bacon agreed to write and publish a pamphlet sullying the good name of his protector.

But the day came, much later, when Bacon paid for his crimes and for his overweening ambition. I witnessed his fall. At that time he had complete control over all legal matters. And the rumour spread throughout the Court that he was trading on this situation. I knew that his behaviour towards King James and his favourite, Buckingham, was that of an obsequious courtier who would stop at nothing to obtain more honours and possessions. But I could not believe that he would push his passion for lucre to the point of selling his verdicts for hard cash. I was wrong. His venality was clearly proved. In 1621 I heard that Francis Bacon had been brought before a Parliamentary committee and accused of bribery and corruption. Many witnesses testified that the Lord Chancellor's men had promised them a favourable verdict if they paid the price of it. He pleaded guilty, in tearful and pitiable terms. He was condemned to pay a fine of £40,000, and to be imprisoned in the Tower during the King's pleasure. He was removed from his offices, declared incapable of holding any other, and banished from Court. The King, out of the goodness of his heart, soon rescinded these penalties, but for me there was nothing more to add: the man and his works would forever more be suspect.

I ought to have told Daniel this story.

28 January 1648

I have seen Heneage Finch again, he came to ask me about the continuation of the medicinal treatment I prescribed for him last year. It seems to me that its effect has been very successful: he is no longer in pain. Shortly after his marriage to my niece Elizabeth, Daniel's sister, he complained of a painful inflammation of the joints. I recognised the signs of rheumatism. That was not his first attack, he had been troubled by the same pains as a young man. It was clear that he had a constitutional pre-disposition to this condition and that energetic measures must be taken. I began by giving him an emollient clyster, followed the next morning by a purge, and the day after by bleeding him of eight or nine ounces of blood. Then, twice a day, he took a decoction of senna, rhubarb, agaric, fennel seed, violet, liquorice and hellebore, the whole infused in water diluted with white wine, syrup and a little cinnamon. I also had some pills prepared with a base of aloes and absinthe, which he was to take at night, once every six days. In the morning, before rising, he was to have gentle massage of the abdomen and flanks for an hour. Finally, I prescribed a light diet, one dish only at each meal, and I told him to abstain from wine, strong drink and all salt meats. The result of these recommendations was excellent. The pain disappeared, the joints regained their suppleness. From that time on, his recovery was maintained without complication. I nevertheless advised him to continue to observe certain precautions, and to resume the treatment at the slightest sign of a recurrence.

What is difficult in medicine is to predict with certainty the effect of treatment. In apparently similar circumstances the same drugs will cure this patient and not that one. This fact should render us modest, and prove to us that our ignorance is still very great. After I have listened to, questioned and examined a sick man from top to toe, I feel a certain idea of his sickness gradually taking shape in my mind, but this idea is only very approximate: it arises from the conjuncture of observed phenomena and the body of one's previously accumulated knowledge acquired from reading or experience. It sometimes happens that this conjuncture is so harmonious that the nature of the trouble becomes apparent and the treatment follows. But it also happens that one cannot fit the observed symptoms into any category of known diseases. In that case, the physician is like a navigator who has been deprived of his compass; he advances by trial and error. Sometimes he brings the patient safely into port, but at other times he runs aground. In these difficult circumstances the best physician is he who is the best visual navigator.

I remember some exemplary cases of this kind of enigma: the sick person's symptoms cannot be fitted into any of the compartments in which we keep what we know, what we have read, or what we have seen. A few years ago, one of the most zealous servants of the College of Physicians told me that his skin was gradually losing its sensitivity. He could be pinched without feeling the slightest pain. He could no longer distinguish hot and cold. He burnt himself without being aware of it. He scratched himself until he bled, without feeling it. And yet he had remained in complete control of his movements and could carry the heaviest loads; he performed his usual duties with diligence, and he could still use his hands with skill. Paralysis of the limbs is sometimes accompanied by lack of sensitivity. But I had never heard that one could become insensitive without being paralysed. I could therefore not give a name to his strange state, and I had to improvise a cure with no authority to rely on. I formulated an electuary inspired by Galen's theriac, with roots of sweet rush, ginger, iris, gentian and serpentaria; with lemon peel; with tops of marrubium and chamaedorea; with dried vipers; with olibanum and opopanax, the whole in a white honey diluted with a fourteenth part of Malaga wine. This remedy produced only a modest temporary improvement.

But this case gave me much thought, for I believe there is a lesson to be learnt from every unusual clinical observation: that is how medicine progresses. In the course of a conversation with Sir Kenelm Digby, a personage who is a little bit of a charlatan albeit very subtle, and who wishes me well (it was he who published a book in Paris, defending my work on the function of the heart against the attacks of René Descartes), Sir Kenelm observed that the case of the College servant contradicted what Descartes and others had written. For Descartes imagined that the nerves are at the same time the bearers of the sensory message and the motive message, that the same nerves inform the brain of the sensations coming from the skin and from the flesh, and transmit the brain's orders to the muscles. Now it is impossible that the path that controls movements should be the same path as that of the sensitivity: if this were so, my patient who has no more feeling should at the same time be unable to move his limbs, whereas he is one of the most lively, alert and vigorous of the College servants. In this way, the careful study of a single pathological case may lead not only to the description of a hitherto-unknown disease, but also to an important advance in the knowledge of our bodies. The nerves of feeling are different from the nerves of movement: that is what Erasistratus suspected twenty centuries ago in Greece, and what my observation proves with certainty for the first time.

Is there any more noble aim than to understand man, to discover, little by little, the secrets of life? I have the feeling that I am present at the beginning of an auspicious period of this eternal journey. If I were to be asked in which century I should like to have lived, I would reply *our own*. For our century is engaged in delivering and enlightening our minds.

29 January 1648

In my notes yesterday I mentioned the story of a patient who had lost his sensitivity. If this patient had been a woman, I would have suspected a particular alteration of the mind, which I know well in that sex. A long time ago I was asked to go to St Thomas's Hospital to see an eighteen-year-old girl called Mary. She too had lost the sense of pain without any loss of motion. When her handkerchief was pinned to her bare neck she walked up and down with it so pinned and seemed to have no knowledge of it. Needles could be stuck into all parts of her body without causing her any pain. Every kind of remedy had been tried, but nothing had had any effect. She had been in St Thomas's for months and I felt that my colleagues were becoming impatient.

I stayed for a long time at Mary's bedside and was soon able to judge her unusual behaviour. For no apparent reason she would pass from laughter to tears, now raising her eyes to Heaven, now making grimaces, and these theatrical attitudes redoubled when one pretended to take no further notice of her, as if she would not bear people to lose interest in her person. I had already observed such women when I was studying witchcraft: women claiming to be under the dominion of spells; women whose strange conduct led people to believe they were witches in service of the Devil. About ten years ago I saw the same mannerisms and the same contortions on the face of the toad-woman.

The toad-woman lived near Newmarket in an isolated house

on the borders of the heath. When passing through the district
with the King, I heard that everyone believed this woman to be
a witch and, as I had been trying for a long time to understand
what might be hidden behind the so-called phenomenon of
witchcraft, I told myself that this might be a good opportunity
to study the subject.

I therefore rode alone on horseback to the house by the heath,
and found the woman in a tumbledown house. She was alone,
and at first very distrustful. I introduced myself as a colleague of
hers, a wizard, desirous of conversing with her about our common trade. As every genuine witch possesses her familiar spirit
who serves as her go-between in her relations with the Devil, I
asked her where hers was, as I had a great desire to see him. She
went and fetched a little milk and poured it into a flat dish,
which she then put down near a chest in a corner of the room,
clicking her tongue in imitation of the call of the toad. I heard a
sound under the chest, and immediately a big toad came from
under it and began to drink the milk. I gave signs of my satisfaction, went over to the chest and quickly withdrew the dish, declaring that I wished to celebrate by offering her a drink of ale.
She had none in the house, but said there was some to be sold
about half a mile away. I gave her a shilling and desired her to
go to fetch some so that we could drink to our meeting, for
brother and sister in sorcery must drink together. She agreed,
and went out. I immediately went over to the chest, under which
the familiar had disappeared. I put down the dish of milk and
imitated its croaking as best I could. The little animal immediately re-appeared, I picked it up, and it seemed to me the most
ordinary toad in the world. Nevertheless, I wanted to get to the
bottom of it and took from my pocket the dissecting knife which
I almost always have with me on my expeditions, opened the
spirit's belly and, remembering the numerous toads I had dissected during my lifetime, found not the slightest originality in
this particular one. The woman must have picked it up on the
heath, tamed it and persuaded herself that it was the messenger
Satan had destined for her.

At this moment she came back with the ale, saw what I had
done and flew into a fit of rage the like of which I had never
seen. She threw the pitcher of ale at my head, rained blows upon

me, scratched my face, tried to tear my eyes out, and I counted myself lucky to escape this Fury with my life. I put up what resistance I could, and taking advantage of a moment's respite I offered her money, trying to persuade her that it had been only a very vulgar toad and in no way a devil, but without success. So I pursued another line, and told her that I was the King's Physician, sent by His Majesty to discover whether she was indeed a witch—for in that case she would be put in prison—or whether she was innocent. She seemed terrified, and gradually grew calmer. She could still not refrain from abusing me, however, and I took my leave to the accompaniment of some very colourful insults.

At the beginning of our conversation, when she was still quite placid, I noticed the same sulky expression and strange look on her face that I had observed in Mary at St Thomas's. All the women I have seen behaving in this way were single women who had no man in their life, and it was as if their uterus, indignant at being deprived of its due sustenance of relations with the masculine sex, were responsible for the paroxysm in the brain. I believe we could talk of uterine melancholy. These women are not fabricating their feelings, they are not simulators, their morbid symptoms are genuine. They have a deranged mind, and it creates some bizarre disturbances that resemble no known disease. It was with these ideas in mind that I suggested an unusual cure for Mary, which I shall call hymeneal. I advised her parents to take her home and find her a husband at once. This was done, and Mary completely recovered from her loss of feeling.

The disorders of the mind assuredly occupy an important place in medicine. By their subtlety, they complicate the task of the practician, who sometimes finds himself envying the greater simplicity of the veterinary art. And that is not all. The physician finally begins to question himself as to the frontiers of these disorders. Between them and what we call mental equilibrium there must be an uncertain zone in which many individuals operate, from a Cromwell to the poorest vagabond. And this uncertain zone may well be what has prevented, prevents, and will prevent men of all ages from living quietly and in peace.

2 February 1648

Anew week is beginning. And, as I do every Monday morning, I am thinking back to the Mondays at St Bartholomew's. For thirty-four years of my life I awoke on this day with a strange feeling, a vague anxiety, such as the actor experiences before going on stage. I knew the reason for it: the most arduous task of the week was awaiting me, an impossible task—that of deciding how many sick people should be discharged from the hospital, and who would be admitted in their place. It is five years since I was Physician to St Bartholomew's, but my mind was for so long accustomed to this Monday morning malaise that even now, when there is no more reason, it is still not free of it. People believe that with age and experience a physician becomes impervious to the misfortunes of his patients. Nothing is more false. I am still not cured of my anxieties; they even pursue my retirement.

The hospital was only a few steps away from my residence. I used to arrive at about seven o'clock and find the Great Hall full of people. The Matron, wearing a red woollen dress with batiste cuffs protected by an apron, her hair gathered up into a cap, was accompanied by some of her eleven Sisters, dressed in blue and white. They began the first selection of the applicants: the group of paupers, old men with families and homeless vagabonds, was separated from the sick, who were groaning, limping, walking on crutches, hunched up on stools or lying on stretchers. Also present at the Monday session were one or two of the hospital's barber-surgeons, the apothecary and some medical students, but the rules did not permit them to sit at the table where I was officiating.

This table was in a corner of the room, partially shielded from sight. I would first receive, one by one, all the inmates of the hospital, with the exception of those too ill to walk, whom I saw at their bedside. Out of a total of two hundred beds I had to release at least fifty, in order not to reduce too many applicants to despair. I had to discharge those who were nearly cured, which was easy, and those for whom I no longer had any hope, which was a difficult decision. The Charter also laid it down that we were to give shelter to the indigent, and not only to the sick, but we could not indefinitely keep the miserable wretches whose only need was bed and board.

For each patient, whether he stayed with us or left us, I myself had to write a prescription; this the apothecary deciphered with ease, as he had finally learned to read my unreadable scrawl.

The sick and indigent who desired admission were brought to me. St Bartholomew's was of good reputation, I believe. The beds were in medium-sized wards; when I was first appointed there were twelve, to which I had two added. Each contained a fireplace which gave out a good heat in winter; each bedstead was surrounded by curtains; the mattresses and bolsters were of both feather and flock, the woollen blankets were of various colours; the patients' linen was carefully washed in wood ash; the food was abundant although a little monotonous (twelve ounces of bread and eight of beef or mutton per day, or cheese and butter, a pint of meat broth or porridge, and three pints of beer brewed on the hospital premises—a diet to which I had added the juice of anti-scorbutic plants). Finally the treatment, it seemed to me, was the best to be found anywhere in England, so much so that the poor who go to hospital are no less well cared for than the rich, who do not go there. After all, these destitute wretches had as their physician the King's Physician in Ordinary.

At various times in my life I have even had the feeling that I was of greater assistance to the simple man than to the great lord. The latter distrusts, whereas the former hopes. The simple man acts on my advice without argument; the great man argues and does not act on it. It is my belief that simplicity of heart aids our remedies. The only desire of the pure is to recover;

complicated people have particular ideas and inner doubts that conspire to prevent recovery. This is already announced in the Beatitudes: Blessed are the pure in heart, Blessed are the meek. I have often meditated upon this state of mind that can be of assistance to the physician: the sick man approaches him, not as a friend or comforter, but as the man *who knows and who can.* He expects him to provide what other men are ignorant of, he wishes him to be of superior, not equal, knowledge. The man of rank distorts things by claiming to be of equal knowledge, and even of greater power. It is only the most elevated of all who escape this rule, and I am happy that King Charles is not one of these patients of little faith.

I have read similar remarks in the strange work of the Reverend Robert Burton, *The Anatomy of Melancholy.* This large volume of quotations from the Ancients is interspersed with very personal annotations touching on the most widely varied subjects: medicine, religion, love, ethics, rules for life. Discussing the sick man and his physician, he writes that the physician is no less than the hand of God, *manus Dei,* that the sick man must be assured of this, that he must have faith in the man who is treating him, just as in order to be cured he must have faith in his cure.

This Robert Burton came to see me, some twenty years ago, at St Bartholomew's. He wanted to visit the hospital because he was interested in everything, and declared in his strong language that he wished to have an oar in every boat, to taste each dish, and to dip his lips in every cup. He introduced himself as "an ecclesiastic by profession and a physician by vocation." But vocation is no guarantee of knowledge, and I know the harm that can be done by those who consider themselves gifted for medicine without having made a proper study of it. I would no doubt have refused to receive him at St Bartholomew's had I not had a great desire to become acquainted with the man who had written *The Anatomy of Melancholy,* which I consider the most astonishing book ever published in England.

I had acquired the book some years before; it had been so successful that it was already in its third or fourth edition. The first strange thing: Burton had published it under the audacious name of *Democritus Junior*—a little as if I were to sign my

books Hippocrates Junior. Yet everyone knew the real name
of the author and, in case of doubt, he had taken the trouble
to have his portrait engraved in a vignette on the frontispiece.
The work began with a poem, with stanzas and refrain on the
order of:

> All my joys to this are folly,
> Naught so sweet as Melancholy.

And he had introduced poetry everywhere into the prose of
this enormous volume. I remember that, speaking of the heart,
he compared it to a pineapple, and dubbed it the sun of our body
and the fountain of our spirit. He said that the left heart contained blood and the right heart air, and that the heart repelled
the blood when the humour turned to joy, but called it back to
itself in sorrow and melancholy. A singular kind of anatomy! He
did not know my work, for which he may be excused as my *De
motu cordis* appeared only a little later. His book had still other
passages that set one's teeth on edge, containing as they did
rather too much of chiromancy, magic, philtres and other spells.
Nevertheless, it was a work of immense ambition, for it was
designed to be an inventory of every human passion and was
classified into parts, sections, chapters and subsections, just as if
it were a herbarium. I had found lively amusement in reading
the hundreds of pages devoted by this vicar to *Love-melancholy,*
in which he expatiated on methods of seduction, or dissected the
causes of jealousy in man and in animals such as swans, ele-
phants and crocodiles, or became so impatient with sodomy
that he suddenly began to write in Latin, whereas all the rest of
the text was in English (with the exception of innumerable Latin
quotations, for it was clear that this man knew by heart the
whole of the Bible and all the classical authors).

From all this hotchpotch, however, there emerged an idea
which I considered worthy of attention: Burton believed that
many maladies—convulsions, cramps, paralyses, gout, sciatica
and other physical tortures—may have as their prime cause
some unbalanced passion. And that sufferers from these maladies might be relieved by the cure of the said passion—as for
instance by distracting the mind onto other objects. There is an

odd chapter on the curative virtues of music. Such ideas may contain some truth. I have always thought that disorders of the mind may take the outward form of a disease of the body. But Burton, through his ignorance of medicine, fell into a trap I know well: that of attributing every malady to a morose or melancholic humour and, with a man suffering in the lower abdomen, of seeking a passion in the mind where there is nothing but a stone in the bladder.

That day, I had before me the author of this bizarre book. His gaze was intense, his gestures nervous, his speech fluent and verbose, and I thought that as a result of dwelling on melancholy and the passions he had allowed himself to be overwhelmed by them. And in any case, I know now that he died a few years later of a decline, just at the time he had predicted when he cast his own horoscope. Above his grave in Oxford is the epitaph he composed for himself: *Hic jacet Democritus Junior, cui vitam dedit et mortem Melancholia*—which I translate freely as, "Of melancholy he died; through melancholy he will survive." (I cannot help feeling, however, that this is an uncertain prediction, for the book has many weaknesses.) At all events, Burton was very lively at St Bartholomew's and seemed to be extremely interested in everything I showed him.

I took him first to St Bartholomew's the Less, the church that adjoins the hospital and was even built before it. Ambulant patients and physicians are required to attend it twice a week. I like the very tall, square tower that forms the entry; above the wooden door the great stained-glass window, amusingly, is not in the same vertical. The vicar received his colleague affably, but Burton had come to see hospital wards, not old churches. So we returned to the hospital. The surgeon John Woodall happened to be looking for me to ask my advice on a difficult case. I allowed Robert Burton to be present at the consultation, as I was sure it would be good for him to see some real medicine.

The patient's name was Ellin French. She was about sixty years old. By profession she was a servant, but she was well known for her depraved habits. She was a thief and an alcoholic, and forever cursing and blaspheming; she was so famous for her vices that *The Sad Ballad of Ellin French* was sung in the streets of London. She stank to high heaven, and it was indeed her

odour that had incited her neighbours to complain: two beadles
had then brought her to us on a stretcher. This was not the first
time that men or women had been picked up in London because
they were fetid: they were taken to hospital.

It was easy to understand why Ellin stank: both her legs were
gangrenous, as were also seven of the ten fingers on her hands.
The gangrenous parts were blackish, sanious and putrid. It was
obvious that all these dead branches must be amputated from a
body whose putrescence could only spread. John Woodall was a
good surgeon for such a case, which he described some years
later in his *Military and Domestic Surgery*. So I gave my consent
to the operation. Robert Burton had become livid: this was a far
cry from bookish medicine and meditations on melancholy. In
the meantime John Woodall, who was always a little simple and
dull-witted, declared that the cause of the gangrene was obvious: it was God's punishment for Ellin's crimes. God was mer-
ciful, because he allowed Woodall to operate successfully, the
patient recovered as best she could, and laments on the misfortunes of Ellin were still sung in the streets of London.

After our consultation I took Robert Burton into the little
physical laboratory where it was my wont to retire in order to
think or to study. Seeing that he had not recovered from his
emotions, I asked him to take a seat and to accept a cordial. I
offered him a beverage that was quite new to England at the time
as I had been one of the first to receive from the Levant Company, to which my brothers Thomas and Daniel belonged, the
beans of the Turkish bush from which it is made. Thirty years
have passed, and the infusion made from these beans is now well
known under the name of *coffee*, its aroma delights my nostrils,
and I consider it to be possessed of analeptic properties that clarify and purge the brain. Since that time, together with watered
cider, coffee has been one of my favourite beverages. I do not
know whether Burton shared my liking for it, but he seemed
revived and started to talk very loquaciously. He was tiring me
rather, and I had work to do. I sent for our apothecary and requested him to take care of my guest, and they went off together.
Our apothecary knew the history of St Bartholomew's better
than anyone, and always took great pleasure in showing visitors
round our hospital and its surroundings. He was better than I at

recounting how there had once been a gallows on this site, and how it had been followed by a Priory, a poor-house, five chapels and a hospital; how, at the time of the Suppression of the Monasteries, the chapels had been demolished and the Priory surrendered to Henry VIII; and how St Bartholomew's had finally triumphed over all these upheavals and had become a sanctuary for the care of the sick poor.

28 November 1648

I have known two kinds of men: the ardent, for whom activity is a vital need and who would suffer if they had to suspend any undertaking that was in train, and the weary, who are attracted and contented by idleness. All my life I have been an ardent man, but I have become a weary one. This must certainly be the reason why I abandoned this diary for some months.

I have to admit that my country retreat, which I enjoyed at first, has now become a burden to me. I miss the College, my patients, the hospital, and I miss even more the almost daily intercourse with the eminent men whom I had the good fortune to frequent in London.

At the same time, my brother's death has drained this house of its joy. He enlivened it with a ferment that made me sometimes long for silence. But death renders some silences unbearable. And there is also the news of the King, which I consider to be very bad. I am told that he is calm, tranquil and respected in his castle on the Isle of Wight; this calm has lasted too long for me to feel re-assured.

Today I resume this diary to record the extreme irritation that a new occurrence has inflicted on me this week. I have received a text, printed by the London publisher Milonis Flesher, which is the most venomous and inept attack on my work that I have ever read. Only a few months ago the author sent me a little *Anatomical Manual* which was full of nonsense about the heart and the circulation but where I was only indirectly challenged.

The new work, which is to be published without delay and to be called *Opuscula anatomica nova,* is a voluminous pamphlet that mischievously attempts to destroy my entire work. Nor am I the only one it attacks: it also arraigns a Leyden physician, Jan de Wale, whom it accuses of being an ardent advocate of my *De motu cordis*—a rather dubious advocate, in my estimation, as de Wale dares to claim that it had all been discovered before me.

And, unfortunately, the author of this scurrilous document is a famous physician, a Paris anatomist who had already published many works and acquired a great reputation throughout Europe: Jean Riolan. I saw a good deal of him in London ten years ago when he came with Marie de' Medici, the King of France's mother, on a visit to her daughter, our own Queen. Riolan teaches anatomy, botany and pharmacy in Paris in an amphitheatre which, as Louis XIII's Physician, he managed to have built especially for him a few years ago. He is an extremely corpulent individual; his enormous, round head, his wide-apart, half-closed eyes, his scornful mouth, have left me with the memory of a man who is violent, self-confident and probably malicious. I know, furthermore, that he is a great drinker of Burgundy: I have been told that he seeks consolation and forgetfulness in wine because he is afflicted with the most bad-tempered, shrewish wife in all Paris. This may perhaps also be the reason for his quarrelsome disposition.

He devotes a large part of both his *Manual* and his *Opuscula* to the movements of the blood. He writes something like this: "I accept that there are certain movements of the blood, but if there is indeed a circulation it cannot be such as is described by the learned Harvey, who talks nothing but nonsense. I propose a very different circulation, whose relationship to Harvey's is that of truth to error."

Riolan is indignant at my comparisons of man with the animals—which he designates as *the brute beasts.* The brute beasts, he writes, incline their heads towards the ground, whereas man looks straight ahead of him. How, then, could the movements of the blood be comparable in the two cases? The use is different, hence the movements must be dissimilar. This affirmation shows Riolan in his true colours: he is *convinced,* he *claims,* he *maintains,* he *knows*—but he does not condescend to verify the ideas he advances.

Nor does he believe that the heart is the prime mover of the blood. He considers it more *reasonable* to suppose that the blood moves of its own accord. He compares the heart to the sail of a windmill that revolves, he writes, "by water power." The heart, according to him, is only of use in bringing warmth to the blood, and "a provision of spirit." For its part, the blood, "that sweet liquor, that vivifying nectar" (what verbiage!) is of use in preventing the heart from drying up. Furthermore, Riolan takes the heart of delicate men and that of women to be a soft organ (as opposed to that of animals, which he thinks is hard). And if, by some wild stretch of the imagination, one were to suppose that the heart might propel a drop or two of blood with each of its pulsations, there would be so many drops that they would have great difficulty in finding accommodation. Quite simply, the man has never himself looked at a beating heart. He would have seen that it is not drops but an imperious jet of blood that the heart expels with every beat. The proof that he has never observed a heart anywhere other than in Aristotle's books is that he asserts that there is an orifice enabling the left and right ventricles to communicate, whereas I, who have looked, and looked carefully, have shown that this orifice does not exist. Moreover, Riolan would find it difficult to accept that waves of blood circulate, as he seems to imagine either that the blood is stagnant in the vessels or that it is only subject to vague backward and forward movements. He declares that only a few organs, chosen by I know not what arbitrary force, are irrigated. I could make ten experiments in front of him which would all demonstrate that, contrary to what he believes, the blood does indeed circulate in our limbs. But I think that in that case he would close his eyes, for love of Aristotle.

Nor does he believe that the blood passes through the lungs. I read: *Itaque Doctissime Harvee, agnosces sanguinis traductionem per pulmones, esse contra naturam*—"Harvey is very learned, but when he says that the blood passes through the lungs, he is going against Nature."

Riolan does not hesitate, either, to make the blood flow backwards in the veins. "In order that the veins in the arms and thighs should not become drained, it is possible that the venous blood descends as I have demonstrated, in refutation of Harvey." He imagines direct passages of the blood between arteries and veins. "No one can deny it," he writes, "since Galen left it in writing for us." And this gibberish, this fantasy, this imaginary circulation—all this, he claims, has the great advantage of existing "without confusion, without troubling the humours or destroying the foundations of Ancient Medicine"!

In truth, I believe that Riolan is the prisoner of a kind of brilliant armature that he has constructed for himself. He has made himself, once and for all, the gallant defender of the Ancients. Hippocrates, Aristotle and Galen are gods, he sees himself as the guardian of the cult, hence every departure from its liturgy is sacrilege, every discovery of new facts is heresy. He is touchy on these points, because any approach to a new understanding would disturb his own image. To undermine the doctrine would be to undermine himself, to doubt his infallibility, and hence his renown. He is unyielding, because he fears collapse.

I have known other men who were similarly enchained by the image of themselves they believe they project. I find it hard to tolerate them because the quest for truth is of far greater importance than stubborn adherence to a theory. To be capable of changing one's mind, to recognise one's error—these are victories, not defeats. But to cling obstinately to a system is probably a natural proclivity. Riolan is adulated by all the anatomists, so why should he suffer contradiction? Even if he is not always sure of possessing the truth, he is sure that his image cannot fail to possess it. A highly understandable temptation: every man constructs his own image, lives with it from morning to night, takes refuge in it when attacked, admires it when complimented, and finally is more in love with his image than with himself.

We have invented altruism, we have invented the love of truth, and these are fine and noble inventions. But a physician clearly sees that it is not in men's nature to allow precedence to others over themselves, or to other men's truths over their own.

I understand Riolan, then, but I do not therefore judge him any the less contemptible. He has only one thought in mind: to be greater than the rest. He claims to be the anatomists' cory-phaeus, hence I must be their heresiarch. Unfortunately for him, scientific truth is an intransigent mistress who only reveals her-self to observation and experiment, and refuses herself to those who wish to make facts dependent on their ideas, instead of making their ideas dependent on facts. My work is built on facts; that of Riolan is built on ancient traditions and *a priori* ideas.

23 December 1648

A messenger has brought me two letters from Ashburnham. They were written at a fortnight's interval but they reached me at the same time. I opened them with feverish fingers for I was sure they would contain news of the King, about whom, in my country retreat, I have heard nothing for several months.

The first letter was terrible. I am still distressed by it. Ashburnham relates that the Army have taken the King by force from his residence on the Isle of Wight and carried him to Hurst Castle. Hurst is a castle in name only. It is, as I well remember, a sinister block-house perched on a desolate rock projecting into the sea, joined to the mainland by a narrow neck of sand covered with stones and pebbles and washed on both sides by the waves. The Governor of the Isle of Wight, who until then had been guarding the King with severity but full respect, has himself been removed and imprisoned, as he was suspected of having felt too kindly towards His Majesty. The new gaoler is a low-ranking officer with brutal, arrogant manners, who has a huge basket-hilted sword at his side and carries a heavy partizan in his hand. The King's apartments are as dismal as a prison, and the only walk allowed him is a long, narrow, stony path terminating in a drawbridge. Ashburnham heard all these details from the King's faithful manservant Thomas Herbert, the only one authorized to go with the King to Hurst. Herbert believes that this imprisonment was organised by a small faction within the Army that professes great hatred of the King. He even believes that some of them would be prepared to assassinate him. He intimates that so sequestered a spot for the reclusion of the King may perhaps have been selected to render the assassination easier.

Even if these extreme fears are without foundation, the King's very solitude must be a torture to him. Reading Ashburnham's letter, I remember Treviso, where twenty days of reclusion taught me the horrors of imprisonment. No one who has not experienced them can truly conceive of them. It was in 1636, at the end of my journey through Europe with the Earl of Arundel. He had asked me to go to Venice, Florence, Rome and Naples, to help the Reverend William Petty choose some masterpieces of Italian art for the King. No sooner had I arrived in Venezia than, at the gates of Treviso, I was asked for my certificate testifying that I had not been in contact with the Plague. I showed it, but was told that as it had not been counter-signed in the towns of Conigliano and Sacile, I must be put into quarantine. I absolutely refused, said I had the pass and recommendation of the King of Great Britain and the Emperor of Germany, but the *Podestà* of Treviso would not hear me. I was surrounded by armed soldiers and shut away, with my horses, my groom and his two servants, in a filthy hole with for all bed and bedding a little straw on the ground. The heat was overpowering (it was in the month of August), and we were devoured by mosquitoes. I told myself that although I had been free of the Plague when I arrived, I might well contract it in this place where dozens of contaminated travellers must have slept. Day after day I sent appeals for help to the English Ambassador to Venice, but I did not know whether my messages reached him. When I was freed, three weeks later, I knew for all time the meaning of incarceration and deprivation of liberty.

I am almost ashamed of remembering this incident of my journey, it is so trivial in comparison with the sufferings of my King. For him, it is not an interrupted journey, it is a severance; he is being deprived of the office with which he identifies himself—the control of the destiny of his beloved England. From compulsory residences to humiliating prisons—the King is being destroyed. Tears come easily to old men's eyes; I wept when I re-folded Ashburnham's first letter.

The second one fortunately allayed my anxieties. Once again, the balance alternates between hopes and fears. On December 17th the King was freed from his prison at Hurst and taken to Windsor Castle. I do believe that of all the royal residences in England it is Windsor that King Charles prefers. There, he is free in his movements, Ashburnham writes, free to come and go in the Great Park, with the illusion of once again being master of his own domain.

Windsor! How many times have I been there with the King, in those happy days I would so like to re-live. I remember hours of festivities, in the 1630s, when the Court received all that England and Europe counted of great thinkers, writers, artists and noblemen. I can see the tall tower that dominates the whole region; the great building that resembles a fortified castle; inside it, the Holbeins, Rubenses, Van Dycks and other magnificent paintings; outside it, the terrace, as extensive as a garden, and beyond the park, the Thames: in those days it provided the exact mixture of animation and tranquillity that I like. The King took a passionate interest in my work, and it was not out of pure courtesy that I dedicated my *De motu cordis* to him. At Windsor, he hunted almost every week, allowed me to dissect the stags, and liked to watch me operate. We had heard of the strange case of Viscount Montgomery, and he asked me to go further into the matter.

The Viscount was a young Irish nobleman. At first sight he seemed sprightly and healthy. But when he removed his shirt and doublet I saw a vast hole in his breast, to the left of the sternum. As a child, he had fallen from a great height and broken several ribs. Far from healing, his wound had begun to suppurate and form a profound ulcer which had destroyed the bony protection of the torso at that place. He now had a cavity into which I could easily put my three forefingers and my thumb. Behind the hole, a simple, soft membrane had formed, and this was all that guarded the organs contained in the breast. The physicians who had seen him before me had declared that behind the membrane they could feel the lung. Hardly had I introduced my fingers, however, than I realised their mistake. What I could feel in the depths of the cavity was something pulsatile; it had just struck my fingers in the rhythm of the heart, not of the respiration.

Behind the delicate membrane that so miraculously protected it, was the heart, the almost naked heart, that I was touching. This observation seemed so remarkable that I wanted the King himself to witness it. I went to the Palace with the young victim and it was clear that Charles was fascinated by what he saw and felt. I was able to demonstrate to the King that I had been right to assert that in contraction, the cardiac muscle causes the organ to strike the chest, while in between the contractions the heart relaxed and retracted. The King declared himself convinced of the truth of what I had been advancing for years: that it is indeed the contraction—the systole—that is the proper movement and function of the heart, responsible for projecting the blood into the arteries.

My last sojourn at Windsor Castle dates back to 1642. There was less splendour and more anxiety. For the first time, the King was becoming aware of the mounting alarm caused by the Parliamentary agitation. He had just sent the Queen to France, as a precaution. There was no laughter at Windsor. Civil war was brewing.

I can imagine the King, today, strolling in the park and thinking back on all these memories. What is the meaning of his relative liberty at Windsor? Why this alternation of persecution and of a certain renewed respect? Everything is happening as if in the Army, in Parliament, and in Cromwell's brain, opposing impulses were at one moment strengthening the will to abolish the monarchy, and at another reinforcing the desire to come to terms with the King, who is still greatly loved by our people and who could perhaps be a master trump in the camp of one ambition or another. For it is certainly a question of ambitions. Revolutions may well be prompted by generous and honest ideas, but impure additions are inevitable. I know men well enough today to be sure of that. There will be a few men of goodwill and noble aspirations in the melting-pot but they will soon be adulterated with a mixture of the embittered, the ambitious, the opportunists, the belligerent, those who have a talent for leadership, and the mass of those who like to be led. Loyalty, fidelity, calm, all these qualities that are so necessary, soon come under threat. In the whole history of the world, has there ever been an entirely pure, clean revolution—even when historians have later regarded it as a healthy, natural sign of the progress of human societies?

At all events, the revolution threatening England today is, I am certain, a dirty revolution. For my part, I who take no sides—I am a Royalist through fidelity of heart rather than through any political position—the forces seeking to bring down the King show no signs of being a spontaneous and unanimous movement. They combine, higgledy-piggledy, the fanaticism of the hot-headed Levellers, the power-lust of an unhinged Cromwell, the wounded pride of the Parliamentarians that Charles refused to pander to, the hatred felt for the Papists, the dissension within the Army, and still other factors. The trouble is that, in my secluded retreat, I am incapable of judging the relative importance of these heterogeneous threats. I think I can guess that Cromwell is torn between two opposing temptations: to make use of the King, and come to power more surely, or to destroy the King, and come to power more quickly. The fellow is in a strong enough position to be able, single-handedly, to weight the scales towards propitious or pernicious decisions. If the King is brought down, thousands of loyal Englishmen will weep, and those who, like myself, were close to him, will see their property, their activities, and perhaps even their lives threatened. My head swims when I think that all this depends on the unstable brain of an ambitious Cromwell. Have I any right to hope that the transfer of the King from the sordid prison of Hurst Castle to the gilded prison of Windsor Castle is an auspicious sign? It sometimes happens that a gravely ill patient suddenly seems to take on a new lease of life, and then dies the next day. I cannot rid myself of my anxiety.

31 December 1648

After a few abominable nights during which attacks of gout and melancholy thoughts alternated, and magnified each other, I asked Dr Charles Scarburgh to come and see me. He came at once.

Charles is thirty-two and I am seventy. And yet there is no doubt that he is today my dearest friend. To have dealings with young, handsome, intelligent men is a great consolation to elderly men, even more so perhaps for those who, like me, have not been able to have a son. Beautiful and intelligent young women would not give me anything of the sort because the age difference would intimidate me: I know too many old men who have been ridiculed by young damsels. But Charles inspires me with a confidence that is free of all fear. I know that he will be faithful to me unto death.

It is barely four years since we met for the first time. He had come from Cambridge, where he had studied mathematics and medicine. But in 1644 Cambridge went over to the Parliamentarians and Charles, a known Royalist, was dismissed from his Fellowship at Caius. Very understandably, he migrated to Oxford, in the same year that the King made me Warden of Merton College. Charles immediately attached himself to me. I was instantly captivated by this very respectful but very enthusiastic boy who was intensely desirous of helping me in my research. His brilliant black eyes, his very long face, beardless but with a delicate, naively swaggering moustache above his sensual lips, his ready smile, gave him a polite yet guileless air. He was fascinated by mathematics, and had gone so far as to make an English translation of Euclid, which had not yet been published. This pleased me, for a modicum of the mathematical spirit (a modicum, but not too much) seems to me to be of great use both to the naturalist and to the physician.

Charles was my assistant in all the work I was able to carry out in Oxford. I had transformed a room adjoining the College Library into a laboratory. Two wide embrasures on either side of the room disseminated a brilliant light, tempered by the pale, carved panelling of the walls. There, Charles and I dissected all kinds of fish, insects and other animals, I showed him what I already knew about their genital organs and what remained a mystery, I felt that he was passionately interested by what I was able to teach him, that he admired my efforts, and had a blind confidence in the new methods of investigation and thought that I tried to describe to him. Perhaps I was fond of him because I felt I was his mentor. To the master, the pupil is always a little like Pygmalion's Galatea.

When the King fled from Oxford I too had to leave, and Scarburgh, in his folly, felt himself obliged to join the Royalist forces. I remember I sent him a brief, imperative message which started with the words: "Prithee leave off thy gunning and stay here. I will bring thee into practice." We were separated for some time, but our friendship did not falter. He arrived here yesterday, only two days after receiving my summons.

I asked his pardon for my need to see him. I told him of the solitude of my retreat, and of my melancholy. Life had heaped its gifts on me, but all of a sudden it had ceased to bring me its joys. Quite the reverse: it was inflicting infirmities and sufferings upon me, as if to make me understand more clearly that the happy—or even merely acceptable—days had come to an end. I confided to Charles that I had a secret stock of laudanum which would enable me, if the need arose, to substitute an easy death for an intolerable existence. I believed this action to be entirely lawful. But it was possible that I might need sympathetic assistance on that day, and it was this assistance that I asked Charles Scarburgh to afford me.

"Did you say lawful?" he asked.

At the same time he drew his chair nearer to mine and placed his long hand with its tapering fingers on my arm. Physical contact may strengthen the exchange of affection communicated by words and looks. I was grateful to Charles Scarburgh for not uttering the banal remarks I feared, such as: you are younger than ever; we need you; you still have it in you to do great things. He simply said:

"Is the right to choose the moment of one's own death as natural as you seem to believe? Through my acquaintance with you I have acquired a certain idea of life: we do not choose to enter it, nor the moment of our entry, we are subject to its joys and adversities, its pleasures and accidents, without having very much say in the matter. One fine day we are removed from it without really understanding why the thread is cut on that particular day. It is clear that the whole business is beyond our comprehension, that it is not within man's grasp. You taught me that science would never provide us with the underlying key to our adventure. Even if we put our faith and hope in God, we have difficulty in understanding his real designs. The only thing we are sure of is that the issue surpasses the feeble resources of our reason. I am your disciple, and I put the question to you: is it our role, have we any right, to intervene in a destiny of which we are assuredly not in control? Is it not to play shamelessly at being a god or a devil if we choose the hour of our own death?"

I replied that man's destiny was precisely to play at being a god, since man is the only living creature who invents his own laws. I said that medicine, which is the passionate desire to heal, is by that very fact a passionate desire to defy death. I said that Kings and men of war never stop playing with fate and upsetting its proclivities. And I said that in my view, man's greatness lay in his power to contest the natural progress of things and their fatality. Charles said that he hoped my state would never warrant my having recourse to a mortal dose of laudanum, but that he would always be prepared to obey me and assist me in all circumstances. I contented myself with these ambiguous promises, and began to ask him about the fate of the King. He lived in London: did he know more than I about the current intrigues?

He confirmed that the two opposing camps, Parliament and the Army, had both had in their midst very many men who advocated coming to an understanding with the King. Parliament did indeed contain some fierce enemies of King Charles, and in the Army, the Agitators accused our sovereign of all the sins in the land. But they did not equal, either in numbers or in force, the Parliamentarians and officers desirous of having the King in their camp, even if it were only in order to triumph more surely over the opposing camp. And then, Charles Scarburgh told me, there occurred a mysterious incident which is being spoken of *sotto voce,* although no one knows how much truth or how much invention there is in what is only a rumour spreading through the streets of London.

Cromwell is said to have intercepted a letter from the King to the exiled Queen in France. He had introduced a couple of his spies among the King's menservants; they had followed the messenger who was secretly conveying the letter and, knowing it to be hidden in the skirts of his saddle, had stolen it from him. No one had any certain information as to the contents of the letter. Everyone thinks he knows, but no one gives the same version. Some declare that the King had written: "You reproach me for the concessions I have made to Cromwell, but you should know that in due time he shall not be fitted with a silken garter but with a hempen cord." I declared to Charles Scarburgh that these words were not in the King's style. He replied that the content of the letter was of little importance; what was certain was that after having read it Cromwell had changed his tune: hesitant up to that time, he had no doubt suddenly decided that he would leave the King out of his calculations.

On the sixth of this month, Cromwell had sent Ireton, his son-in-law and general factotum, to "purge" Parliament. Colonel Pride's regiment began by turning out the guards of the House of Commons, and then Pride himself had forty-seven Royalist members arrested as they were entering the Chamber. Some eighty others were debarred or, fearing prison, fled. None remained in the Chamber but safe men who could be relied upon to bring down the King. In my opinion this month of December, Charles Scarburgh concluded, marks the end of our hopes.

Night was falling. We went on speaking for several hours more. We did not pronounce the King's name again, but all our thoughts were with him. We suffered the same torments. I invited Charles to stay until the next morning, and Daniel had the blue room on the second floor prepared for him. As dawn broke this morning, Charles left for London. I went with him to the stables where his horse was saddled and waiting for him. During the night the garden had become covered in snow. Today, the 31st of December, I said to Charles, it is traditional to wish people a happy new year.

2 February 1649

The King is dead. His death is murder and, even though he remained in the background, I hold Cromwell to be his murderer.

3 February 1649

There was the semblance of a trial which, by its cynical effrontery, makes a mockery of England's honour. A High Court of Justice was formed by a House of Commons that had been purged by Cromwell last December 6th of all its members favourable to the King. Those who remained must have felt some shame, for on the day of the trial nearly half the members designated to constitute the High Court failed to answer when their names were called. The charge against the King accused him of being a "tyrant, traitor, murderer, and a public and implacable enemy of the Commonwealth of England." I was told that when the Solicitor for the Commonwealth pronounced these epithets the King burst out laughing. He refused to answer this senseless charge and confined himself to the dignified declaration that he denied his judges the right to judge him, for this Court had been constituted in total violation of English law. If such courts might be improvised in our country, he cried, then the liberty of the people of England was threatened. What they might decide for his person was of indifference to him, but were he to recognise such an assembly as a court, it would be to deny the laws that protect every English citizen against arbitrary judgements. Some of the crowd dared to cry "God save the King," but they were promptly arrested and the officers ordered their soldiers to shout "Justice, justice!" I was told that after the charge was read, a masked woman stood up in the gallery and called out: "It's a lie. Oliver Cromwell is a rogue and a traitor." A Colonel was for firing into the gallery, but the lady had already left. I was also told, under the seal of secrecy, that the masked woman was none other than Lady Fairfax, the wife of the Army's Commander-in-Chief. The death sentence was voted by forty-four to twenty.

The most extreme of the horror and contempt aroused in me by this so-called Court of Justice is reserved for its Chaplain, Hugh Peter. I know him well, for he was in perpetual trouble with the Archbishopric. He was always vilifying the Anglican liturgy, and he answered any call to order with insults. Archbishop Laud, after having taken counsel with the King, decided to exile him for a time. A long enough time for his bile to accumulate, and we have now seen the result: the hatred he exudes from his every pore would be degrading to any man; in a clergyman it is scandalous. Last Sunday, two days before the execution, he took as the text for his sermon: "Bind your Kings with chains, and your Nobles with fetters of Iron." In passing, he termed King Charles "The Rabble of Princes," and gave other no-less-eloquent signs of his Christian charity.

It is thanks to Thomas Herbert that we have been able to learn everything about the King's last moments. Herbert is His Majesty's faithful Groom of the Bedchamber who did not leave the King for an instant. The day before the execution the Bishop of London had been given permission to spend several hours with the King. On his arrival, Bishop Juxon had expressed his grief. The King cut him short with a smile, telling him that they had no time for such thoughts. They should forget the coxcombs who thirsted after his blood, and who would have it, and let God's will be done: he forgave them most sincerely. He and the Bishop should rather think of his whole business, which was a serious preparation for death: he had to prepare himself to appear before God, to whom he would shortly have to give account of himself. It was his hope that he would acquit this task with calm, and that the Bishop would help him to do so.

That evening the King asked Herbert, who was sleeping near him on a pallet, to wake him at four in the morning. At the arranged hour he awoke of his own accord, opened his curtain and knelt down to pray. Then he asked Herbert to dress him. As the groom seemed to be combing his hair with less care and more agitation than usual, he said: "Though it be not long to stand on my shoulders, take the same pains with it as you were wont to do, Herbert, this is my second marriage day: I would be as trim today as may be, for before night I hope to be espoused to my blessed Jesus."

The Bishop then arrived and prepared what was necessary for the King to receive Communion. It was very cold. Some food had been brought in but the King did not touch it, not wishing to take anything after having received the Eucharist. The Bishop remarked that he had been fasting for a long time, that the weather was bitter, and that he might suffer a malaise on the scaffold. This observation struck him, because of the interpretation that might be put on such an incident, and he decided to eat a little bread and drink a glass of claret.

A little later the King declared that he was overcome with joy, for he had just been told that his son Charles had sent a message offering his life in exchange for that of his father.

When the King was finally led to the scaffold, he asked the executioner to allow him to pray for a few moments, saying that he would give him a sign to show him when to strike. His only anxiety was that the axe might be blunt, and he added: "Take care they do not put me to pain." To Bishop Juxon, who was with him, he said: "I go from a corruptible to an incorruptible crown, where no disturbance can be, no disturbance in the world." Then he asked Juxon to tuck his hair under his white cap, to leave his neck free of obstruction. He told the Bishop that he had a good cause and a clement God. Then, casting a watchful eye on the block, he asked the executioner to raise it a little. Stretching out his hands, the King said to the headsman: "When I put out my hands this way, then!" He lifted his eyes to Heaven, fell on his knees, and laid his head on the block. The executioner bent over to tuck some remaining strands of hair into his cap and the King, thinking he was going to strike, said: "Stay for the sign!" The headsman said he would await His Majesty's pleasure. After a few minutes the King extended his hands and the executioner separated his head from his body at a single stroke. Then, holding up the severed head, he cried: "Behold the head of a traitor!" When the blow was struck, a deep groan went up from the crowd. The soldiers soon dispersed them. The Bishop and Herbert carried the body away, had it embalmed, and placed the remains in a lead coffin which was taken to Saint James's Palace, covered with a black velvet pall.

Unhappy England! My country used to be one of moderation, it used to hate excess and the public display of emotion, it used to detest the unrestrained Latin cry, it showed the world the path of wisdom, it did not experience the martyrdom of the Inquisition. Heresy, for which such men as Giordano Bruno and Michel Servet were burnt at the stake in Rome and Geneva, was practically unknown. But now we have seen an agitated, ambitious clique decapitate a man for no other reason than that his political conduct inconvenienced them. I accept the principle that a King may be judged. I accept the principle that he should be reproached for his errors (and Charles did perhaps commit errors, but certainly not crimes). If he has made serious mistakes, I agree that his powers should be curtailed, or that he should be dethroned or, as a last resort, exiled. But to condemn him to be beheaded, to determine on the death of a man because his conception of his own task is an obstacle to the view of others—I can think of nothing more odious. It may be my profession that gives me so acute a sense of the gravity of any action that threatens the life of a human being, whether King or yokel. Medicine is an unremitting battle for life. The physician comes to see life as a permanent miracle that must not be allowed to flee before the normal hour; he comes to be in love with this miracle, and the idea that men may cut it short in order to appease their political or religious passions causes him suffering.

All I have just written, though, is but a device to hide my pain. The truth is that I had the greatest veneration for my King. The man they have just put to death was as dear to me as my closest friend. I hardly dare say I loved him, because one does not love a King as one loves one's brother. There was a distance between us. Nevertheless, my respect concealed an almost tender attachment. This feeling was all the more lively in that I was always as aware of the man's weaknesses as I was of his glory. I believe that he too loved me. I do not remember a single occasion when he did not make every endeavour to encourage my task. His face, which was so frequently severe, lost some of its coldness when I was telling him about my work. I remember some days when he had a way of taking my arm and giving me a gentle look that suddenly filled me with emotion. I loved him because there was in him an affinity with what, ultimately, was the meaning of my life: the attempt, imperfect but ardent, to know, to understand, to aid.

4 February 1649

Two days ago, the House of Commons created a new Court of Justice whose duty it is to sit in judgement on the King's loyal followers. They have rid themselves of the head; now they wish to amputate the limbs. Should I feel anxiety on my own behalf? My attachment to the King is common knowledge. I was on the list of the forty-two privileged persons who every year received a message and present from him.

But it would be a great mistake for me to worry about it. It happens that men who know they are nearing their end, and who sometimes even desire it, cast ridicule upon themselves by becoming terrified of a cold, fearing it is a fever. I want none of this kind of ridicule.

I have also seen men assuaging the end of their existence simply by nourishing themselves on their memories. Alas, happy memories please me, but do not appease me. I have too great a thirst for present joys, and even for future hopes, for the past to satisfy me. This time it is I who am ridiculous. I know that I have no future, and yet I cannot prevent myself from hoping for one. This lack of logic may well be what enables us to tolerate the intolerable. No doubt this failure of reasoning is a gift from Providence, a gift that helps us to bear life and that even lends it an astonishing attraction. It is an identical failing that enables men, knowing that they are going to die, nevertheless to live and act happily as if they had an eternity before them.

From the contradiction that thus dwells in me—the desire to

have done, combined with the desire for new endeavour—there arises a kind of inner conflict whose outcome I do not know. But I suspect that the incredible forces of life, which abandon us only with our last breath, are once again going to lead me to attempt action rather than to accept renunciation. *Endeavour* is a word that I would willingly have chosen for my motto. Endeavour may not be the secret of happiness (the secret of happiness exists no more than the secret of staying the sun in its course), but it is most assuredly the principal source of our joys, a shield against lassitude, as the aegis was the shield of Zeus and Athena. And if I wish, I may allow myself to be tempted by a multitude of endeavours.

In the first place, I shall produce a written refutation of the malevolent criticisms of that old drunkard, Riolan. I have never taken the trouble to reply to those who denigrated my work on the circulation of the blood. For the most part, they did not deserve the honour of a reply. But the celebrated Parisian is spreading throughout Europe the detestable lampoon he has thought fit to address to me. He opposes my discoveries with bitter venom, maliciously enveloped in compliments. He is amazed, he seems to say, that so remarkable an anatomist as I could be so much mistaken about the movements of the blood. But I know as well as he does how to interlard with praise and adulation a demonstration that will be unanswerable, and a condemnation from which there can be no appeal. This Riolan's mind is warped; I cannot redress it for him. But he is also given to dangerously false affirmations; I intend to rub his nose in his errors, and I shall publish my reply so that the truth shall become glaringly apparent to everyone.

I might also once again take up my old idea of writing a treatise on morbid anatomy. None of any pertinence exists. And I am convinced that the description of the organic lesions of a man who has died of a disease is far more useful to medical science than the autopsy of ten men who have no other morbid past than their crimes.

And above all, if I am allowed to return to London, I would like to devote my remaining strength to the College of Physicians, that illustrious company to which I have belonged for forty-five years. I have a desire to endow it with a new library and with a museum. And there are other ventures that could make the College what it should be: a temple of medicine, and a friendly meeting-place for its members. I have no more needs, I have no direct heirs, and I want my money to be used for this great project.

25 February 1650

Thomas Hobbes has written me a long letter from Paris; it is almost like a gazette, it contains so much news. He is in exile, and yet he is less cut off from the world than I am in my outlaw's retreat.

He tells me first that he was recently struck down by an extremely severe fever and was sure he was going to die. He is courteous enough to write that he missed my care, for he had to content himself with French doctors who are much less knowledgeable. During his illness, Father Mersenne visited him daily. Hobbes believes that he wanted to get hold of his soul before it flew away, having determined that he must die a good Catholic rather than a dreadful Anglican. But Hobbes gently replied that as all religions are excellent, the best thing for the order of the world was that everyone should persist in the religion of his youth and of his country. Mersenne, whose function as a priest obliges him to recruit souls to Papism, was nevertheless delicate enough not to press a fellow-philosopher farther than was necessary, smiled, did not insist, and afterwards proved himself the most obliging of friends. After these severe alarms, Hobbes finally recovered. Some time later, Father Mersenne fell ill in his turn and, being put in the hands of unskilful surgeons, after atrocious suffering, he died. Hobbes tells me of the great grief he felt because, he writes, Gassendi and Mersenne were his two best French friends. This death saddens me too; I remember the lively, smiling little man who, when I was in Paris, gave me such a warm welcome to his convent in the Place Royale and who introduced me to Gassendi. Both men won me over by their knowledge of my work and their very sound remarks about the changes in science that our century must bring about.

Hobbes's letter next speaks of a movement which is all the rage in France and which is popularly called the *Fronde*. Its target is Cardinal Mazarin, the absolute master of the Kingdom whose heir to the throne, young Louis, is only eleven years old. The French seem unanimous in their detestation of this prelate from the Abruzzi, who has managed to become the most intimate favourite of the Regent, Anne of Austria. Dozens of pamphlets hold him up to ridicule; whole volumes of them may be bought in the bookshops. One of their descriptions of Mazarin reads something like this:

> Filthy felon, fawning fake
> Scheming, swindling, slimy snake.
> Murd'rous, mealy-mouthed, malicious,
> Pimping, profligate, pernicious.

And there are many others, employing similarly choice epithets. This unrest has been shaking France for the last two years. There was fighting last year in a Paris bristling with barricades. Today there are increasing numbers of assassination attempts, the prisons are full, and Parliament is rebelling against the power of the monarchy. Mazarin has just had the Prince de Condé, whom he sees as his rival, shut up in Vincennes. Carriages crossing the Pont Neuf are fired upon. No day passes without news of some new blow struck by the *frondeurs,* who are the enemies of Condé, as well as of Mazarin and Anne of Austria. Hobbes amuses himself by making jest of this French turbulence, but he hints that the Royal Family might well suffer the same cruel fate in France as in England.

Had I not devoted all my efforts to works of anatomy, medicine and natural philosophy, I should have liked to study these historical movements. Why, after so many centuries, are peoples and States still shaken by perpetual convulsions? Why can we in no way feel that they are gradually progressing towards equilibrium and stability? What little I know of the history of Greece, Rome and the Christian era makes my head swim: there is not one country, not one form of society which, after a certain time, does not experience discord and unrest, revolt, attempts to overthrow it, prisons and deaths. No living organism would be able to withstand such inner struggles and turmoil. For the naturalist, it is clear that this perpetual quest for a new equilibrium is inherent in the human soul, or rather in the soul of human groups. The phenomenon apparently seems to depend, here on an unbearable tyranny, there on the ambition of a few; in some cases on the misery of the people, in others on the revolt against injustice. The historian always finds a ready explanation. But this business has been repeating itself too regularly and in too many forms for dozens of centuries and in dozens of countries for it not to have a more constant cause. This is evidently a fact of Nature, as it is in the nature of the volcano to spew out its lava periodically. The underlying mechanics are always the same, no doubt, however diverse may be the mechanics of the moment. Those who are fascinated by man's nature should give this their attention.

Hobbes also tells me of the death of René Descartes. The French philosopher was in Sweden where he had been invited by Queen Christina, who treated him with great respect. She desired his presence at the castle every day, plying him with questions, wishing to learn how to philosophise well, even asking him to take sole responsibility for creating a Swedish Academy. One day, after a long conversation with the Queen, he returned exhausted to the house of the friends who were offering him hospitality, took to his bed with inflammation of the lungs, refused to accept treatment from the Dutch physician they sent him (who, by an unfortunate chance, had been a party to the attacks Descartes had suffered at the University of Leyden), and, in short, he died on the eleventh of this month. Hobbes did not like Descartes, he had fought the man and his ideas, but in his letter he avows himself distressed by his death. The demise of an adversary may have the sadness of the end of a combat; some adversaries serve as a goad. If that idiot Riolan had not existed, I should never have published my two letters in answer to his attacks, and I believe those letters to be important.

I remember having received, several years ago, a volume of Descartes' *Metaphysical Meditations*, followed by *Objections* written by various philosophers, among whom were Mersenne, Gassendi and Hobbes. Hobbes had sent me this work and asked me to read his own sixteen personal objections, as well as Descartes' replies. I have just re-read this book, and I am once again amazed at what these great minds write. For example, in his second objection, Hobbes says that Descartes is wrong to say "I am thinking, therefore I am a thought," or "I am intelligent, therefore I am an understanding," for I might equally well say "I am walking, therefore I am a walk." And, farther on: "It is not another thought that I infer when I think. For even though someone may think that he has thought (which thought is no more than a memory), it is nevertheless completely impossible to think that one thinks, just as it is to know that one knows. For this would constitute a never-ending interrogation: how do you know that you know, that you know, that you know, etc.?"

This kind of controversy apparently angered Descartes; at all events, their disagreement dates from that year. All this apropos of the famous *I think, therefore I am,* an invention whose success astonishes me and which I consider inept—in the same way as, I must admit, I consider Hobbes's objections obscure. How is it possible to doubt one's own existence, except by a play upon words? I give the name existence to my life, it is an appellation like any other, one could have chosen a hundred different ones, but once the choice has been made I cannot begin to doubt my feeling that I am living by pretending to doubt the word I have chosen to convey this feeling. If I suffer from the gout and agree to call that pain, is it appropriate to ask whether pain exists? If I had arbitrarily decided to designate my feeling that I am living not by the verb *to be* but by the verb *to mump,* would it be appropriate to doubt thereafter that I *mump*? One has to be a professional philosopher to argue about words and not facts. Many of these thinkers are dear to me, and Hobbes more so than any other. But it seems to me that they are expending their efforts on games rather than on serious matters. These gentlemen are playing with language rather than occupying themselves with objects. They become the slaves of the awkward, imprecise word we have wrought, instead of working to gain a better knowledge of the object, and abiding by the results of our observation. The creation of words to designate things is one of the great achievements of the human race, but this achievement becomes a pitfall if we forget that it was only a temporary convenience, and that science only applies to the object concealed behind the name we have given it.

Nevertheless, I had very much liked the idea of the *methodical doubt* of which Descartes, I believe, had made himself the herald. This idea is the foundation of the honesty of the sciences. To doubt what one sees, to doubt the accuracy of one's reasoning, to doubt what the Ancients asserted, to remain on the *qui vive* for possible illusions—this is what I have always taken to be the essential rule. If I had not doubted what I was formerly taught about the heart and the path of the blood, I should never have discovered anything.

And then, I am not forgetting that Descartes was one of the first to declare that my demonstration of the circulation of the blood was correct and important. Although he was wrong to add a few idiocies concerning my study of cardiac contraction, about which he understood nothing. Finally, he was a man who defended doubt with intelligence, but handled it at random, describing a good method but not knowing how to apply it, a suspicious dreamer but a dreamer all the same, doubting my experiments on the heart instead of doubting the false traditions, going so far as to call into question the existence of the world without perceiving that he was quarrelling with the words *I am* rather than what is concealed behind them, and which is certainly beyond the understanding of human reason.

LONDON
1 June 1650

Two years, seven months and twenty-three days of exile from London. A voluntary exile at first, and then a compulsory exile. On March 20th last, Parliament (or rather what remains of it, a Rump Parliament of seventy members) ordered all "delinquents" to reside more than twenty miles from London, and I am on the list. Daniel's house, where I found peace, is henceforth prohibited. My nephew took me in at his home in Coombe, south of Croydon, beyond the illegal perimeter. There I found neither the comforts nor the warm-hearted care I had at Little Valley. The Act of Parliament provides for a lifting of the ban on March 20th, 1651, but who can tell whether the period will not be equally arbitrarily extended? I had given way to despair when an unexpected event occurred, which is the reason for my presence in London at the moment.

The widow of Sir Thomas Thynne, whom I attended a dozen years ago, was suddenly taken so ill that she had the idea that I alone could save her from death. This fortunate illusion caused her to request the Parliamentary Council to permit me to move to London, notwithstanding the Act of March 20th. No doubt I still retain a certain prestige among some of the Parliamentarians, for the request was made on April 23rd and permission arrived only two days later. It was granted for a period of fourteen days; on May 6th it was without difficulty extended by a month, and I have reason to believe that I shall be allowed longer. I am staying in my brother Eliab's house in St Lawrence Pountney Hill, in the city. I have already been able to see several of my friends from the College of Physicians, and I feel that the London air is making me several years younger.

During my long months of exile I came to realise how invaluable to man is the freedom to move wherever he wishes. Compulsory residence may seem a mild penalty, but it can be more painful than corporal punishment. I did not stay long at Coombe, but several days were sufficient to plumb the depths of solitude. I had with me only my manservant John Raby and my pretty young maid Alice Garth. Seeing me so unhappy, Alice would sometimes come up to my armchair, sit down on the floor, and dare to place her arm or even her head upon my knees. She reminded me of what the Bible says of the old age of King David, for whom they searched throughout the Land of Israel for a girl "to lie in his bosom so that he might get heat." My servant Alice was like a pet kitten that comes and nestles against its master to provide him with a little of its living warmth. I let her do this, being more grateful than embarrassed, merely feeling the benefit of the warmth she transmitted to my chilly carcass. But at such moments I sometimes felt my solitude even more acutely. All my life I have believed that I like solitude because I have disposed of it freely. I used to interpose it at will between periods of numerous and animated company. I prolonged it or interrupted it as I wished. I am not, of course, speaking of the secret feeling every man carries with him from birth to death—the certainty that he will always be fundamentally alone despite all the agitations and attachments that surround him. No, the solitude I am speaking of is simply that of silence, of perpetual rumination, of the ceaseless movement of a thought that goes round in circles without any other interlocutor than oneself, of a longing for questions and answers, of the disappearance of all human echo. I admire the hermit who shuts himself away forever in such solitude, but I am not of his stamp, I do not exist without other people (I mean without being recognised by other people), I need them even when the sound they make inconveniences me. I am made more for the city of London than for country retreats.

It is much easier to be informed of the state of the country

here than it was at Coombe. What I have learnt about Cromwell
does not surprise me, although it shatters me. God knows how I
hate the civilian *Levellers* and the military *Agitators,* who
preach subversion and who rejoiced at the King's death. But I
have been shown the latest pamphlet by Lilburne, the leader of
the Levellers, *England's New Chains.* And I have to admit that
he is telling the truth when he writes that one can barely speak
to Cromwell without him clapping his hand to his breast, raising
his eyes and calling God to witness. He will weep, groan, repent,
and while so doing he will strike you under the fifth rib. This is
an accurate portrait, but I must add that Cromwell is a mentally
unbalanced man, as I have long known. Unbalanced and calcu-
lating, that is a combination whose dangers are proclaimed by
the whole history of the world. Cromwell began by having several men put to death without any form of trial, their only crime
being that they had dared to voice their admiration for Lilburne.
What an outcry there would have been if the King had done as
much! Then Cromwell went off to Ireland at the head of an
army of twelve thousand men because Ireland too had ideas of
revolt. When he left, he made a fine speech in which he declared
that it was not he but God who was leading the expedition. And
it was in God's name that he besieged the fortified town of
Drogheda and, having made himself its master, slaughtered
more than two thousand of its inhabitants, both military and
civilian. Whereupon he announced: "This is a righteous judgement of God. It was the Spirit of God who gave my men the
courage to win, it is good that God alone have all the glory." He
then took Wexford, after which he exterminated a similar number of Irish men and women. Then, to extirpate the Papist spirit
which, he claimed, sullied the country, he arraigned the priests,
evicted the Irish from their lands and forced them to submit to
the Puritan credo, distributed two thousand five hundred acres
of these lands to his ruffianly soldiers who were complaining of
their meagre pay, and uttered harangues declaring that with
God's help he had upheld the Faith and Glory of England in the
face of a people who behaved like an enemy of the human race.
Everything I have been told leads me to believe that Ireland will
never forgive England these crimes. Cromwell has created a gulf
between the two islands that is far deeper than the Irish Sea and

St George's Channel. He has returned to London this month, and I wonder what new follies he has in store for us.

George Ent, who shares my fears, paid me a long visit. He is still young and eager, his mere physical presence does me good. The publication of my *De generatione,* which he has taken in hand, is under way. I told him in confidence of my desire to endow the College of Physicians with a new library and a museum, a project which filled him with enthusiasm. The very next day he asked the present President of the College, Dr Francis Prujean, to come with him to visit me, and I unfolded my plans at length.

I first declared that until further notice I wished to remain an anonymous donor. I do not wish my reputation as a proscribed Royalist to prevent the members of the College from accepting my gift. I shall allow the origin of the project to be made known when it has, as I hope, been unanimously adopted. President Prujean will first announce that a benefactor, who wishes to remain anonymous, is offering to present the College with a library worthy of its illustrious company.

Next, I unfolded my plans. I knew that my friend Dr Hamey possessed a piece of land adjacent to the College and I was sure he would donate it to us. I wanted a two-storeyed building to be erected there. On the ground floor there would be a large, magnificent hall for friendly meetings among the members of the College. Above, would be the library and museum. The library would not be confined to books on medicine. The proper exercise of our art requires us to have views on many other facets of science. There would be books on optics and geometry, studies on the heavens and the earth, essays on natural philosophy, books on music, accounts of voyages to far-distant countries. The culture of a physician must never be narrow. It must encompass the most diverse moulds; it must never be concerned solely with the knowledge of man's body and miseries, but also with the world he lives in. The best fertiliser for medicine is the progress of other and quite different sciences.

I also announced an endowment that would enable the College to add friendly meetings to working meetings. I hoped, with fifteen grammes of pure gold, to provide sufficient funds for the organisation of meetings to which all the members of the

College would be invited each month and where they would partake of a light collation. I also wished to reserve the equivalent of forty grammes of pure gold for an annual Feast, during which an Orator would commemorate the great events of the College, celebrate the honour of the profession, exhort the members to study the secrets of Nature by way of experimentation and, finally, remind them of the benefits to concord and the ravages of discord. These plans seemed to delight George Ent and President Prujean. They felt, as I did, the need to give new life to this College which had started with six members in the last century but which now counts nearly fifty. And a society with fifty members soon loses all sense of a corporate soul, if one does not take care.

I profoundly believe that in order for there to be mutual understanding between men, and consequently for them to have power to act efficiently, they must have common interests. What unites them must have more weight than what divides them. If my neighbour and I are quarrelling over the same piece of land, we shall avoid war only when a third robber comes and attacks us both. Two peoples or two heads of State will choose either to join forces or to fight against each other according to whether they feel more or less under pressure from the same external threat. It is, alas, my opinion that their fears do more than their affections to bring dissimilar men together. And as their fears always come from other people, I despair of men ever being able to live in total peace.

Medicine, however, does not have far to look in order to feel attacked. As the old proverb has it: Physicians' faults are covered with earth. As long ago as Antiquity, Aesop and Aristophanes were making people laugh at the expense of our art, and Alexander the Great exclaimed on his death-bed: "I die, succoured by too many physicians." Nor have I forgotten the agreeable aphorism concocted by my illustrious patient, Francis Bacon, in his Essays, in which he claims that the physician cures the disease but kills the patient. A Chinese saying even declares that a conscientious physician should either die with his patient or recover with him. The list of such quips is interminable.

We may laugh at them. We may despise the scoffers. We may take refuge in our honour, and in the certainty of having done our duty. But I believe we should go farther. A corporation, of whatever nature, does not do all the good it is capable of if it is working on barren ground. Men are so made that they work badly when surrounded by hostility or indifference, whereas they can surpass themselves when accorded confidence, esteem and gratitude. An entire country, with its customs, its prevailing ideas, its principles of coercion or liberty, may be either propitious or pernicious to what is produced on its soil. This is true for its physicians, but also for the progress of its science, the wealth of its inventions, the originality of its artists, the fruitfulness of its writers and philosophers. Some soils are fertile for the spirit, and others infertile; the government of peoples may turn the scale to one side or the other. But the professional guilds are equally responsible, it is their duty to demonstrate the effort and dignity of their art, to prove that their success is the success of all, to explain that the independence and respect accorded to them are not privileges they claim for themselves, but the conditions of their work from which the others will benefit. That is why I consider that the College of Physicians must become even more strongly united, and use the friendship of its members to spread these ideas amongst them.

Before he left me, the President of the College showered me with compliments. He declared quite simply that I was the most eminent physician and the most generous man he had ever met. These excessive epithets only half-pleased me for I knew Francis Prujean too well to take them literally. He is one of those who are skilled in the manipulation of the dithyramb and the panegyric, and who compliment everybody upon everything. His sole condition is that he be treated with the reverence he knows to be his due. But I am wrong to ironise at his expense, for he is a good President and an excellent physician. I like him just as much as I detested his predecessor, a violent anti-Royalist, or at least one who pretended so to be. Furthermore, I know that Prujean is a sagacious, prudent man, and that if he praises me in so flattering a way it means that in his view the College will no longer be in any political danger if in the near future it once again welcomes me with open arms.

Prujean went ever farther: he desires, said he, that the library I am to give the College should contain a bust of me, or even a full-length statue. He wants the statue to be carved in white marble, and asks me if I would agree to it being fashioned by the

celebrated sculptor Edward Marshall of Fetter Lane. I did not
hide the pleasure he was giving me, although at the same time I
was wondering why I was so pleased at the thought that from
now on the College would contain my sculpted image.

I must admit that I have always liked having portraits made
of me. There now exist more than a dozen, and I retain indelible
memories of each sitting. Every time a famous painter came to
Court I hoped that I would be on his list of models. The illustrious Mierevelt stayed only a few weeks in England, for he almost never left his studio in Delft, but he agreed to paint my
portrait in which, as was his wont, he would surround me with
objects connected with my profession or my tastes. Young Peter
Lely, who was the King's portraitist, asked a great price for
painting my face. But it was my sittings for Anthony Van Dyck
that I found the most picturesque of all. This was in 1634, he
was only thirty-five years old, but no painter living in England
had acquired such renown. Rubens had introduced him to Lady
Arundel when she was taking the cure at Spa, and it was she
who persuaded the young Flemish painter to go to London. He
came for the first time during the reign of King James, but His
Majesty did not appreciate his talent and Van Dyck promptly
returned to Antwerp. It was Charles I, advised by Lord Arundel,
who brought him back to London, made him Court painter and
set him up in style. He knighted him, and gave him an annual
allowance of two hundred pounds, together with a summer residence in Eltham and a winter residence in Blackfriars. It was in
a magnificent studio there that I posed for him.

Van Dyck had a cherubic appearance, curly red hair, a pink,
beardless face, a straight nose, and fleshy, strongly outlined lips.
He wore an elegant black jerkin adorned with a large golden
chain over his left shoulder, under which could be seen the wide-
open collar of his white lace shirt. Even though he had adopted
England and England had adopted him, he had very little of the
appearance of an English gentleman, although some of my compatriots also have baby faces and curly hair.

All the aristocrats and persons of consequence desired to have
their portraits painted by Van Dyck. His sittings lasted for exactly one hour, never longer. It was the task of a few musicians
in a corner of the studio to divert the model. The sound of a

clock striking soon announced that the time was up, the painter
bowed low, arranged the day for the next sitting, and passed on
to the next model.

Between two sittings one was requested to send a manservant
with one's apparel. I believe that Van Dyck confined himself to
making a rough sketch of the work, to choosing the pose, the
proportions and the arrangement of the portrait, and himself
painted the details of the features of the face. He then had the
clothes painted by his pupils and the hands as well, for which he
kept a few paid models on the premises. Then he added the
finishing touches, and this was where his genius became apparent. The first time I saw my finished portrait I thought it very
handsome, much more handsome than my natural features,
which are not to my taste. And yet the resemblance was striking.
Therein lies the immense talent of the painters of our century
who possess the art of embellishing the model, although no one
can discover any visible difference between the model and the
portrait.

Van Dyck lived in luxury, and more than once he invited me
to dine at his table. He had married the most attractive of the
young ladies at Court; she was of small fortune but of an aristocratic family. She gave him a daughter, who was born at
Blackfriars, but when I visited him at that time I found him ill in
bed; in spite of all that medicine could do, he died a week later.
He was forty-two. The next day, December 10th, we buried him
at St Paul's. Nearly nine years have passed since then, but he was
a man of so great a presence that he is still very much alive in my
memory. And the considerable body of his work, which collec-
tors and museums are already wrangling over, will no doubt
long remain a posthumous witness to his passage on this earth.

How I too should like my work to survive me, and future
generations to know that I discovered the circulation of the
blood. Even if they forget that I, like them, was a creature of
flesh and blood, animated like them by desires and sorrows,
those who see one of my many portraits may perhaps imagine
that a life was hidden behind that now-immobile face. These are
proud thoughts, and as vain as can be; a stupid way of defying
one's own death, when the challenge is lost in advance. How
stupid is this temptation not to disappear completely from this

earth, since it is a natural event! How can posthumous glory possibly interest me?—for glory is something to be enjoyed like good wine, and when I am dead I shall enjoy neither good wine nor celebrity. And yet this is the only way I can explain my wish to see my features delineated on canvas, and the pleasure I felt today about the business of the statue.

3 February 1654

Like a draught of honey to which a few bitter drops of gentian have been added, I found the great day yesterday very sweet, and only barely tinged with melancholy thoughts. It was the day of the inauguration of the library and museum at the College of Physicians of London.

The new building has majesty. The Corinthian pilasters, standing out against the white stone wall, give it the appearance of classical architecture. Above a flight of some ten steps is a portal standing within a wide embrasure of sculpted stone. This gives access to the entrance hall, and thence to a room large enough to contain about a hundred people. The walls are in a light-coloured wood, as I like them. The furnishings are welcoming.

At the far end of the entrance hall and in the centre of the building, a beautiful, dark-red carpeted staircase leads up to the library floor. On the upper landing, *the* statue is ensconced. It shows me in my Doctor's robes. I find it difficult to recognise myself in this man of marble, who has a far greater presence and nobler face than his model. But when I read the inscription engraved on the plinth, it was hard for me to remain unmoved. It is in Latin, the language of the scientific world, and may be translated more or less as follows:

To William Harvey
The College of Physicians of London
has erected this statue

As an eternal sign of its gratitude
For his work on the movements of the blood and the
generation of animals

So now I am recognized, at least by the most eminent physicians of my country—and I believe that elsewhere in Europe the bitter critics of recent years are gradually losing some of their virulence. The circulation of the blood, from now on, is William Harvey. So my life has a meaning, and my efforts will leave an indelible trace. This is what Francis Prujean affirmed in his opening speech to the Fellows gathered round me. And in saying that, I thought him right, just as I thought unreasonable the emphatic epithets he thought fit to add, in his usual manner. He declared that my munificence, my worth, my perspicacity, my knowledge, surpassed those of all the physicians in the world; he compared me successively to Hippocrates, Aristotle, Galen and a few other personages of that order, and he decided categorically that I was "the prince of all the doctors in England." This speech, designed to please me, caused me on the contrary some embarrassment, for extravagance is not to my taste. I replied, nonetheless, with the most courteous thanks I could summon up.

I do not at all like making such speeches. I find it easy to speak seriously of serious matters, but on occasions such as this, the College tradition is that one should adopt a bantering tone and avoid any grave remarks; I have no talent for that. I told them that my marble statue was no doubt an invitation to a cold manner and to the renunciation of the passions, but not to the cold of death, and that they would not rid themselves of me so easily. Moreover, the warmth of their friendship would protect me. And I added that the new building would in any case be protected from inclement weather by that same friendship among the members of the College, all the more so in that the habitual source of storms—women, that is—would be absent from it. I uttered a few more equally dunderheaded quips, and was warmly applauded. Next, George Ent spoke of my work in moving terms. Finally, tables were prepared for a Great Banquet at which they never stopped toasting me. After the feast there was a meeting at which I asked the members to choose my successor to the Chair of Anatomy, and Francis Glisson was elected.

Why, then, as I went back to St Lawrence Pountney Hill after so glorious a ceremony, was I still prey to melancholy thoughts? It is useless, no doubt, for me to pretend that I have made my peace with the idea that everything is going to finish for me and that I am going to disappear, for this peace stems more from rationality and reasoning than from profound feeling.

20 June 1654

This morning the sky is grey, and it is raining. I have heard that Queen Christina of Sweden has abdicated. In Rheims, young Louis XIV has been crowned King of France. In China, the Manchu dynasty has been recognised by the Chief Lama. In my country, were I in a mood to jest, I would write that all goes well. Parliament, that eternal nuisance, no longer exists. We now have an absolute monarch, a Lord Protector of England named Cromwell. He has just enacted two new statutes: one forbids cock-fighting, the other bans itinerant singers.

Here, Harvey's diary breaks off. He died three years later, on 3 June 1657, at ten o'clock in the morning.

Postface

William Harvey was one of the most remarkable personages of the seventeenth century. His discoveries of the circulation of the blood and of the function of the heart were not his only contributions to his century, in which new forms of thought were beginning to arise. He brought to it a profound renewal of medical reasoning, which up to that time had been the slave of the formidable influence of the traditions of antiquity. This was a time when the University of Paris refused all propositions that dared question the assertions of Aristotle and Galen. Harvey was one of the first, if not *the* first, to dare to question them. Modern scientific thought was in the painful process of being born.

Many documents on Harvey's life have come down to us, although there is a total lack of information about certain periods. I have been as strictly accurate as possible in my accounts of the events, and I have allowed myself a certain liberty only when dealing with those circumstances that have remained totally obscure. Even if we lay all the historical evidence end to end, that does not bring the man back to life. Yet it is his thoughts, his reflections, his joys, and his sorrows that we would like to know, just as much as, if not more than, the episodes of an eventful life.

Shall I be forgiven for having had recourse to the form of an imaginary diary to solve this difficulty? The William Harvey of this diary is the one I felt I could glimpse between the lines of the few hundred texts available to us today. The following pages contain the most important references to these texts. I have been greatly helped by many specialists on seventeenth-century England and by the Royal College of Physicians of London and the Royal Society of Medicine, of which I am a Fellow.

The Diary of William Harvey owes a great deal to the collaboration of Hélène Bourgeois. Not only did she suggest the idea of the book, but throughout the documentary research and the preparation of the manuscript I found her help and advice of inestimable value. I am also most grateful to I. Bernard Cohen, Professor of the History of Science, Harvard University, who was kind enough to revise the English version and make useful suggestions.

Notes and Comments

A good many biographies of William Harvey have been published. Among the most interesting are the following: Geoffrey Keynes, *The Life of William Harvey*, 2nd ed. (Oxford: The Clarendon Press, 1978); Kenneth D. Keele, *William Harvey, the Physician and the Scientist* (London: Thomas Nelson & Sons, 1965); Louis Chauvois, *William Harvey, His Life and Times; His Discoveries; His Methods, Etc.* (London: Hutchinson Medical Publications, 1957); W. Herringham, "The Life and Times of William Harvey," *Annals of Medical History* 4 (1932): 109–125, 249–272, 347–363, 491–502, and 575–589; D'Arcy Power, *William Harvey* (London: Fisher Unwin, 1987); Walter Pagel, *William Harvey's Biological Ideas: Selected Aspects and Historical Background* (Basel and New York: S. Karger, 1967); Jerome J. Bylebyl, ed., *William Harvey and His Age: The Professional and Social Context of the Discovery of the Circulation* (Baltimore: The Johns Hopkins University Press, 1979).

Harvey's own works, which were written in Latin, have been translated into English and sometimes also into French. His *Exercitatio anatomica de motu cordis et sanguinis in animalibus* (Frankfurt: Guilielmi Fitzeri, 1628) was first published in English translation in 1653. The *Exercitationes de generatione animalium* (London: Octavian Pulleyn the Elder, 1651) was first published in English in 1653. Both these books have had several subsequent editions—for example, *The Works of William Harvey*, trans. and ed. R. Willis (London: The Sydenham Society, 1847). The best French translation of the *De motu cordis* has been established by Charles Richet: *William Harvey, La Circulation du sang* (Paris: Masson & Cie, 1879), with two letters from William Harvey to Jean Riolan (originally published at Cambridge in 1649). A new edition of the latter book appeared in 1990 (Paris: Christian Bourgois) with a foreword and comments by Jean Hamburger.

The best English versions of Harvey's work are, in my opinion, those by Gweneth Whitteridge. Her translations of *De motu cordis* and *De generatione* were published as *An Anatomical Disputation Concerning the Movement of the Heart and Blood in Living Creatures* (hereafter cited as *De motu cordis*) (Oxford: Blackwell, 1976) and *Disputations Touching the Generation of Animals* (hereafter cited as *De generatione*) (Oxford: Blackwell, 1981). Both contain valuable notes by the translator.

Dr. Whitteridge has also deciphered and translated Harvey's lecture notes (*Prelectiones*), the manuscript of which is in the British Museum: *William Harvey, The Anatomical Lectures* (London: Livingstone, 1964). She is also the author of *William Harvey and the Circulation of the Blood* (London and New York: Macdonald & Elsevier, 1971).

1 April 1647

Page

1   Harvey's state of health at age seventy is described in F. D. Zenman, "The Old Age of William Harvey," *Archives of Internal Medicine* 3 (1963): 829. Harvey suffered frequent attacks of gout which he treated, curiously enough, by immersing his feet in ice-cold water.

As Charles I's physician in ordinary, Harvey followed the king to Oxford during the Civil War. The king and his army had tried to march on London in order to subdue a Parliament that was becoming more and more hostile, but they were stopped at Newbury by Oliver Cromwell's Ironsides. The king then settled in Oxford, on October 27, 1644. Harvey was made warden of Merton College, Oxford, on April 7, 1645. A year later, on April 27, 1646, the king had to flee Oxford, which was being threatened by the parliamentary troops. Harvey was dismissed from his wardenship and returned to London. See M. Hudson, "An Account of King Charles 1st's Escape or Departure from Oxford in the Year 1646," in W. Hemingford, *Canonici de Gisseburne* 2 (1731): 551–583; and Isaac D'Israeli, *Commentaries on the Life and Reign of Charles the First, King of England* (London: Colburn & Bentley, 1831), vol. 5, pp. 190–205.

2   Many diaries were written in England at this time. Elisabeth Bourcier has found and analyzed seventy-three: *Les Journaux privés en Angleterre de 1600 à 1660* (Paris: Publications de la Sorbonne, 1976).

4   Charles I stayed in the Newcastle Scottish camp between May 1646 and February 1647. To try to understand the king's state of mind and guess at the subjects of his conversations with Harvey, I have consulted, in addition to D'Israeli's *Commentaries*, the French translation of Eikon Basilike, *The Purported Memoirs of the King, Said to Have Been Written During His Captivity,* trans. Le Sieur de Marsys (Paris: F. Preuveray, 1649), chaps. 22 and 23;

and of Sir Thomas Herbert's *Memories of the Two Last Years of the Reign of King Charles* (Paris: Bechet Aîné, 1823).

6   William Harvey studied at Padua from the beginning of 1600 until the spring of 1602. All details of Paduan life at this time are taken from Maria Borgherini-Scarabellin, *La Vita privata a Padova nel secolo XVII* (Venice: Miscellanea di Storia Veneta, 1917), vol. 12, p. 3.

8   Girolamo Fabrizi d'Acquapendente (1533–1619), better known under the Latin name of Fabricius (of Aquapendente), was a famous anatomist whom some consider to be the founder of comparative anatomy. This science compares the structure of the organs in different animal species, a comparison to which Harvey was to attach so much importance. Fabricius discovered the valves in the veins in 1574, but did not publish his discovery until 1603, in a little work called *De venarum ostiolis*.

Harvey's memory is mistaken. He probably had very little idea about his future work when he was in Padua. The keys that led him to plan his research took place later on (I. B. Cohen, personal communication). There was a pump near his house in London, and hearing its clack he suddenly understood the role of the valves in the vessels. In the *De motu cordis* he also states another clue: quantitative measurements indicated that the liver simply could not produce enough blood to account for the observation.

9   In chapter 13 of his *De motu cordis* there are two plates illustrating Harvey's experiment with the compression of the veins. In these plates the anatomist's hands are shown emerging from white linen double cuffs and pointing to the place where the vein should be observed.
   Andrea Cesalpino (1519–1603) was a famous Italian physician and naturalist who discovered the sex of flowers.

Fabricius's *De formatione ovi et pulli* was published in Padua in 1621, two years after the author's death.

15 April 1647

Page

11   On Cromwell I have consulted, among other books, Antonia Fraser, *Cromwell, Our Chief of Men* (London: Weidenfeld & Nicolson, 1973); and George R. S. Taylor, *Oliver Cromwell* (London: Jonathan Cape, 1928). It is in the latter book that I found

the details of Cromwell's grandfather accusing a whole family of witchcraft.

12   Sir Theodore Turquet de Mayerne, born in Geneva in 1573, was successively a professor of medicine in Paris, physician to Henri IV of France, and physician to James I in England; he was one of the most highly esteemed physicians of Harvey's day. He died in 1655, two years before Harvey.

13   Milton, who was thirty-nine in 1647, had published his *Areopagitica* in 1644. He had met Galileo during his Italian journey in 1638. Back in England, he sided against the king and the Anglican church. In 1649 he became Cromwell's "secretary to foreign tongues." There is no proof that he ever met Harvey or sent him his works, but it is a plausible hypothesis. D'Arcy Power, in his *William Harvey*, shows that English men of letters and philosophers of the time rather curiously took Harvey to be an expert critic of literature.

15   James Primrose (1592–1659) was the author of the first published attack on Harvey's *De motu cordis*, in 1630. The excerpt in my text is taken from a passage of extreme violence, quoted by Chauvois in his *William Harvey:*

> Thou hast observed a sort of pulsatile heart in slugs, flies, bees and even in squill-fish. We congratulate thee upon thy zeal. May God preserve thee in such perspicacious ways. But why dost thou say that Aristotle would not admit of small animals possessing a heart? Dost thou declare then, that thou knowest what Aristotle did not? Those who mark in thy writings the names of so many and diverse animals will take thee for the sovereign investigator of nature and will believe thee to be an oracle seated upon the tripod and dictating thy decisions. I speak of those who are not physicians and have but a smattering of the science. But if we read the works of real anatomists, such as Galen, Vesalius, the illustrious Fabricius and Casserius, we see that they have provided us with engraved plates representing the animals they dissected. As for Aristotle, he made observations of all things and no one should dare contest his conclusions. [*Exercitationes et animadversiones in librum G. Harveii de motu cordis et circulatione sanguinis*, London: 1630].

> Primrose had studied in Paris under Riolan, another of Harvey's virulent adversaries. Harvey's two famous letters to Jean Riolan were published at Cambridge in 1649, under the title *Exercitatio anatomica de circulatione sanguinis. Ad Joannem*

Riolanum filium Parisiensem. While the content of the letters is
severe, their form is exquisitely polite. On the title page, Harvey
describes Riolan as a "skillful physician, Coryphaeus of anatomists, royal Professor of the University of Paris, supreme Savant
of that University, personal Physician to the Queen Mother of
Louis XIII." In the text, the aggressive book that Riolan had published in 1648 and that Harvey had refuted point by point is
called "a work worthy of the highest praise, a work such as only
a great intellect could produce," written by "the Prince of anatomists."

28 April 1647

Page

17   The king was held at Holdenby House, near Althorpe in Nor-
     thamptonshire, from February 1647 until June 4 of the same year
     (see works already cited concerning this period of Charles I's life).

18   Sir Thomas More (1478–1535), Lord Chancellor to Henry VIII,
     refused to renounce Catholicism and was later canonized. His op-
     position to Henry's divorce from Catherine of Aragon resulted in
     his execution on a charge of treason. In *Utopia* (1516) he criti-
     cized the English as well as the European political systems and set
     forth his concept of the ideal state.

29 April 1647

Page

22   Among the numerous works on the Levellers, I have consulted O.
     Lutaud, *Cromwell, les Niveleurs et la République* (Paris: Julliard,
     1967; rev. ed., Paris: Aubier-Montaigne, 1978).

23   On October 14, 1609, Harvey was made physician to St. Barthol-
     omew's Hospital. At this time St. Bartholomew's and St. Thomas's
     were the only two institutions in London for the needy and the
     sick poor. The hospital's structure and organization were very dif-
     ferent then from what they are today; they are described in detail
     in Keynes, *Life of W. Harvey,* pp. 49–62. See also the references
     provided under 2 February 1648, below.

24   Almost all the details Harvey writes here may be found in his *De
     motu cordis,* including the dove's heart story.

2 May 1647

Page

27 On November 24, 1604, Harvey married Elizabeth Browne, the daughter of Dr. Lancelot Browne, of the College of Physicians. The story of his wife's parrot is authenticated by Harvey himself in *De generatione,* where he describes how the bird obeyed its mistress. The date and cause of Elizabeth's death is not known with any certainty, but it is known that she died between 1645 and 1651.

28 Pope Sixtus V called Elizabeth of England "un gran cervello di principessa." The expression I have just quoted is repeated in all the histories of the queen. I presume it is authentic.

29 Thomas Harvey (1549–1623), William's father, married as his second wife Joan Halke (1555–1605). Thomas was a rich Folkestone merchant who imported goods from the Levant and who was interested in maritime problems. He had been administrator of the port of Folkestone and was mayor of the town in 1600. He belonged to the yeoman class. Joan, William's mother, was the daughter of John Halke, who was probably a very pious man; he had been a churchwarden of his village, Hastingleigh, not far from Folkestone. William was born in Folkestone on April 1, 1578, the first of a family that was to count six more sons and two daughters.

5 May 1647

Page

32 John Harvey, William's younger brother, was "footman to the king," a post which in those days was of greater importance than its name might imply today.

   In February 1609, Harvey was able to present the governors of St. Bartholomew's Hospital with a letter of recommendation from King James I. Thanks to this letter, Harvey was appointed physician to the hospital on August 18, 1609, at first "in reversion," which meant upon departure of the then holder of the post, an event which occurred on October 14 that same year.

   In 1623 Harvey received another letter from King James, which is preserved in the British Museum under the number 6987. The king tells Harvey that he will appoint him his physician in ordinary in the event of one of the four actual holders of the post dying or resigning. He adds: "In the meantyme, your attendance upon our Person shalbe at as gratefull and with asmuch freedome to waite as our other physitians doe."

Later, Harvey was one of the principal physicians attending James I during his last illness in March 1625.

33   Witch-hunting was rife in England during the sixteenth century and the first part of the seventeenth. Reginald Scott, an Oxford graduate, denounced witch-hunts and cast doubt on the existence of sorcery in *A Discovery of Witchcraft,* published in 1584. Shakespeare is said to have taken his inspiration for the witches' scenes in *Macbeth* from this book. But far more numerous were the works that dealt with witchcraft as an indubitable reality and that discussed ways and means of confounding and combatting it. One such was published in 1597 by the king when he was still only James VI of Scotland and had not yet also become James I of England. It was called *Daemonologie in Forme of a Dialogue.* James also published theological treatises and two books of political doctrine: *Basilikon Doron* and *The True Law of Free Monarchies.* He considered himself a theologian first and foremost, and he believed that the king is God's representative and is consequently not required to give an account of himself to any mortal.

34   The Edmund Robinson affair, many details of which I have omitted, is far more fully recounted in Keynes's *Life of W. Harvey,* "Harvey and the Witches," pp. 206–216.

David Webster was to publish in London in 1677 *The Displaying of Supposed Witchcraft,* a denunciation of the abuses of witch-hunting.

36   Harvey knew Sir Kenelm Digby well. He was a curious personage who combined an imaginative charlatanism (which dazzled James I) with more serious researches, which he described in his *Two Treatises on the Nature of Bodies and the Nature of Man's Soule,* published in Paris in 1644. This book shows him to be an ardent defender of Harvey's discoveries.

38   Thomas Hobbes (1588–1679) probably met Harvey during the years 1621–1626, when he was working as Sir Francis Bacon's secretary.

In the article on "Hobbism" in Diderot and D'Alembert's *Encyclopédie,* Diderot describes the friendship between Harvey and Hobbes after the latter returned to England. I decided to write about the exchange of ideas between the two men after reading a recent French edition of Hobbes's *De cive* which contains a long commentary by Simone Goyard-Fabre (Hobbes, *Le Citoyen ou les fondements de la politique,* Paris: Flammarion, 1982).

I also consulted several other works on Hobbes, including Raymond Polin, *Politique et Philosophie chez Thomas Hobbes* (Paris: Presses Universitaires de France, 1953). Reading a series of texts on Hobbes was yet another demonstration of just how difficult is the task of the historian of science or philosophy: each commentator sees Hobbes's personality and actions in a different light. In his search for a "rational" construction of the organization of societies, Hobbes came to the conclusion that to be effectual, every government must be supreme. Certain of his affirmations, such as that the basis of all government is force, that the spiritual must ever give way to the temporal, and that the people must implicitly accept not merely the laws but the mode of faith that the king or his ministers have seen fit to ordain, caused Hobbes to be accused of defending dictatorial regimes. Other people, however, see him as advocating that the rights of citizenship form a diptych with the powers of sovereignty and can thrive only through the mediation of civil law (Simone Goyard-Fabre).

What is certain is that, in Harvey's time, Hobbes's loyalty to the English crown was sufficiently doubted by the Monarchists to impel him to leave England for a time. Equally certain is that Hobbes's original approach toward politics ranks with that of Harvey toward scientific procedure, in that both men thought to pursue their research in a logical manner free of all passionate belief in received ideas. Similar ideas were defended at this time by others, including Descartes with his theory of "mechanism," even though Descartes and Hobbes were on extremely bad terms. All this was perhaps the faltering start of what we today call the scientific method.

The famous book of Hobbes, *Leviathan* (1651), on the opening page, mentions rather explicitly Harvey's discovery of the circulation of the blood, and the entire book is probably influenced by the physiological ideas of Harvey (I. B. Cohen, personal communication).

According to the terms of Harvey's will, Hobbes was one of the legatees.

11 May 1647

Page

42   Descartes was one of the first to write that Harvey was correct to believe that the blood circulates. For Descartes, Harvey is "a physician of England, who has the honour of having broken the ice on this subject, and of having been the first to teach that there are many small passages at the extremities of the arteries, through which the blood received by them from the heart passes into the

small branches of the veins, whence it again returns to the heart, so that its course amounts precisely to a perpetual circulation" (*Discourse on the Method of Rightly Conducting the Reason, and Seeking the Truth in the Sciences,* trans. John Veitch, London: Sutherland & Knox, 1850). Descartes, however, had erroneous reservations about the active role of the heart demonstrated by Harvey.

Sir Francis Bacon (1561–1626) strongly criticized doctors in *The Advancement of Learning* (1605), saying that in medicine "I find much Iteration but small Addition," and he declared that "Empiriques and Old Women" were often happier in their cures than physicians. John Aubrey (1626–1697), who knew Harvey well, wrote in his *Brief Lives* (a marvelously readable book, available in a Penguin edition) that Harvey had "been physitian to the Lord Chancellor Bacon" but did not like him, and said that "his Eie is like the Eie of a viper," and also: "He writes Philosophy like a Lord Chancellor."

43 The phrase "There is no science that does not derive from an *a priori* idea, but there is no solid and reliable knowledge that does not have its origin in the senses" comes from the first paragraph of Harvey's first letter to Jean Riolan (cited above).

Andreas Vesalius (1514–1564) was professor of anatomy at the University of Padua sometime before Harvey's arrival there. He stressed the importance of basing knowledge of the "construction" of the human body upon the evidence of direct dissection, rather than on the books of Galen and his commentators, as most sixteenth- and seventeenth-century doctors did. Vesalius stated that he found "blind pits" in the wall that separates the two ventricles of the heart and no passage or orifice that forms a communication.

In August 1615, Harvey was appointed to the Lumleian Lectureship, an important chair of anatomy founded by Lord Lumley in 1582. Harvey's lectures began on April 16, 1616. They were given either in Latin or English, according to the occasion, and he continued to give them biennially for nearly thirty years. His notes for these lectures, which he prepared with great care, have fortunately not been lost and are preserved in the British Museum. Even though Harvey wrote them, with a view to their presentation, under Latin headings written in red ink, these *Prelectiones* are almost illegible. They have been well translated into English by Gweneth Whitteridge (*Anatomical Lectures,* cited above). I have found in this source almost all the lecture material Harvey presented in the anatomical theater.

12 May 1647

Page

49   The book by Eckard Leichner that wounded Harvey was published in Arnstadt, in 1645, under the title *De moto sanguinis. Exercitatio anti-Harveiana.*

      James Primrose has already been mentioned (see notes under 15 April 1647, above). Aemilius Parisanus (1567–1643), whose real name was Emilio Parigiano, was a doctor from Venice. In that city he published (in 1635) long extracts from Harvey's *De motu cordis*, accompanied by a methodical refutation, paragraph by paragraph, of all Harvey's arguments. Marcus Aurelius Severinus (1580–1656), Marco Aurelio Severino in everyday life, was a professor of anatomy at Naples. The book by Severinus to which Harvey alludes was called *De recondita abscessuum natura* [Of the Hidden Nature of Abscesses]. The exchange of letters between him and John Houghton is reported in J. C. Trent, "Five Letters of Marcus Aurelius Severinus," *Bulletin of the History of Medicine* 15 (1944): 306–323.

50   Jean Riolan the Younger (1580–1657) was a professor of anatomy in Paris, the son of another Jean Riolan (1539–1606) who had been the dean of the faculty. We shall have more to say later about this obstinate opponent of Harvey's work, one of whose utterances (though I do not know whether it is authentic or apocryphal) has come down to posterity: "There is no reason to believe that the blood circulates and to trample tradition underfoot merely to indulge the whim of an English physician."

20 May 1647

Page

52   On Sir Kenelm Digby, see the notes under 5 May 1647, above. Descartes's three letters on the circulation were published in Johann Beverwijk's *Epistolicae quaestiones, cum doctorum responsis* (Rotterdam: 1644), pp. 118–149.

53   John Evelyn (1620–1706), whose name is mentioned in Thomas Hobbes's letter, is a British traveler who, in his diary, gives us the most valuable information we have about the Paris of the time as

seen by an Englishman. Passages of this diary relative to Paris may be found in Martin Lister, *Journey to Paris in the Year 1698, Followed by Extracts from John Evelyn's Works on His Journeys to France from 1648 to 1651* (London: 1699). The whole of Evelyn's diary was published for the first time in 1818; a 2nd edition, in 4 volumes, was published in 1859 (London: John Forster).

54   James Stewart, Fourth Duke of Lennox, was the grandson of the first duke, who was a first cousin of James I. At the end of 1629 Harvey was commanded by King Charles to accompany this "illustrious Prince . . . in his travels beyond the seas." So Harvey resigned from the treasurership of the College of Physicians and awaited a summons from the duke, who had left for Paris in July 1630. The dates of Harvey's stay in Paris are not known with any certainty. Sir Geoffrey Keynes (*Life of W. Harvey*) advances several hypotheses and suggests that Harvey might have made the journey either at the beginning of the summer of 1630 or between December of that year and February 1631. The dates I have chosen, then, are arbitrary.

Paris is said (in Roland Mousnier, *Paris, capitale au temps de Richelieu et de Mazarin*, Paris: A. Pedone, 1978) to have contained 20,000 houses in 1637, whence it was concluded that it must have held between 412,000 and 415,000 inhabitants. According to the same source, London contained 270,000 inhabitants in 1636.

55   "Residents" was the name given to diplomats sent by a state to a foreign government. In Pierre Chevalier's *Louis XIII* (Paris: Fayard, 1979) it is made clear that the English residents in Paris were among the best informed about French affairs: the author frequently relies on their dispatches to describe this period of French history, in particular concerning "The Day of the Dupes" (November 11, 1630).

57   Ambroise Paré's *Discours* was published under the title *Discours d'Ambroise Paré, conseiller et premier chirurgien du roy, ascavoir de la mumie, de la licorne, des venins et de la peste* (Paris: Gabriel Buon, 1582). There exist very many documents on the plague in England, France, and Italy at the beginning of the seventeenth century. Bubonic plague was rife in northern Italy from 1629 to 1631, counting more than a million victims; the Duke of Lennox therefore abandoned his projected journey to Venezia. The epidemic spread to France, reached Lyon, and then moved to Tours and Blois. *L'Ordre public pour la ville de Lyon pendant la mala-*

die contagieuse, the Chevalier pamphlet cited by Harvey, appeared in 1628. The horrors of the 1630 plague are the subject of one of the famous chapters in Alessandro Manzoni's historical novel *I promessi sposi,* which appeared in 1827. On the plague in France, I have also consulted Jean-Noël Biraben, *Les Hommes et la peste en France et dans les pays européens et méditerranéens,* 2 vols. (Paris: Mouton & Cie, 1975–1976), with its 228 pages of bibliographic references. I could not find detailed studies of the plague in the city of Blois, except for a short communication by F. Baillet, "La Peste à Blois en 1627," *Mémoires de la société archéologique et historique de l'Orléanais* 16 (1911–1913): 465. Everyday life in French cities during the epidemic is well described in Louis Porquet, *La Peste en Normandie du XIV^c au XVII^c siècle* (Vire: Imprimerie René Eng, 1898).

59   There is no proof that Harvey actually visited Mersenne during his stay in Paris. We can say only that Mersenne knew Harvey's work well and helped to make it known, as his correspondence shows (see below). What is certain is that many meetings between men of letters, savants, and scientists took place in Paris during this period; it is very likely that Harvey, who already had a considerable reputation, was invited to some of these "academies." But my choice of the Dupuy brothers' house and the convent of the Order of Minims, where Mersenne lived, is arbitrary.

On Father Marin Mersenne (1588–1648), I have consulted Robert Lenoble, *Mersenne ou la naissance du mécanisme* (Paris: Librairie Philosophique J. Vrin, 1943). Most of Mersenne's words recorded by Harvey are taken from that book. But still more interesting is Father Mersenne's correspondence, published by Mrs. Paul Tannery with comments by Cornelis de Waard (Paris: Beauchesne & Fils). I found especially useful vol. 1 (1617–1627), published in 1932, and vol. 2 (1628–1630), published in 1937; they give information not only on Mersenne himself, but also on Gassendi, Descartes, and Peiresc and on the way Harvey's work was understood. The physical description of Mersenne was inspired by a Latin text reproduced on pp. lviii–lix of vol. 1.

On Pierre Gassend (usually called Gassendi) (1592–1655), I have also consulted A. Koyré, G. Montgredien, A. Adam, and B. Rochot, *Pierre Gassendi, sa vie et son œuvre* (Paris: Centre International de Synthèse, 1955).

61   Théophraste Renaudot (1586–1653) studied medicine in Montpellier and then settled in Paris, where protection in high places enabled him to acquire the title of "physician to the king." Full of imagination, cunning, and generosity, he managed to obtain from

Richelieu the post of *commissaire général* for the poor of the kingdom. In 1630 he opened his Bureau d'Adresses ("Le Coq d'Or,"
rue de la Calandre, Paris), an advertising center where anyone
wishing to sell or buy anything, to give or obtain employment, or
to obtain information could make known his wants. He founded
the first pawnshop, offering loans at 3 percent. He published the
Feuille du Bureau d'Adresses, the first example of commercial
publicity and small advertisements. Following on from this *Feuille*
he produced, on May 30, 1631, *La Gazette,* a journal offering
political and general news. (In the following centuries it became
the *Gazette de France.*) More details can be found in Mousnier
(*Paris, capitale*). L'Institut de France possesses a complete collection of the *Gazette* dating from the year 1631. What Harvey
writes about it does not reflect the amazement of the present-day
reader, for it is not a mere local paper but a journal that gives,
with an honest attempt at truth, both foreign and domestic news.

25 May 1647

Page

62   Infant mortality was considerable during this period, and miscar-
riages and stillbirths were very frequent. In England "it was an
ordeal that terrified every woman. . . . Births and deaths, bap-
tisms and burials, followed one another without causing the least
astonishment. One child dies, another will be born, and he will
bear the first one's name until he too dies. All the diarists, without
exception, are content to record, in a few laconic phrases, these
never-ending bereavements" (Bourcier, *Journaux privés,* p. 304).
It was from this book that I took the story of Mrs. Thornton's
sister, Lady Danbury.

Harvey's criticism of "giddy young midwives," the clinical cases,
and all the succeeding anecdotes are taken from Harvey himself,
in his *De generatione.* In the English version by Dr. Whitteridge,
pp. 393–441 are devoted to parturition and "the membranes and
humours" of the uterus. This section, which comes almost at the
end of the book, constitutes a sort of obstetric manual and contains a thousand curious (not to say unbelievable) stories, mixed
with much good practical advice and common sense.

64   Gregorius Nymannus (1594–1638), whose 1628 book Harvey re-
fers to, was a professor of botany and anatomy at the University
of Wittenberg; he believed that the fetus has an autonomous life
in the womb through its "personal vital principle" and that the
mother merely serves as a dwelling place.

28 May 1647

Page

67   The message the army sent to the king in April 1647 is described
in detail in D'Israeli's *Commentaries,* p. 246, (citing the *Clarendon State Papers,* vol. 2, p. 365). The king was requested to place
himself at the head of the army and under its protection, when it
"would restore him to his honour, Crown and dignity." Charles
replied that he was sure of the loyalty of this petition, but that he
had a horror of the idea of "engaging the poor people in another
war." What he did not know, according to the same source, was
that it was Cromwell and his son-in-law Ireton who were behind
the army's protestations of loyalty to the king. In the fight—
which by then had become open—between the army and Parliament, Cromwell had gradually chosen his camp—the army—and
he thought it would be to his advantage to have the king on his
side, even if only temporarily. Harvey may have suspected Cromwell's duplicity, but he could not know the extent of his genius,
which was both Machiavellian and perverse (see, for example,
Taylor's *Cromwell*).

69   All the details about what Harvey did during the Battle of Edgehill are consistent with the various documents available today.
The Battle of Edgehill is somewhat differently described in histories by the king's admirers and in those by his detractors. The Earl
of Clarendon, a strong supporter of the king, gives an account
favorable to the king in his monumental *History of the Rebellion
and Civil Wars in England Begun in the Year 1641;* in the 1907
edition, published at Oxford in 3 vols., the battle is described in
vol. 2, p. 34ff. The king is more severely judged in François Gui-
zot's *Histoire de la révolution d'Angleterre* (Paris: Leroux &
Chantpie, 1826); the battle is described in vol. 1, p. 302ff. The
episode of the cannonball falling near Harvey and the two young
princes is told by Aubrey (*Brief Lives*), who claims to have heard
it from Harvey himself. William Dobson's painting, which the
king gave Harvey as a token of his gratitude, is today in the National Portrait Gallery, Edinburgh.

70   All accounts agree that Harvey kept with him a preparation of
opium which he intended to use to put an end to his days if his
infirmities rendered life intolerable; this fact is vouched for by several contemporaries, including Aubrey and Sir Charles Scarburgh,
author of the Harveian Oration pronounced in 1662. Sir Charles
is even said to have been given a bottle of poison by Harvey and
to have promised to help Harvey die, if need be. Keynes (*Life of*

W. *Harvey,* p. 411) quotes other accounts current in later generations; these, too, suggest that Harvey was in favor of euthana-
sia—for himself at any rate.

8 June 1647

Page

72   The abduction of the king by the cornet, George Joyce, is related
      hour by hour in D'Israeli's *Commentaries.*

73   The case of Mrs. Bennet is described by James Alsop in his article
      "A Private Consultation by Dr. William Harvey in 1642," *Medi-
      cal History* 24 (1980): 93.

74   The case of Sir William Smith is known in some detail because of
      a lawsuit, about which Harvey prefers not to speak in his diary.
      The minutes of this suit were discovered by Professor C. J. Sisson,
      who reported them in his "Shakespeare's Helena and Dr. William
      Harvey," in M. St. Clare Bryden, ed., *Essays and Studies* (London:
      Murray, 1960), vol. 13. More information is to be found in the
      long study by Edmund and Susan Hey, "William Smith v. William
      Harvey, the Revealing Story of a Law Court Case," *Journal of the
      History of Medicine* 24 (1969): 3–21. After Sir William Smith's
      death, Harvey sued his family for the last quarterly installment of
      the annual sum of £50 his patient had agreed to pay him. The
      family put in a countersuit in the Court of Chancery, addressed to
      the Lord Chancellor, John Williams, who was also bishop of Lin-
      coln. The action seems to have been interminable, and its outcome
      is not known with any certainty.
           For the description of an operation for cutting the bladder in
      the seventeenth century, I relied on the *Encyclopédie française
      d'urologie* (Paris: Doin, 1914), vol. 1, pp. 135–176.

9 June 1647

Page

77   The College of Physicians' dealings with the barber-surgeons are
      described in detail by Keynes (*Life of W. Harvey,* p. 62). I took the
      portrait of John Woodall from the same source (pp. 66–72).
      Harvey describes Woodall as master of the Barber-Surgeons'
      Company, but this he became in reality only in 1633. On the fron-
      tispiece of his book *The Surgeon's Mate* (1617), Woodall seems to
      me to bear an astonishing resemblance to another celebrated sur-
      geon, Ambroise Paré, a sixteenth-century Frenchman who like-

wise had a great deal of trouble with the physicians of his country, although he later became a surgeon to Henri II.

The draconian rules that Harvey got the governors of St. Bartholomew's to accept on October 15, 1633, were partially moderated by King Charles in 1635, on the demand of the surgeons (J. F. South, *Memorials of the Craft of Surgery in England*, London: 1886).

31 August 1647

Page

82   John Ashburnham, Groom of the Bedchamber, a rather colorless but very well bred character, had followed Charles I in his peregrinations. On April 27, 1646, at the time of his flight from Oxford, Charles disguised himself as a servant and Ashburnham played the part of his master (see Harvey's diary entry, 1 April 1647). In the summer of 1647, although the king was in fact the prisoner of Cromwell and the army, they nevertheless left him the illusion of being entirely free, "in the full state of Royalty." At this time, the king's two closest advisers were John Ashburnham and a brave officer, Sir John Berkeley. Both wrote their memoirs: the information Ashburnham gives to Harvey, which is a résumé of complicated, not to say confused, transactions, is taken from Berkeley's *Memoirs Containing an Account of His Negotiations with Lieutenant-General Cromwell, Commissary-General Treton and Other Officers of the Army for Restoring King Charles the First to the Exercise of the Government of England* (London: A. Baldwin, 1699) and Ashburnham's *Narrative*. The latter (*A Narrative by John Ashburnham of His Attendance of King Charles the First from Oxford to the Scotch Army and from Hampton-Court to the Isle of Wight*, 2 vols., London: 1830) was published by one of his descendants.

The Agitators were military delegates elected within the army, where they formed a kind of parliament. Originally, the term was in no way synonymous with "Seditionmongers"; it should rather be understood as meaning "Agents" or "Representatives."

84   Harvey describes both his research into the generation of various species of deer and the interest King Charles took in it in his *De generatione*. That work reveals the author's uncertainty about the role of the sperm, but it must be remembered that spermatozoa were not discovered until 1677—by the Dutch naturalists Johan Louis Ham and Antonie van Leeuwenhoek, thanks to the microscope. (The first microscopes did already exist in Harvey's day,

but he seems not to have had recourse to them.) Harvey's text gives the curious impression of being a mixture of rigor and inaccuracy. At times we have the feeling of being present at the birth of the experimental method and of modern scientific reasoning, but these passages alternate with the vaguest, most confused, and fanciful affirmations. Harvey is harking back to the prescientific era from which he is still not as free as he thinks. The sentence comparing the action of the sperm with the action of the brain, both being capable of responding to action at a distance, is almost literally taken from Harvey's text. Harvey believed that the egg is neither the work of the female nor the semen of the male, but rather of a "soul" which the egg contains:

> In dogs, conies [rabbits] and many other animals, I have discovered that nothing at all can be found in the uterus after copulation for the space of several days. In so much that I consider it certain that in viviparous animals also, as I previously decided for the oviparous, the foetus does not arise from either the male or the female sperm emitted in coitus, nor from both of them mixed together, as the physician thinks. . . . What it is that makes an egg fertile, whether it should be called the soul? or a part of the soul? or something of the soul? or something having the soul? [Whitteridge, *De generatione*, pp. 353 and 138]

In contrast to these lucubrations, Harvey's observations on the uterus of does after copulation are almost a model of the modern experimental method. Alas, Harvey was unfortunate in his interpretation of these observations, for the ovum in the fallow and red deer hunted by Charles I develops differently from that in most other mammals. The embryo is not a rounded, easily visible formation; in its first stages it resembles a thin, elongated object which can easily remain unnoticed. In Harvey's eyes it took the form of "mucous filament like spiders' threads," and he wrongly concluded that the uterus was empty during the first seven weeks.

1 September 1647

Page

87   The story of the tobacco affair has been reconstituted from the minutes of the College of Physicians of London dated October 13, 1628. I found all the details of the crisis in relations between Charles I and the British colony of Virginia in W. Robertson, *The History of America*, bk. 9: *The History of Virginia to the Year 1688* (London: Strahan, Cadell, Davies & Balfour, 1796); and Thomas Jefferson Wertenbaker, *Give Me the Liberty: The*

Struggle for Self-Government in Virginia (Philadelphia: The American Philosophical Society, 1958).

The pamphlet against tobacco written by James I in 1604 is entitled *A Counter-Blaste to Tobacco*. It can be consulted in *The Workes of the Most High and Mightie Prince, James, by the Grace of God, King of Great Britaine, France and Ireland, Defender of the Faith*, collected in 1616 by James, Bishop of Winton, pp. 214–222. Harvey's diary provides only a pale reflection of this extraordinarily bombastic text, with its authoritative reliance on the most extravagant medical assertions.

4 September 1647

Page

91 We now possess many details about William Harvey's family. A very full account is given by Herringham (*The Life and Times of William Harvey*, pp. 500–502 and 575–588), who includes the story of Daniel Harvey's dealings with the parliamentary authorities. Daniel Harvey Junior, born 1631, became a member of Parliament in 1660. Charles II, on the very day he returned from exile, knighted him.

5 September 1647

Page

94 Harvey has already mentioned in his diary (11 May 1647) that he saw in 1605 the play wherein (Act V, scene 5) Macbeth, talking of life, exclaims:

> It is a tale
> Told by an idiot, full of sound and fury,
> Signifying nothing.

95 Harvey's work on the egg and the development of the embryo in birds takes up no fewer than sixty-two chapters of *De generatione*. Harvey's amazement at the mechanism of reproduction and embryologic phenomena often provokes him to write in an astonishingly lyrical style that is very different from the concise, rigorous exposition of *De motu cordis*. Several passages in the diary are taken almost verbatim from *De generatione*.

20 November 1647

Page

98 The whole of the account of Charles I's flight is taken from Ashburnham's *Narrative*. D'Israeli (*Commentaries*, pp. 331–347), in

a careful analysis of this account, finds that it occasionally contradicts other contemporaneous reports, but the text I have written for the diary of William Harvey describes the way in which Ashburnham lived through these events. His relationship with Harvey was such that it is legitimate to suppose that Ashburnham wrote him a detailed account of the vicissitudes of the king's flight; the letter in the text, however, is a pure invention.

25 November 1647

Page

102   All the descriptions of life in London during Harvey's lifetime are taken from Bourcier's doctoral thesis on private diaries in England from 1600 to 1660 (*Journaux privés*). The mass of information contained in her book has been useful to me for the whole of Harvey's diary.

26 November 1647

Page

104   Lord Arundel's journey to the Continent is known down to the last detail owing to the account published by the delegation's official chronicler, William Crowne: *A True Relation of All the Remarkable Places and Passages Observed in the Travels of the Right Honourable Thomas Lord Howard, Earl of Arundel and Surrey* ... (London: 1637). See also Francis C. Springell, *Connoisseur and Diplomat: The Earl of Arundel's Embassy to Germany in 1636* (London: Maggs, 1963).

106   Harvey's demonstration in the anatomy theater of the University of Altdorf and the subsequent exchange of correspondence between him and Professor of Medicine and Anatomy Caspar Hofmann are fully reported by Keynes (*Life of W. Harvey,* pp. 232–238). Hofmann's letter, which is shortened in the diary, deserves to be quoted at length:

> Your unbelievable kindness, my Harvey, makes me not only like you but love you. Hence you have more readily obtained from me my fulfilment today of what I promised you yesterday, namely my opinion of your circulation. I hope, moreover, that you will accept it in the spirit in which I give it to you, with no malice to vex you, and without any conceitedness to make it appear that I know more than you. But simply and frankly. For this reason I guarantee you that if, after the clouds have been dispelled, you

will show me the truth which is more beautiful than the evening and the morning stars, I will with Stesichorus publicly recant and retire from the field. . . .

I will first deal with you rhetorically.

I. You appear to accuse Nature of folly in that she went astray in a work of almost prime importance, namely, the making and distribution of food. Once that is admitted, what degree of confusion will not follow in other works which depend on the blood.

II. You appear to disapprove in fact of that which you praise in word, namely the universally accepted view of Nature, that she is not lacking in the essentials but does not, however, abound in unnecessary things. . . .

To discharge my pledge, I wish you to receive these messages from my own hand. Fare you well, my Harvey, and walk well with your most illustrious Count, my most gracious Lord, whose hands I humbly kiss.

Harvey's reply ran to more than two thousand words and cannot be reproduced here, in spite of its being a remarkable example of a style of scientific correspondence that no longer exists, mixing dithyramb with rigorous, if not always sober and well-ordered, criticism.

28 November 1647

Page

108   There are several documents from which we may form a good idea of the personality of Thomas Howard, Earl of Arundel and Surrey, Earl Marshal of England (1585–1646). He was the greatest English connoisseur of the arts and the richest collector of the period. He was an adviser to both James I and Charles I, and his name is still famous because of the Arundel (or Paros) marbles. There are many accounts of his friendship with Harvey, all carefully collected by Keynes (*Life of W. Harvey*, pp. 219–263). Keynes also quotes *in extenso* (pp. 222–225) an English translation, done by Arnold Muirhead in 1939, of Harvey's Latin report of his postmortem examination of Thomas Parr on November 16, 1635.

The deciphering of the inscriptions on the Arundel marbles was entrusted to John Selden (1584–1654). He was a great scholar, but he was also a Parliamentarian and the author of various writings that were rather hostile to the crown and that earned him two years' detention; the Earl of Arundel's choice seems curious, then, at least on the basis of the documents I have been able to consult. After Selden's publications, several other translations of the Greek inscriptions were made, enabling us today to have a precise knowledge of these valuable texts.

1 December 1647

Page

112   The Earl of Arundel was not received by Ferdinand II at Ratisbon but at Linz. As he feared, the earl was not able to persuade the emperor, and Maximilian von Wittelsbach was finally confirmed as the Elector Palatine. The journey of the earl and his suite was not cut short, however, and that was how Harvey was able to stay a whole week in Prague, where he arrived on July 6, 1636.

His meetings with Joannes Marcus Marci of Kronland, the Hippocrates of Prague (1599–1667), are fully described by Marci in his *Philosophia vetus restituta* (1662). Marci described how he gave Harvey his book on the generation of living beings "into his hands, here at Prague, talking to him familiarly," and he complains bitterly that Harvey did not quote him in his *De generatione*. Their encounter is analyzed by Walter Pagel and Pyrali Rattensi in "Harvey Meets the 'Hippocrates of Prague,' Johannes Marcus Marci of Kronland," *Medical History* 8 (1964): 78–84, and in V. Kruta, "Harvey in Bohemia," *Physiologia Bohemoslovenica* 6 (1957); 433–439.

According to several studies I consulted on Marci, he was an astonishing personality. I did not find it easy to read his *Idearum operatricium idea sive hypotyposis et detectio illius occultae virtutis, quae semina faecundat, & ex ijsdem corpora organica producit* (1635), and Harvey's diary gives only a faint approximation of the unimaginable gibberish sometimes written on biological and medical problems in those days. Marci's prose shocked Harvey, although he himself is not entirely exempt from similar failings in *De generatione*. Marci's work is adorned with a frontispiece, vignettes, and tailpieces of great delicacy, as well as with a portrait of the author that inspired the description of him in the diary.

Marci's work on mechanics and optics seems to be far more rigorous than his medical and philosophical writings. In particular, he seems to have discovered the unequal refractivity of different-colored rays in 1648, before Huygens and Newton.

12 December 1647

Page

116   All contemporary accounts speak of the friendship between Marci and Archbishop Ernst Albrecht von Harrach (1598–1667). He

was the son of Count Karl von Harrach, a favorite of Emperor
Ferdinand II. Contrary to what Marci's measured words might
suggest, the younger von Harrach was known for his animosity
and aggressivity toward Protestants.

117   On Marci's concept of a "soul of the world," see Bedrich Bau-
       mann, "Un Philosophe tchèque oublié, Jean Marcus Marci," *La
       Pensée*, n.s., 65 (1956): 95–102.

13 December 1647

Page

119   Robert Fludd (1574–1637) had frequent dealings with Harvey; it
       was he who advised Harvey to publish *De motu cordis* in Frank-
       furt, where a young Englishman, William Fitzer, was the son-in-
       law and successor to Johann Theodore de Bry, who had published
       Fludd's books and who, like Fludd, was a Rosicrucian. I took the
       list of Fludd's machines and automatons from Serge Hutin's *Rob-
       ert Fludd, alchimiste et philosophe rosicrucien* (Paris: Omnium
       Littéraire, 1971). Fludd seems to have preceded Denis Papin in the
       discovery of the virtues of water vapor under pressure as a driving
       force. His "pantheistic" ideas were the object of virulent attacks.
       The exact titles of the publications cited in the diary of William
       Harvey are as follows: W. Foster, *Hoplocrisma Spongus; or, A
       Sponge to Wipe Away the Weapon-Salve* (London: 1631); *Doctor
       Fludd's Answer unto Mr. Foster; or, The Squeezing of Parson Fos-
       ter's Sponge* (London: 1631); M. Mersenne, *Quaestiones celeber-
       rimae in genesim* (Paris: 1623); R. Fludd, *Sophiae cum moria
       certamen* (Frankfurt: 1629); P. Gassendi, *Epistolica exercitatio,
       in qua principia philosphiae Roberti Fluddi Medici reteguntur*
       (Paris: 1630).
       Fludd's singular mixture of traditional medicine, "magic"
       practices, and esoteric interpretations was the subject of his book
       Medicina catholica (*catholica* here meaning "universal"), pub-
       lished in Frankfurt in three volumes and two supplements be-
       tween 1629 and 1631. His "weapon salve" is described in several
       of his works, but particularly in *Discursus de unguento armario*,
       which appeared in a voluminous anthology of various "powders
       of sympathy" (including that of Sir Kenelm Digby) by S. Rattray:
       Theatrum sympatheticum auctum (Nuremberg: 1662). The im-
       portance Fludd attached to demons as a cause of diseases is par-
       ticularly marked in his *Pathologia daemoniaca*, which was
       published in Gouda, Holland, in 1640.
       In order to give an idea of Robert Fludd's style, I should quote
       a few lines of his *Theologo-philosophical Treatise of Life, Death*

and Resurrection, Dedicated to the Rosicrucian Brotherhood (Leyden: 1616):

> In every century, Light and Knowledge have been seen, in the midst of darkness, by a few Chosen ones. And, in all Ages of Church, there will be some men to whom will be given weapons of victory, the wood of God's paradise, or the hidden manna, or the morning star, or the domination of peoples, or white clothes to put on, or the gift preventing removal from the Book of Life, and they will be the Temple Columns and given the name of New Lamb. Moreover, Truth itself has promised that the Hidden will be known and the Secret open to knowledge. Truth is guarded by an élite and will be revealed before the world cyclic revolution, by permission and will of our Lord Jesus-Christ. . . . From my careful research I have concluded that you, illuminated Rosicrucian brothers, are really illuminated by the Spirit and by divine warning.

20 December 1647

Page

126   Dr. George Ent (1604–1689), though younger than Harvey by twenty-six years, became his valued friend and supporter. Ent was educated at a school in Rotterdam and at Sidney Sussex College, Cambridge, and spent five years studying medicine at Padua, where he took his M.D. on April 28, 1636. Later, he became one of the first members of the Royal Society. He was knighted by Charles II in 1665, following a lecture in the Harveian Museum at which the king had been present. Ent is the author of various publications on the circulation and the respiration. His complete works were published in Leyden in 1687.

The friendship between Harvey and Ent later inspired the poet and playwright John Dryden (1631–1700) to write his *Epistle to Dr. Charleton.* See N. Moore's biography of Sir George Ent in the *Dictionary of National Biography* (London: Smith, Elder & Co., 1889), vol. 17, p. 377.

127   The two Raphael frescoes that caught Harvey's attention are to-day (probably wrongly) entitled *Disputation Concerning the Blessed Sacrament* and the *School of Athens.* They are in the Stanze di Raffaello in the Vatican Museums.

128   Lord Arundel played an important part in the purchase of the works by Leonardo da Vinci possessed by England. Before 1630 he acquired a volume of 234 folios of drawings which Pompeo

Leoni had managed to procure from an erudite Barnabite monk by the name of Mazenta, who had them from Lelio Gavardi, who had stolen them from the son of Francesco Melzi, a disciple of Leonardo. Leonardo had bequeathed all his manuscripts to Melzi. There is little doubt that Leonardo da Vinci defended empirical research and criticized those theoreticians who neglect observation and experimentation. His *Codex Atlanticus* as well as his *Trattato della pittura* commend experience as the "mother of both sciences and arts" and as the "source of every certainty."

129   Emilio Parigiano (Parisanus) has already been mentioned (see notes under 12 May 1647, above). His pamphlet against Harvey (*Nobilium exercitationum de subtilitate pars altera de cordis et sanguinis motu singularis certaminis, ad G. Harveum,* published in Venice in 1635) is signed Emilius Parisanus. In Ent's reply, published in London in 1641 and republished in 1685, the Venetian physician is called Aemilio Parisano. Parigiano had the same anatomy master as Harvey: Fabricius of Aquapendente. Yet, he attacks Harvey very violently in his book. Apropos of heart sounds, he writes: "Our poor deaf ears, nor those of any physician in Venice, cannot hear them; thrice fortunate those in London who can."

130   The residence of the viceroys of Naples was built in 1600 by the viceroy, a Spanish "Maecenas" and patron of Cervantes, the Count of Lemos. The building, called the Royal Palace, must have had flower-filled gardens leading down to the sea, but they were replaced by fortifications. This same Count of Lemos was responsible for the completion of the Naples Museum, begun in 1587 by his predecessors.

　　　The chapel of San Gennaro, an annex of the Santa Restituta Basilica (the former Cathedral of Naples), was built in 1608 at the expense of the people of Naples, in order to fulfill a vow made during the 1526 epidemic of the plague. San Gennaro's relics were already in Naples, where they had been taken by Ferdinand in 1495. Since that date, the phials containing the saint's blood had been taken through the streets of Naples in procession every time the people wanted to implore the saint to protect their town. The episode of the miracle performed by order of the army is authentic, but I have changed its date. It actually took place in 1799, at the time of the town's conquest by General Jean-Antoine-Etienne Championnet at the head of a French army.

28 December 1647

Page

132   George Ent's visit at Christmas 1647 (or, some say, 1648) is described in detail by Ent himself in his preface to Harvey's *De generatione*. He had chosen the publisher, Octavian Pulleyn the Elder, and the printer, William Dugard, whom he considered the best craftsman of the day and who was also a very well educated man. The book was published in London in Latin—a language in which Dugard was extremely proficient—in 1651, but an English edition had already appeared by 1653.

136   Bernard Palissy's book was published in Paris by Martin Le Jeune in 1580; its complete title is *Discours admirables de la nature des eaux et fontaines, tant naturelles qu'artificielles, des métaux, des sels et salines, des pierres, des terres, du feu et des émaux, avec plusieurs autres excellents secrets des choses naturelles; plus un traité de la marne, fort utile et nécessaire à ceux qui se meslent d'agriculture; le tout dressé par dialogues, esquels sont introduites la théorique et la pratique; par maistre Bernard Palissy, inventeur des rustiques figulines du roy et de la reyne, sa mère* [Admirable Discourses on the Nature of Waters and Fountains, Whether Natural or Artificial, on Metals, on Salts and Salt-springs, on Stones, on Earths, on Fire and on Enamels; with Many Other Excellent Secrets of Natural Things; Also, a Treatise on Marl, Very Useful and Necessary for Those Who Are Concerned with Agriculture; the Whole Drawn Up in Dialogues, Wherein Are Introduced Theory and Practice, by M. Bernard Palissy, Inventor of Rustic Figulines to the King and to the Queen, His Mother]. A modern translation into English by Aurèle La Rocque has been published under the title *Admirable Discourses* (Urbana: University of Illinois Press, 1957). The sentence that Harvey remembered was: "Ceux qui besognent impatiemment de l'art de terre perdent beaucoup bien souvent par leurs impatiences." Lord Arundel's collections contained some of Palissy's works. Sixteenth-century English connoisseurs of art had in any case closely followed the misfortunes of this Huguenot who was in turn protected by Catherine de' Medici and persecuted for his faith. He died in 1590 in the Bastille, to which he had been committed for refusing to abjure Protestantism.

137   The hypothesis has been presented that the concept of an egg being the common origin of all animals might have been suggested to Harvey by the printer's mark of Gilles Gourbin, the famous French publisher of medical books who was to publish Harvey's *De generatione* four years later. The mark showed Pandora open-

ing a spheroidal box from which there emerges a cloud of living creatures. A similar image is to be found on the frontispiece of Harvey's book, with Jove instead of Pandora and a bisected egg-shell in place of the box. The reader can find a detailed discussion of this point in I. Bernard Cohen, "A Note on Harvey's 'Egg' as Pandora's 'Box,' " in M. Teich and R. Young, eds., *Changing Perspectives in the History of Science* (London: Heinemann, 1973).

29 December 1647

Page

139   The detailed description of William Harvey's journey to Edinburgh, where Charles was to be crowned King of Scotland was taken from several sources. A complete list of the king's suite was found in the *Mercure françois, ou suite de l'histoire de nostre temps sous le règne du très chrestien roy de France et de Navarre, Louis XIII* (Paris: Estienne Richer, 1636), vol. 19, pp. 871–874. Another source was Edward, Earl of Clarendon, *History of the Rebellion and Civil Wars in England* (London: Oxford University Press, 1958), vol. 1, pp. 97–108. On the means of transport for the period, I have consulted with profit Maurice Ashley's *Life in Stuart England* (London: Batsford, 1964). Useful information on masques is to be found in *The New Oxford History of Music*, vol. 4: *The Age of Humanism*, ed. Gerald Abraham (London: Oxford University Press, 1968). The letter in which Lord Arundel describes how Lord Portland's state of health prevented them from leaving with the rest of the procession, despite Harvey's efforts, is preserved in the *Calendar of Domestic State Papers: Charles I* (1633), CXXIX, fol. 37, and also quoted in Keynes, *Life of W. Harvey*, pp. 196–201, which also provides many other details, such as the "Freedom of the City" conferred on Harvey and the king's touching a hundred people for the "King's Evil," or scrofula.

    Harvey himself tells of his visit to Bass Rock in *De generatione* (p. 53 of the 1653 English edition), doing so in his typically precise yet racy style.

5 January 1648

Page

144   Inigo Jones (1573–1652), besides being an architect, was a painter, stage designer, mathematician, and man of letters. He traveled abroad a great deal. His talent for drawing was noticed

by William Howard, Third Earl of Pembroke, who sent him to Italy to study painting. The depth of his knowledge of Italian art and Renaissance theory was uncommon in England, and his revolutionary buildings brought the classical style to that country. He began his career as a designer of masques in 1605. In 1615 he became "surveyor of the king's works." His most famous buildings are the Banqueting Hall of Whitehall; the Queen's House, Greenwich; and Wilton House, the seat of the Earl of Pembroke, whom the king was visiting at the time of Jones and Harvey's expedition to Stonehenge.

145   The origin of Stonehenge was hotly disputed in the seventeenth century. Inigo Jones's opinion, that it was a Roman monument, was published in 1655 by his pupil John Webb, who described in detail the expedition mentioned in Harvey's diary. Jones's conclusions were attacked by Walter Charleton, who was one of the king's physicians at the same time as Harvey and who published a pamphlet in 1633 stating that Stonehenge was a ritual site of the Danish court! It is now known to be prehistoric and may have been erected as long ago as 2000 B.C.

146   Apropos of Harvey's remark about the symbolism of the circle, it must be said that several authors have been struck by the importance of this symbol in Harvey's work: the circulation of the blood; the circular image of generation (the cycle of seed–fetus–child–adult–seed, etc.). Walter Pagel, in "The Philosophy of Circles," *Journal of the History of Medicine* 12 (1957): 140–158, defends the idea that if Harvey is attached to the figure of the circle, it is so that his work shall fit better into the Greek philosophers' vision of the classic world, where circular forces act both on the "macrocosm" of the universe and the "microcosm" of living man.

25 January 1648

Page

153   If Harvey had been granted the wish he expresses at the end of this diary entry, he would have known that his nephew Daniel was knighted by King Charles II and became ambassador to Constantinople in 1668.

26 January 1648

Page

154   As previously mentioned, Harvey had little respect for his famous patient Francis Bacon. Aubrey says (*Brief Lives*) that Harvey told

him as much in very strong terms, and all the later biographers repeat Aubrey's remarks. It is certainly true that Bacon behaved contemptibly and was a servile, ambitious courtier, greedy for money and honors. In the many works devoted to Bacon over the past three centuries, I have found some indulgent commentators and others who were more severe, but none denies the facts reported by Harvey in his diary.

Bacon's philosophy also contained much that displeased Harvey, but he is being unfair when he says that Bacon never experimented. In fact, Bacon made several observations on the reflection of light, the incompressibility of liquids, the density of bodies, and the elasticity of air; but it is true that he did not draw original conclusions from those experiments.

Joseph de Maistre (*Examen de la philosophie de Bacon,* Paris: Poussielgue-Rusand, 1836, vol. 1, pp. 168–169) wrote:

> Bacon's incompetence outrageously contrasts with the contempt he exhibits for all his predecessors. . . . Why, it was asked for centuries, why does water rise in suction pumps. And for centuries the answer was that Nature abhors a vacuum. And here comes Bacon who says: "You are all wrong, don't you understand that the phenomenon simply results from the fact that bodies that like touching each other refuse to part. The School that sees only the effects and ignores the real causes asserts that NATURE ABHORS A VACUUM. Idiots! It is the LOVE OF THE PISTON."

Many other commentators, however, see Bacon despite his errors, as one of the founders of modern epistemology. When Harvey reports Gassendi's favorable opinion of Bacon, he does so in Gassendi's own terms: "With heroic determination, Bacon dared open an unknown path; one may hope that, if he valiantly continues his undertaking, he will found and give us a new and perfect system of thought" (Gassendi, *Œuvres complètes,* Lyon: Montmort & Sorbière, 1658). There is a bibliography of the principal (and very numerous) works devoted to Francis Bacon in Anthony Quinton's little book in the Past Masters series (Oxford University Press: 1980).

The experiment Harvey chose in order to refute Bacon's methodology is taken almost word for word from *De motu cordis.*

28 January 1648

Page

160   Heneage Finch, a lawyer, had married Harvey's niece Elizabeth, the daughter of his brother Daniel, in 1646. He later became Lord Chancellor and Earl of Nottingham. Keynes (*Life of W. Harvey,*

p. 443) reproduces Harvey's prescriptions for him, which Finch copied into his commonplace book, now in the library of the College of Physicians of Philadelphia. I have greatly simplified the formulae for the decoction and the pills, just as, farther on, I have considerably shortened the list of the constituents of the theriac electuary which, in Galen's formula, contains no fewer than sixty ingredients and was later known in ever more complex variations. Reading the medical prescriptions of Harvey's day, one is stupefied by the extraordinary number of products used, their variety (which ranges from crayfish eyes or extract of viper to the rarest plants), and by the plethora of details on how to use them.

The English pharmacopoeia of the time (*Pharmacopoeia Londiniensis, 1638*) would be enough to drive a present-day pharmacist mad.

161   The case of the servant at the College of Physicians is considered by Harvey's biographers to be an early observation of syringomyelia (not labeled until 1824, by Charles Prosper Ollivier), a disease of the spinal cord in which cavities form in the gray matter. This retrospective diagnosis is plausible, but not certain. As for the discussion of "the sensory message and the motive message," it was Sir Kenelm Digby (*Two Treatises*, p. 282) who described how the case observed by Harvey inspired the distinction between motor and sensory nerves.

29 January 1648

Page

163   The case of Mary and her cure by the "hymeneal exercises" advised by Harvey is reported by several authors, among them Robert Boyle (*Some Considerations Touching the Usefulness of Experimental Naturall Philosophy,* Oxford: 1663, p. 72). Harvey described other cases of hysteria, notably in the obstetric chapter in *De generatione.* The word "hysteria" (from the Greek *hustera,* uterus) reflects the belief of Harvey and the doctors of his day in a close connection between women's hysterical manifestations and their genital functions. In two cases in *De generatione,* Harvey even reports that a prolapse of the uterus coincided with the disappearance of a woman's neurosis. He also reports, in his 1616 *Prelectiones,* the story of two women suffering from "nervous pregnancy," which was then called pseudocyesis, or "false conception." There is, therefore, not the slightest doubt of Harvey's interest in psychiatry and, in particular, female neuroses.

The story of the Newmarket "toad-woman" is described in detail by Keynes (*Life of W. Harvey,* p. 213) from contemporary documents. It is a good example of Harvey's passion for direct observation, experimentation, and even the dissection of living animals.

2 February 1648

Page

166   All the details about St. Bartholomew's Hospital in Harvey's day are taken from the following two books: Sir Norman Moore, *The History of St. Bartholomew's Hospital,* 2 vols. (London: 1918); *The Royal Hospital of Saint Bartholomew,* ed. V. C. Medvei and J. L. Thornton (London: 1974).

168   The visit of Robert Burton (1577–1640) to William Harvey is hypothetical, but it is certain that Harvey could not have been unaware of *The Anatomy of Melancholy,* which Burton had published in 1621 and which had enjoyed a very great success. There are still those today who consider Burton the English Michel de Montaigne. I worked from the 8th edition (Oxford: Henry Cripps 1628). Its complete title is

THE ANATOMY OF MELANCHOLY
What it is, with all the kinds, causes, symptomes
prognostickes and severall cures of it

In three Partitions, with their severall
Sections, members and subsections,

Philosophically, Medicinally, Historically,
opened and cut up

By
Democritus Junior
With a Satyricall Preface
Conducing to the following Discourse
Omne tulit punctum, qui miscuit utile dulci

The title page contains ten vignettes. The "Argument of the Frontispiece" describes them:

Ten distinct Squares here seen apart
Are joyn'd in one by Cutters art

One contains a portrait of the author, and among the other nine

are: "The Inamorato"; "A Superstitious man"; "Hypocondria-
cus"; "The Madman"; "A landskip of Jealousie"; and "of Soli-
tariness, A portraiture."

This very large, hefty book of 655 pages is a treatise on medicine, psychology, and correct conduct whose riches are only
faintly reflected in the few lines Harvey devotes to it. Some of the
very first references to what we now call psychosomatic medicine
may be found in this book; it also extols the therapeutic qualities
of the game of chess, of singing, dancing, comedy, pantomime,
music, and so on. If it seemed useful to confront Harvey with
Robert Burton and his book, it was in order to elicit Harvey's
thoughts on the subject. Harvey writes: "For although it be a new
and difficult way to find out the nature of things by the things
themselves rather than by the reading of books to take our
knowledge from the opinions of Philosophers, yet must it needs
be confessed that the former is a much more open way to the
hidden secrets of natural philosophy and one which leads less
into error" (*De generatione*, Whitteridge trans., p. 9).

170   The case of Ellin French, reported by John Woodall in *The Surgeon's Mate* (p. 398), is analyzed in detail by S. Epstein, "The
Case of Ellin French. . . . Peripheral vascular . . . with amputa-
tion," *Angiology* 5 (1954): 391–413. Epstein amused himself by
reconstituting Woodall's presentation of the history of the illness
rather as it would be done today during the visit of a consultant
in a hospital.

171   Harvey's love of coffee is described by Aubrey in *Brief Lives:* "I
remember he was wont to drinke Coffee; which he and his
brother Eliab did, before Coffee-houses were in fashion in London." Harvey must have been among the first in England to adopt
this drink, which he did as early as 1616; his brothers imported
coffee beans from Turkey. As for watered cider, that too was one
of Harvey's favorite drinks, according to Sir Kenelm Digby (*The
Closet of Sir Kenelme Digby Opened*, 1671) and Geoffrey Keynes
(*Life of W. Harvey*, p. 406).

28 November 1648

Page
174   Jean Riolan (1580–1657), the son of another Jean Riolan who
was dean of the Faculty of Medicine in Paris, was himself physician in ordinary to Henri IV, and then to Louis XIII, before becoming personal physician to the Queen Mother, Marie de'

Medici. His singular personality is very well described by Th. Vetter in "Jean Riolan, second du nom, qui ne fut pas doyen des écoles de Paris," *Presse Médicale* 73 (1965): 3269–3274. That is where I found the details of Riolan's excessive indulgence in Burgundy wines and of the shrewish wife who poisoned his existence.

Riolan's habitual aggressiveness was sometimes exercised in a happier fashion than in his fight against Harvey's work; for instance, Riolan wrote a book ridiculing a surgeon from the Hôtel-Dieu, one Nicolas Habicot, who had mistaken the bones of an elephant, discovered in a grave in the Dauphiné and labeled *Teutobocus Rex,* for the skeleton of a giant king of the Teutons, thirteen feet tall. In his *Anthropographie* (1616) Riolan devotes several pages to the human heart, and these already contain the essentials of the errors and nonsense he would stubbornly persist in later, although he does not yet refer to Harvey, whose *De motu cordis* had not yet appeared. Harvey is attacked for the first time by Riolan in his *Encheiridium anatomicum et pathologicum,* published in Paris in 1648, and even more forcefully in the *Opuscula anatomica nova,* published in London in 1649. Later editions of the *Encheiridium* even contain a supplement, *Discourse Touching the Movement of the Blood,* which returns to the attack in an extraordinary mixture of venomous compliments to "the most illustrious English anatomist" (whose work is thereafter judged "ridiculous") and which puts forth theories that today seem fantastic and incomprehensible. For the sake of clarity, Harvey's diary presents a very much simplified synthesis of these criticisms. Harvey replied in 1649 in his two famous letters to Riolan: *Exercitatio anatomica,* cited above.

Jan de Wale (1604–1649), whom Riolan attacked under the name of Joannis Wallaei at the same time as his attack on Harvey, was a Dutch physician who accepted Harvey's theories of the circulation of the blood; however, de Wale claimed that those ideas had their origin in texts from antiquity, and he attributed a perfect knowledge of how the blood circulates to Fra Paolo Scarpi and Fabricius of Aquapendente, which is demonstrably incorrect. In his *Epistolae de motu chyli et sanguinis* (1641), de Wale merely allowed Harvey the honor of having definitely confirmed the circulation of the blood.

23 December 1648

Page

178   The last moments of Charles I's stay in Carisbrooke Castle, the ambiguous attitude of the governor of the Isle of Wight, Colonel

Robin Hammond, the colonel's dismissal by the army, the king's transfer to Hurst Castle, and so forth are fully described in most histories of the period, among them Charles Carlton's *Charles I* (London: 1983) and D'Israeli's *Commentaries*, vol. 5, pp. 393–411). I also found some details in the memoirs of the King's Groom of the Bedchamber, Sir Thomas Herbert (*Memories*).

179 Harvey himself described the misadventures he suffered when quarantined for more than two weeks in Treviso, in a series of letters he wrote from there to Lord Denbigh, King Charles's Ambassador Extraordinary to the Republic of Venice, and to Signor Francesco, whom he had been asked by Lord Arundel to visit. The letters to Lord Denbigh are kept in the British Library. They were published in 1911 by the Historical Manuscripts Commission under the title *Eleven Letters of William Harvey to Lord Feilding*. (Basic Feilding was the Earl of Denbigh.)

I have taken everything Harvey writes in his diary from these letters. They offer a glimpse of a desperate, fearful, suppliant, unfamiliar Harvey.

180 The dates of Harvey's stay at Windsor Castle are those given by Kenneth D. Keele in his *William Harvey: The Man, the Physician, and the Scientist* (London: Thomas Nelson, 1965). The strange case of the young Irish viscount, Hugh Montgomery, is described by Harvey himself in *De generatione*. He uses this observation as proof of the insensibility of the heart to the touch.

31 December 1648

Page

183 Sir Charles Scarburgh, born in 1610, was a very close friend during Harvey's last years. All biographers agree on this point. The portrait from which I drew my physical description is in the Royal College of Physicians of London; it was painted by an unknown artist when Scarburgh was forty-two. Harvey's suicidal inclinations and the help promised by Scarburgh—if Harvey were ever brought to that extreme—are attested by the Earl of Egmont, who writes in his diary (cited by Keynes, *Life of W. Harvey*, p. 369):

> The first attempt he made to do it was unsuccessful, as Dr. Scarborow, his intimate friend, related it, who agreed in opinion with the other that suicide was lawful. One day, Harvey being in great pain (he was then about 72 years old) sent for Scarborow, and acquainting him with his intention

to die by laudanum that night, desired he would come next morning to take care of his papers and affairs. Scarborow, who had long before promised him that friendly office when occasion called on him, did accordingly come next morning, but was surprised to find Harvey alive and well; it seems the laudanum he had taken, instead of killing him, had brought away a considerable number of stones, which effect caused a suspension of his design to destroy himself for some years.

186   The story of the king's letter intercepted by Cromwell and of the parliamentary purge appears in many histories of the time. In particular, an excellent book by Gérard Walter, *La Révolution anglaise, l'exécution de Charles Ier et l'ascension de Cromwell* (Paris: Albin Michel, 1963 and 1982), enables the reader to understand, insofar as this is possible, the complicated forces at work during this confused period.

3 February 1649

Page

189   The words attributed to Charles I during his last days and hours are reported by many historians, among them Carlton (*Charles I*).

The King's Groom of the Bedchamber, Thomas Herbert, who is the source of Harvey's information, obviously gives a version of these events that is entirely favorable to the king and unfavorable to his enemies. It was natural for Harvey to share this interpretation. A less favorable version is given by others, especially Lord Bradshaw in his argument for the prosecution during the king's trial. But it was easy for me to imagine Harvey's feelings, for they were shared two centuries later by a historian who also defends the king with a sort of posthumous passion: namely, D'Israeli, in his *Commentaries*.

25 February 1650

Page

197   The events reported in Hobbes's letter took place between 1647 and 1650. Hobbes's serious illness dates from 1647; a notable account of it is given in Sir Leslie Stephen, *Hobbes* (London: Macmillan, 1904), p. 40. Stephen offers various versions of Mersenne's efforts to convert Hobbes to Catholicism; the text in the diary is inspired by the version provided by Hobbes himself. Father Mersenne died in September 1648.

198   The parallel between the English Revolution and the anti-Monarchist threats of the *Fronde* has been drawn by many historians.

199   The details of Descartes's last illness and death in Stockholm are well described in Elizabeth Haldane, *Descartes, His Life and Times* (London: John Murray, 1905), pp. 339–357. The quotations chosen by Harvey from Hobbes's "Objections" to Descartes's *Meditations* are taken from *Les Méditations métaphysiques de René Descartes touchant la première philosophie, suivies de six séries d'objections* (*par MM. Caterus, Mersenne, Hobbes, Arnaud, Gassendi et un groupe de philosophes, géomètres et théologiens*) (Paris: Soly, 1641).

   The mixture of admiration and criticism of Descartes that Harvey expresses reflects, I think, the ambiguous feelings the French philosopher inspired in many English intellectuals. Both Harvey and Hobbes were fascinated by Descartes's methodical doubt, anti-Scholastic stance, and some of his mechanistic concepts, but they did not follow him in his analysis of the relation between soul and body; they also complained that he did not give enough weight to experiment. René Descartes, in fact, experimented very little himself, although he had very decided views on the organic functions of living beings.

1 June 1650

Page

202   The account of Harvey's successive domiciles, at Coombe in Surrey and then in the city of London at St. Lawrence Pountney Hill, is probably accurate, but absolute certainty is not possible here. There exist very few reliable documents for this period. We know that the Coombe estate belonged to Daniel, William Harvey's young nephew; he had inherited it in 1642 at age eleven from another of his uncles, Matthew Harvey. The estate was in actual fact within twenty miles of London. The house in St. Lawrence Pountney belonged to Eliab Harvey, another of William's brothers; Eliab owned several other houses, and some people think that William may have stayed in Eliab's house in Hempstead, Essex, which was beyond the boundary laid down by Act of Parliament in 1650. The question is discussed in detail by Keynes (*Life of W. Harvey*, pp. 375–376). His main source, however, is John Aubrey (*Brief Lives*); and Aubrey, though brilliant and amusing, can be wildly inaccurate.

203   The same source (with the same reservations as to its veracity) is
      the origin of the rumor that Harvey had a weakness for his maid,
      Alice Garth. Aubrey writes: "I remember he kept a pretty young
      wench to wayte on him, which I guesse he made use of for
      warmeth-sake as King David did." Harvey himself, in his notes
      for the Lumleian Lectures, writes that certain organs warm the
      abdomen just as a kitten does, and he adds: "Thus an old man
      uses a cat to warm him, and David uses the servant." The allusion
      to King David is from I Kings 1:1–4: "Now King David was old
      and stricken in years; and they covered him with clothes, but he
      gat no heat. Wherefore his servants said unto him, let there be
      sought for my lord the king a young virgin: and let her cherish
      him, and let her lie in thy bosom, that my lord the king may get
      heat. So they sought for a fair damsel throughout all the coasts of
      Israel, and found Abishag a Shunammite, and brought her to the
      king. And the damsel was very fair and cherished the king, and
      ministered to him; but the king knew her not."

206   The alleged Chinese proverb is in actual fact an invention of Eu-
      gène Ionesco, but Ionesco's aphorisms sometimes resemble mar-
      velous Chinese proverbs; it seemed to me that this one was so well
      turned that it could stand for all the sarcastic remarks that have
      ever been made about doctors, and I could not resist the tempta-
      tion of presenting it as a traditional Chinese maxim.

208   Throughout his life, Harvey commissioned portraits of himself
      from many different painters. In a paper entitled "Dr. William
      Harvey as a Man and an Art Connoisseur" (2nd Congrès interna-
      tional d'histoire de la médecine, Paris: Imprimerie Herissey, 1922,
      pp. 452–456), D'Arcy Power notes that in 1913 he and Sir Wil-
      liam Osler traced thirteen portraits in oil by the most varied paint-
      ers and one engraving by William Faithorne the Elder. It is from
      this article that I have taken the names of Michiel Janszoon van
      Mierevelt (1567–1641), Peter Lely (1618–1680), and Sir An-
      thony Van Dyck (1599–1641). The description of Van Dyck's
      features was inspired by a self-portrait he painted circa 1621, now
      in the Munich Pinakothek.

3 February 1654

Page
211   The library and museum, Harvey's gift to the College of Physi-
      cians, were inaugurated on February 2, 1654. The building was at
      Amen Corner, near what is now the Stationers' Hall. The details

of the ceremony are recorded in the *Annals* of the college. The precise inscription engraved on the plinth of Harvey's statue was as follows:

GULIELMO HARVEO
Viro monumentis suis immortali,
hoc insuper Collegium Medicorum Londinense
posuit.
Qui enim sanguinis motum
ut et
Animalibus ortum dedit, meruit esse
stator perpetuus.

Despite these last words, the statue was not eternal; it was destroyed, along with the building, in the Great Fire of 1666, nine years after Harvey's death. Aubrey tells us (*Brief Lives*) that Harvey was represented in his doctoral robes and that above his statue there was an inscription giving his date and place of birth and the names of his father, mother, brothers, and sisters. Keynes (*Life of W. Harvey*, p. 417) thinks that the statue was probably the work of Edward Marshall of Fetter Lane, the sculptor of the bust of Harvey still to be seen in Hempstead Church, where Harvey is buried.

20 June 1654

Page

214   It was in fact on June 16, 1654, that Queen Christina of Sweden, who was barely twenty-nine years old, abdicated in favor of her cousin, Karl Gustav. The coronation of Louis XIV, then age sixteen, took place on the seventh of the same month. The Manchu dynasty of the Tai Ch'ing (the "Great Pure") had taken possession of China a few years earlier, but their Emperor Shun Chih was not formally recognized by the chief lama until 1653.

After the dissolution of Parliament, Oliver Cromwell was made Lord Protector of England in December 1653. Between this date and the formation of a new Parliament, Cromwell promulgated eighty quite varied statutes. Not only did they prohibit cockfighting and itinerant singers but also dueling, the "excesses" of horseracing, gaming, blasphemy, and travel on Sundays. They also established the death penalty for adultery and prison sentences for the "frivolous or dissolute."

The time of Harvey's death on June 3, 1657, is that given by John Aubrey in his *Brief Lives*. Aubrey says that it was caused by an attack of paralysis, which deprived Harvey of speech very shortly before an apparently peaceful end. Harvey had no need of recourse to the "preparation of Opium ... which he kept in his study to take, if occasion should serve, to putt him out of his paine. . . . The Palsey did give him an easie Passeport."